# BLOOD IN THE SAND

Emily Slate Mystery Thriller
Book 15

## ALEX SIGMORE

Dark Woods Press

BLOOD IN THE SAND: EMILY SLATE MYSTERY THRILLER
BOOK 15

1st Edition

ebook ISBN 978-1-957536-63-7

Print ISBN 978-1-957536-64-4

## Prologue

HER TORN DRESS flutters in the wind as her feet carry her as fast as they possibly can.

*Just another few feet. I'll find someone. Someone can help.*

She's barefoot, but her adrenaline is pumping so fast she can't even feel the small rocks that cut at the bottoms of her soles as she runs. She's immune to pain at this point. Past it. All that matters is getting away.

*I just need to find a road. Something.*

The dense jungle surrounds her on all sides, blinding her to a direction. The sun, high in the late morning sky isn't much help. She can't tell which way is which, but all that matters right now is that she gets *away*. Away from there, from *them*. Do they know she's escaped? Are they coming after her?

The thought speeds her pace beyond what she thought was physically capable of. She hasn't run like this since college. Since those days when she would don her headphones and set out on a trail or a greenway, training for some marathon or another. And she always had her mother's voice in her head:

*Always be aware of your surroundings, Marian. There are nasty people out there who want to do you harm. You can't just turn yourself off to what's going on around you.*

What she wouldn't give to be back on one of those trails right now. Back then she'd carried a small can of mace and an emergency whistle. And she never had to use it. In the four years before she hurt her back, she never once had someone jump out of the bushes or try to corner her. The worst she ever experienced was someone coming up to ask her for directions, and while she'd been on edge at the time, that's all it had been. Someone just looking to find their way.

An errant branch slapped at her face, causing her to wince and slow down for the first time. She was tired, dirty and thirsty beyond all belief, but she'd seen an opportunity and wasn't going to waste it. They had let their guard down, and Marian had taken off.

Maybe they thought because they hadn't fed her much over the past week she wouldn't have the strength to run. Or maybe they were just that arrogant. Whatever the reason, it didn't matter. She was free of them now. She could see in her mind's eye finding some house on the side of the hill, maybe even a family out on their patio enjoying the day. She would come running up, explain what had happened, and ask to use their phone.

After that, everything would be okay.

She stopped a second to catch her breath. Her lungs were on fire and sweat poured down her brow. It was hot as blazes, even under the canopy of trees. Momentary dizziness overcame her, and she had to steady herself against a nearby tree until it passed. She needed water. Ironic that on an island surrounded by it, she was denied the one thing that her body craved the most.

She heard the snap of twigs somewhere behind her. *They're catching up.* Marian took off running again, this time in another direction. Why hadn't she seen any houses yet? Wasn't this a vacation paradise, after all? Where were all the pretty little white homes on the hills with the gorgeous views of the Caribbean? Where were the roads? She remembered something about the island being some kind of national forest, but that couldn't be the *whole* island, could it? She'd been on the west side when they'd taken her. There had been plenty of homes over there. So many that it almost bordered on crowded.

As she ran, her foot snagged a strong vine of some sort and Marian went face first into the dirt. More noise behind her forced her to get up, despite the fact she was now bleeding. She wouldn't go back, no matter what. Every word out of their mouths so far had been a lie. And the others...the looks on their faces...

The thought was the only thing that powered her on. Because this wasn't just about her. This was about all of them. Her legs faltered again, and again she went down. Cursing the earth, she tried to get back up, but found her body wasn't responding like it was supposed to. She was completely out of fuel, running on what little fumes she had left.

Marian crawled forward, finally breaking the tree line only to find herself looking out on a small cove a hundred and fifty feet below her. The sheer face of the cliff dove straight down to a small hill which eventually flattened out into something of a beach. The cove was bright blue, the water sparkling in the mid-day sun. But all Marian could think about was how she couldn't drink any of that water.

Then she spotted it. A small dirt road close to the beach at the end of the cove. There weren't any vehicles visible, but she could see clear tire tracks. Tire tracks that looked almost fresh. If she could just find some way to get down to that road, she could follow it to civilization.

To freedom.

*Voices.* Voices behind her. They were getting closer. She hadn't made it as far as she'd hoped. They were well fed and rested. She was starved and malnourished. Her brain had only made her think she'd made it farther than she actually had. Marian looked down at the cliff, her exhausted brain trying to figure out how far the jump would be. Could she make that distance and live?

Her brain was foggy, throwing conflicted answers back and forth. Part of her said yes, the other part said no way. But they were coming fast, and Marian didn't have another way out. She wasn't going back with them. That was the only thing she was absolutely certain of.

As the voices grew louder and angrier, Marian forced herself to stand on shaky legs. She peered over the edge of the cliff, looking down at the clear blue calm water. It looked so inviting. How could it ever hurt her? Just one step and she would be free.

One step and this would all be over.

# Chapter One

I FEEL RIDICULOUS.

And anyone who knows me knows this is about as uncomfortable as I can get. My hair pulled up so taut that I'm getting a headache. A thin, black dress so tight it threatens to cut off my circulation. Six-inch heels that cost two month's salary, and a clutch embroidered with real diamonds that would bankrupt me if I lost it. No gun, no sensible shoes in the event I need to make a quick break for it, not even a coat. The idea is to make sure everyone sees and notices me going into the hotel. For once in my life, I am actually trying to stand out.

Which I hate.

Thanks to Zara, all I can think about as I climb the stairs to the hotel is that I look like the main character from one of those damn animated princess movies. She would not quit fawning all over me as she put me in this godforsaken getup. I swore the last time she did this to me that was it. And yet, here I am, back where I said I would never be.

It's not all her fault. I mostly attribute this to Theo. This operation was his idea—just the latest in a long string of operations FBI intelligence has considered actionable, with the only caveat being they don't ask where he sources his information, which bothers me. Despite the fact he and Zara have been an item for almost a year now and we still don't know a lot about him is…difficult. I don't trust easily, and Theo isn't doing himself any favors to change that. But Zara seems to revel in it. For her, not knowing everything about someone is something of a relief. But for me, it's a red flag.

Not that I can complain. His help has allowed us to pull off some pretty major operations that would have been much harder otherwise—taking down a human trafficking ring that was using a traveling carnival to cover its tracks, breaking up a smuggling operation that was bringing in tons of contraband to the states every month, disrupting an inter-state cocaine supply chain. None of it would have been possible without him. And I have to admit, it's has been something of a relief being able to actually do my job for once and not have to worry about the personal consequences. It's been nine months since the woman pretending to be my mother was caught and arrested. But the justice process has been slow. She's still awaiting trial and still sending me letters from jail, all of which I tear up the minute they arrive at my house.

"Evening, miss," the doorman at the hotel says, opening one of the double doors for me. I nod to him, thankful to be inside from the cold. I shiver once as I take in the lobby of the Montague, one of the most elite hotels in the city, and thus fancier than what I can normally afford.

I marvel at the floor bathed in marble. The checkered rose and white pattern reminds me of a chess board, and for one fleeting moment, I think of myself as a queen on the board, moving in any direction I like. Crystal chandeliers burst above my head like fireworks frozen in time. The fact that everyone is not craning their necks up, simpering oohs and ahs, is down-right astounding. I have to remember all of this is "normal" for my persona and not to gawk.

Passing through the lobby, velvet tufted chairs and well-worn leather sofas frame the center of the room around free-standing, crackling fireplaces, welcoming the frigid evening politics dressed in suits and stilettos.

As I reach the bar, a soft melody from the piano touches my ears and patrons sit perched on the barstools, warming themselves with Manhattans despite this being DC. Few are paying attention to the tickers running across the two televisions over the bars, instead hunched in conversation, speaking over cocktails named after the founding fathers, complete with large ice cubes and small garnishes. Tiny masterpieces all their own.

It's impossible not to notice the famous faces. The restaurant is open to the lobby, and there are some powerful people here, no doubt making the deals that run the country. I can't even imagine how much money is exchanging hands at some of these tables. What I wouldn't give to wire this entire place just to listen in on the conversations. But that's not my goal this evening.

I have one target in mind, and one target only. But just as Zara taught me, I give every other red-blooded male I pass a sly smile and a wink, making sure they turn their heads as I pass. I need to make this look good, despite being way outside of my element. Undercover work used to come so easily for me, but after being out of it for a good twelve months, I lost some of those skills. Like anything else, it's a muscle, one that needs to be worked to maintain. And even though I've been "under" for the past four weeks, it's all been building up to this.

I make my way to the bar, keeping my eyes peeled for Mr. Big, aka, Joaquin Fletch. But there's no sign of him yet. Right on cue, Zara chirps in tiny device nestled in my ear.

"See him yet?"

"Not yet," I mumble, taking a seat at the bar, though I keep my posture open and turned outward. "I'm waiting at the bar."

"Are you—"

"Yes," I hiss. "I'm looking as alluring as I can here. I'm only human."

She chuckles. "Cross your legs."

"What?"

"It shows them off. As well as those Louboutin beauties I picked out for you. He'll be able to spot you from across the room."

"How do you know I don't already have them crossed?" I ask.

"Because I know my best friend," she says. "You're not a leg crosser."

I huff and cross one leg over the other. If I had a piece strapped to my thigh, it would be completely exposed. I argued over and over that I needed to be armed, but apparently it would have been too obvious. "You owe me big time once all this is over. Do I have to remind you I'm doing *your* job here?"

"No you're not," she retorts. "I told you I'm never going undercover again. And one of us had to do it. It isn't like we could have sent Liam in there in your place."

I chuckle at the thought of Liam in a tight dress and heels. "I dunno. I might have paid to see that."

"What can I get for you?" the bartender asks as he walks over. I don't miss the fact his eyes give me a quick once-over. That's a good sign at least.

"Vodka on the rocks," I say, sliding my eye to the side as I look for any other familiar faces.

"Lime?" the bartender asks, but I barely hear him. The man I've come here to see has just exited the restaurant, and he looks very pleased with himself.

"Got him," I whisper as the bartender heads off to make my drink without the lime. The man is tall and well-built with a dark moustache and beard. He's dressed immaculately in a dark suit, which he's buttoning. I can see why Zara made sure I was dressed to the nines. Anything else he would have ignored. But I manage to catch his eye and I keep the eye contact until a small smirk quirks the edge of his mouth.

I look away as he begins making his way over. "Hooked," I mutter.

"Good luck," she says. "You got this."

I silently thank her. This is the moment. Four weeks of work, tailing him, learning his movements, watching his schedule and doing background checks on his bodyguards. Of inserting myself into this world, building a persona, of showing up at events, at making the smallest movements to make him notice me, but not so much that he felt the need to introduce himself; manufacturing relationships that all needed to be in place before we could attempt something like this. I just hope the intel we've been working off is worth it. If this all turns out to be for nothing, that'll be a full month down the drain.

"Ms. Agostini, I'm surprised to see you here. You look…in a word, stunning," the man says, approaching. I smile and hold out my hand delicately for him. He takes it in his and makes a deliberate show of leaning down and kissing the top ever so gently, maintaining eye contact with me the entire time. I narrow my eyes in a playful reciprocation, though it turns my stomach. He gently releases my hand.

"Mr. Fletch. We all have business in the city at some point or another, don't we?" I do my best purring impression, just like Zara taught me, though it comes out as a half growl. That only seems to incentivize him and he takes a seat at my side.

"Double bourbon, neat," he says to the bartender, never taking his eyes off me. "I have to say, I didn't expect to see you again so soon. That ceremony last weekend was just so *boring*."

"Agreed. I just finished a *very* lucrative dinner with some clients across the street. But I can never resist this hotel. Every time I pass I have to come in and soak it up," I reply. *It's a role, play the part.* But I know what kind of man Fletch is. I know what he's done…some of it anyway. It would be easier if I were ignorant, though not by much. Flirting has never been one of my strong suits. Another reason I argued against taking this assignment. Besides, I've never done this kind of undercover work before and I'm not a hundred percent sure I can pull it off. Zara spent a solid week coaching me on how to handle this without tipping him off, and I had to practice on Liam, which was only the most embarrassing thing I've ever had to do.

AND YET HERE I SIT.

The bartender brings both of our drinks at the same time. I don't touch mine but Fletch already has his in hand and knocks it back without even blinking. His eyes are all over me; if they were hands I would have needed to call the police. But that was the idea. Zara made sure my bust was front and center, accentuated with a little extra tape and a few well-placed socks to give the impression I'm locked and loaded. God, I wish I had my gun.

"Have you seen Ambassador Repola?" he asks. "He's in the restaurant. I'm sure he'd love to say hello."

"Frankly, now that you're here, I don't give a shit about Ambassador Repola," I reply.

Fletch's eyes flash and he motions to the bartender for another. He's having a hard time restraining himself; that much is clear. But I can't forget about the two men seated near the hotel's entrance, both of their eyes on us, as hard as they're pretending otherwise. Fletch isn't stupid, he's not about to be caught alone anywhere, but that's something we've prepared for. It's taken Zara weeks of surveillance to figure out this man's routines. The two men seated about twenty feet from us are named Raphael and Augustus. Both from Italy, and both expert mercenaries trained in hand-to-hand combat. On a good day I'd have trouble taking one of them out, much less both. Which is why this has to go one way. It just so happens that way makes me want to puke.

"Not thirsty?" Fletch indicates to my drink, which I still haven't touched.

I make a show of examining him, hopefully giving him the impression I'm trying to imagine him with his clothes off. And while nothing could be further from the truth, I think I succeed when he gives me a wicked grin. "Alcohol dulls the senses. I'm not sure I want to miss anything." Still, to show that I'm a good sport about it, I take a quick sip of my drink. "Then again, it can also remove any...inhibitions."

"Are you asking me for something?" he says.

"I would never presume to ask," I reply. "I'm the kind of girl who *demands*."

That seems to almost send him into overdrive. Outside there is a loud horn and the sound of screeching tires. Everyone, including Fletch's two muscle boys turns at the sound of the commotion, giving me just enough time to tap the tiniest bit of white powder into his low ball. It dissolves immediately and by the time he turns back, I'm pretending like I've just been startled as well.

"I wish people would learn how to drive in this city," I say, taking another sip of my drink. "Fucking idiots."

Fletch takes his glass in hand, all his attention back on me. "Cheers to that. You should see Barcelona during a *football* match. Worst traffic of your life."

"Speaking of which, I understand you just purchased a new car," I say. I need to stretch this out a little. It won't do me any good if he's so revved up to jump me that he doesn't finish his drink.

"Ah, doing a little spying on me, huh? Naughty girl." He knocks the drink back just like the first.

"I just like to know who my friends are," I say, maintaining my coyness and looking away for a brief moment before locking eyes with him again. "It's what…one of only a hundred made?"

He nods. "A Pagani Huayra Roadster. Six years from concept to production. And a bargain at only three million."

I pretend to be impressed. "You'll have to take me for a ride sometime." Doing my best not to grit my teeth as I do, I place one hand on his thigh.

"I can take care of that right now," he growls back.

The stuff is in his system. Theo said it would only take a few minutes to take effect. I have no choice but to hope it works like everyone keeps assuring me it would. I'm not worried about Fletch; I can take care of him as long as he's on his own. But I need him to get away from his security for a while. "Yeah?" I ask, then quickly glance at the elevators. "Show me."

He produces a fifty from seemingly nowhere and drops it on the bar before taking my arm. His grip is strong, but not overpowering and nothing I couldn't turn back on him if I wished.

Out of the corner of my eye I notice his two guards stand, but he stops them, shaking his head. I don't even bother looking over, instead I keep my gaze on Fletch as he leads us to the elevators. My heart is pumping with the speed of a jackhammer. If we manage to make this elevator ride without me breaking something of his, I'll call it a success.

The doors open and he steps into the car, pulling me along with him. I act like I'm pretending to resist when every bone in my body is telling me to get out of here. How long until these drugs take effect?

Finally, I'm forced to shit or get off the pot and I step in after him. As soon as the doors are closed his mouth is on mine and his hands are all over me. My body reacts without me telling it to and stiffens, going completely rigid and I know I'm freezing up. Then I hear Zara's voice in my head:

*You are Emily* fucking *Slate. You have chased down child molesters, beaten literal serial killers, gone up against the worst organized crime has to offer. You can do this.*

I relax and allow Fletch to take the lead. His hands find their way up my dress and for a half second I think we might not make it to his hotel room. But then I feel one of his hands go slack and his body lurches forward as he pulls his mouth away from mine. He holds his hand to his head for a second.

"Are you okay?" I ask, breathless.

"Yeah," he says. "Just got a little dizzy for a second." Thank *God*.

The door dings for the seventh floor and I put my arm around him, though I can tell he's having more trouble than he's willing to admit. "Here, let me get you to your room. I'll make you more comfortable once we get there."

"Yeah," he replies. "Sounds...sounds good." By the time we reach his room he's stumbling. He presses his card to the room and the door opens into the dark space. I flip on the light, but I'm almost carrying him at this point. "I need...to call..."

"You said you'd take care of me," I say. "Or should I just do back downstairs?"

"No, no," he says. "I just..." But before he can finish, his entire body goes slack and he falls face first to the floor. I only just manage to get under him to keep him from breaking his nose on the wood floors.

I close the door behind us and stare at the man lying in front of me.

"Okay," I say to Zara. "I'm in."

## Chapter Two

"GOD, HE'S *HEAVY*," I say, pulling Fletch by his legs toward the bedroom. Thankfully, his absolutely massive hotel room features polished wood floors which make the job slightly easier.

"That was amazing! You absolutely nailed it! See, I told you you could do it," Zara says on the other end. "You got yourself all worked up for nothing."

"I think I have a few bruises from where he was trying to get under my dress so hard," I reply, grunting again as I pull him back. "Theo couldn't have had better timing with the horn. No one saw the powder."

"He's good like that," she replies.

"How am I supposed to get him on the bed?" I ask as I drag the man into his bedroom. "He has to weigh two hundred pounds."

"You'll figure something out. It'll give you something to do while I work. Do you see his computer anywhere?" Zara asks.

I take quick stock of the room. In my haste to get Fletch into the bedroom in the event someone happened to come by, I hadn't really paid much attention to the room. But as I look around, calling it a "room" would be a disservice.

We entered into a small entryway, which opens up into a large living space, complete with a long table, couch, four additional seats and a massive television, all of it framed on the opposite side by large picture windows looking out onto the city, one of which opens up to a balcony. The bedroom is off to the left, and it has its own primary bathroom attached. I flip on the light to the bathroom and am greeted with every fixture gilded in gold. It's like a leprechaun threw up. What is it with rich people needing to show off their wealth? If I were rich, the last thing I would want would be for anyone to know about it. That's how we're in this situation. If Fletch weren't such a show-off, we might not have even noticed him. But it was his penchant for showing off that put him right in Theo's sights, leading him to us.

I return to the bedroom and step over the splayed-out body on the floor, my heels clicking against the wood floor as I make my way into the other "wing" of the suite. Connected to the other side of the living space is another bedroom and an office, with yet another opulent bathroom. I'm so over the gold.

But my target is sitting right on the desk in the office, which also has a window looking out onto the city. "Bingo," I tell Zara, and fish around inside my clutch for the USB she gave me, along with a pair of gloves. The last thing I need to do is leave fingerprints for someone to find.

"Is the computer plugged in to anything?" she asks.

"Just a wall socket," I reply. "Why?"

"Making sure," she says. "Go ahead and connect the remote to any open port."

I pull on the gloves then remove the small rectangular device and plug it into the port on the side. All of a sudden, the monitor lights up and asks for a password. "It wants a password."

"Let me worry about that from here," she says. "You make sure to stage the scene."

I groan and head back into the bedroom, removing my shoes. If I'm going to lift this behemoth, I'm sure as hell not about to do it in six-inch heels.

Using a combination of the bedframe and some creative leverage, I finally manage to get Fletch up on the bed. He's still breathing, which is a good thing, but he's completely out. According to Theo, he shouldn't be awake for a few more hours. As I stare at the man on the bed and catch my breath, I can't help but want to reiterate that this job should be firmly within the realm of the CIA, though I've already been shot down three different times.

"Any luck?" I ask Zara.

"Working on it. How about you?"

"He's on the bed." I stare at his legs which are still off the end. "More or less."

"Open his pants."

"*What?*"

"Open his pants. He needs to think something happened," she says.

"I'm not touching *his pants*. Or anything else for that matter," I say, gathering my shoes and slipping them back on, despite how much my feet already ache. I'm going to have to take the stairs to get out of here without Fletch's men seeing me and the thought of descending seven flights on the balls of my feet isn't appealing. But then again walking down barefoot isn't much better.

"Em, you gotta. Otherwise he'll suspect something. But if you can—"

"Okay, okay, fine. But his underwear stays on." I grit my teeth as I tentatively reach for his belt. As I'm undoing the loops I hear Zara chuckling in the background. "Shut up."

"I would pay anything to see your face right now."

"Oh, you'll get to see it," I say, unbuttoning his pants and unzipping the zipper. He's wearing dark boxer briefs underneath. I pull his shirt up some and try to pull the pants down a bit. Hopefully he'll wake up in a fog and just think he passed out after the main event. Unfortunately, I can't burn this bridge entirely if we need to hit him up again in the future.

"How's the view?" she asks.

I roll my eyes.

"C'mon, aren't you a little bit curious? This might be your only chance."

"I think I'm good," I say. "If I expose any more I'll be too tempted to twist it off."

"You're no fun," she says. "Hey, I need you to do something. It's requiring a fingerprint scan. Can you bring the computer to him and press his index finger on the pad?"

I sigh and head back into the office, unhooking the computer and bringing it back into the bedroom. I press his finger to the pad and the computer unlocks.

"Thank you," she says, still chipper.

"I still say you should have just done this yourself." I head back into the office with the computer. "It would have been quicker. And your feet would be killing you instead of mine."

"Boo hoo. My name's Emily, I get to go to fancy hotels and dress up," Zara mocks on the other end.

"Yeah, and I hate it. This is your scene, not mine."

"That reminds me, save that dress. You're going to need it when you get back." I roll my eyes. I'm sure she's concocted something that will not only embarrass the hell out of me, put me in yet another uncomfortable situation. Then again, nothing could be much worse than this.

"Tell me what you're seeing on the screen."

As I plug the computer back in, I watch the screen. "It's a bunch of numbers, rolling in ten different segments. I think I have to stop them all on the correct number to gain access."

"That's a digital cypher. Damn, he's smarter than he looks. This is going to take a minute. Good thing you've got some time. Why not take a bath in that excessive tub while you wait?"

"I'm fine here," I grumble.

"Your loss," she replies. "See if he's got anything else interesting there. Maybe you'll get lucky."

I huff, stepping back from the computer. I check Fletch on the bed, he's still sound asleep.

I can't believe I'm even doing this CIA bullshit. I'm a field agent, one who is used to confronting a problem head on, not sneaking around, seducing men and breaking into their hotel rooms. Caruthers, though, is much more open than his predecessors on what types of operations we need to be running. He believes, and I tend to agree, that the FBI has been too myopic in the past, too steeped in tradition and structure. So if he's willing to work outside the box a little, I guess I need to be too. I just hope this operation bears fruit. But our intel on this guy has been solid. He's been involved in the sale of some high-end black-market information, some of which we believe is a threat to national security, even if we don't exactly know what the information is yet. We need to get a look at it first, to make sure, which is the reason for all the cloak and dagger. Once we know what he's doing and who his known associates are, I can have Fletch in an interrogation room where I'm much more comfortable to take him on. Let's see how smarmy he acts then.

As I wait for Zara to work her magic, I begin checking the rest of the room. The place is more than gaudy—unreasonably so.

I start by going through the drawers, finding little inside. Fletch travels light, preferring only the best rooms, but carrying little luggage. A small suitcase and a valise sit in the closet, but the suitcase only has clothes inside. The valise contains a few travel documents and not much else.

Dismayed, I sit back on my heels and stare at the snoring suit on the bed. As much as I'd like to deliver a gut punch to his stomach, I have to let him be.

"Hey, Em, we have a small problem," Zara says. I glance

up and return to the computer. The remote device is still working, and the cursor is moving quickly over the screen as Zara continues to operate it from six miles away. "Look at this."

The screen changes, and database of hundreds of documents pops up. "What am I looking at?"

"That's the question. Everything is encrypted, and without the key it's going to take me weeks, maybe longer to break through this stuff. I can copy it over, but we can't read any of it unless you happen to see an encryption algorithm anywhere."

"I don't even know what that looks like."

She pauses. "Screw it. I'll copy all this over and we can decrypt it later."

"And if it turns out to be nothing more than betting scores or restaurant menus?"

"Then we have wasted the Bureau's time," she replies. "But knowing this ass, I doubt that's the case." Fletch is a known information dealer, working as a middleman between nefarious organizations. Theo got a tip he was dealing in classified documents, which has been what this whole operation was about. We just don't know what *kind* of classified documents yet. Hence the need for all this subterfuge. If Zara can figure out what he's been holding, we can bring charges against him.

"Give me about two more minutes, then you can get out of there."

"Good, because my feet are about to fall off. How I ever let you convince me to wear these things—"

"Quit whining, you big baby," she chides. "It's only a couple of hours. You'll survive."

But as Zara finishes and I remove the remote from Fletch's computer, there's a knock at the door. "Mr. Fletch? Sir, are you all right?"

"What the hell are they doing here?" I ask in a hushed voice. "They're supposed to be downstairs."

"He might have some kind of timer where he's supposed to check in," Zara suggests. "But none of the surveillance suggested that."

The knock comes again, more urgent this time. "Sir, I need you to give me a verbal response that you're okay, otherwise we're coming in."

I glance around the room even though I already know there is no other way out.

Dammit, I knew this was a bad idea.

# Chapter Three

I'M TRAPPED on the seventh floor of one of the most expensive hotels in Washington, DC. with a passed-out traitor on the bed and his security ready to tear down the door.

And I'm in *heels*.

The hotel room may be made up of six different rooms, but there is only one entrance and exit to the main hallway. No other way out.

"Z, his security is at the door. I'm cut off," I say, a slight panic in my voice.

"What are you worried about?" she asks. "Just get undressed and get into bed with him," she says like it's the most natural thing in the world. "You are undercover, remember?"

"And if they decide to search me and find the earpiece and the hard drive?" I say. Not to mention I wouldn't get in bed with this pig if I had a gun to my head. Which I nearly do.

"Okay, hang on," she says.

This is why I got out of undercover work. It's too unpredictable. I got used to playing everything straight, to looking people in the eye and telling them exactly what I was about to do. But there is no explaining this away. If I'm caught, it's going to cause an international incident, and I'm pretty sure Caruthers isn't going to be very forgiving. He's been a good boss for the past eight months, but even he can't shield me from the wrath of a powerful foreign country.

One thing is for sure: the next time I see Theo, I'm going to *strangle* him. This was supposed to be a clean operation.

"Mr. Fletch, we're coming in," the guard on the other side of the door warns.

"Z..." I say with an impatient whine.

"I'm working on it," she says, matching my tone. "I can't access the fire suppression system. There's some kind of fire-wall in place."

*Dammit.* I chance a look at the bed, but immediately reject that option. Even if I could convincingly play a drunk mistress, I'm not sure I could go through with it. There has to be another way.

My eyes land on the door to the balcony. I curse under my breath. But given my options, this is about as good as it's going to get. As I hear them working on the lock of the door, I dash to the balcony, opening then closing the double doors behind me.

It's freezing and my skin goosepimples as soon as I'm outside. With little more than a thin dress to protect me against the cold, I'm not exactly prepared to stay out in thirty-five-degree weather for very long. Not only that, but the wind up here is gusty, making what I'm about to do even more dangerous.

"Em?" Zara asks in my ear. "What's going on? I've got you out on the balcony."

"Extreme measures," I say.

"Do *not* do what I think you're about to do," she says. "It's too dangerous. We'll find another way."

I press my back against the cold stone of the wall beside the door as I hear Fletch's security team make their way inside the room. No doubt they saw him come up with me, so they'll be wondering where I've gone and it won't take them long to check out here. I glance at the next balcony over. It's about six feet, give or take, but already my stomach is doing somersaults.

Pulling off my heels, I chuck them in the direction of the balcony, but the wind catches one of them and blows it askew where it falls the hundred and fifty feet to the ground below, landing beside a small fountain that has frozen over.

Well, Zara won't be happy about that.

The other problem is my clutch. What genius decided to design evening gowns to be as impractical as possible? No coverage for warmth, no pockets, and not even a strap where I can attach this damn thing. Grumbling, I toss the clutch to the next balcony, where thankfully it lands safely.

Still, my heart is pounding in my chest. There is a flurry of activity in the room behind me as Fletch's guards are searching everywhere, no doubt having already check the bathroom and found it empty.

I stare at the balcony. It's either this or face an inquiry at work and expose everything I've been working on for the past four weeks. I close my eyes, take a deep breath, and climb up on the concrete railing for the balcony. Before I can talk myself out of it, I jump with all the force my shivering legs can muster.

I see the patio in my mind's eye, and I see myself landing there, but as I fly through the air, it seems like it's taking forever for me to get anywhere. Part of me thinks I've misjudged it, that the wind will catch my dress and whip me out into nothingness, just like my shoe.

But then I hit the balcony. It's not a pretty landing; my upper chest strikes the concrete and I feel it tear the dress as I struggle to pull myself up. Thankfully, I've kept up with my pull-ups and I manage to pull myself onto the balcony with ease, though it shreds the dress in the process.

As soon as I recover, I can hear the guards opening the doors to Fletch's patio. I scramble and grab my clutch and remaining shoe and flatten myself up against the alcove of the balcony, breathing hard. The cold doesn't seem to be bothering me anymore. I listen closely as they shuffle around out there, but finally I hear the patio doors close again.

"Em, what just happened?" Zara asks.

"I'll tell you when I see you," I whisper and pad my way to the doors of this patio. Of course, they're locked from the inside and I don't see any lights on in the room they belong to. I crack open my clutch again, and with shaking hands, I go to work on the lock with a lockpick set, managing it after only a few minutes.

As soon as I'm in the warm room I take a sharp breath, not realizing just how cold I had been. My naked feet are practically blue. The room isn't occupied, but looks to be as large as Fletch's along with all the amenities. I run to the bathroom and start the tub, filling it with warm water before placing my feet inside. For a second nothing happens, but then the pins and needles start and it's like little spiders crawling up the inside of my legs. At least I'll keep all of my toes.

As soon as I'm warmed up, I take a look at myself in the mirror. My dress is completely shredded from my little stunt, and I'm still missing a shoe. I head to the closet and pull out one of the two large fluffy robes inside, along with the matching slippers. *This* is more like it. The robe even has a large enough pocket for my clutch.

"I'm going to need an extraction," I mutter to Zara as I wrap the robe around me, pulling the belt tight.

"Where?" she asks.

"Front entrance. As soon as you can manage it." I pull the pins from my hair and let it fall down before pitching forward and dunking it in the tub. I then wring it out and wrap another towel around my head. A minute and a few makeup wipes later, and I've removed all the color from my face.

"Theo is on the way," Zara says. "He'll be there in five."

"Good," I say as I check my reflection now. Without all the accents, I look like just a normal hotel guest, which is the whole point.

Fluffy slippers and warm robe on, I make my way to the door and take a second to control my breathing. I'm just another guest on her way to the spa. I open the door and immediately I see a group of men in dark suits standing around Fletch's door, deep in discussions. They look up as I exit my room, but I don't pay them any attention. Instead, I close the door and walk towards them, acting like I don't have a care in the world.

"Excuse me," I say softly as I pass by. As expected, men rarely pay attention to a woman without any makeup. From their perspective, I don't look anything like the bombshell that brought Fletch up to his room earlier. And thanks to the towel, they can't even tell what color my hair is. I manage to make it in the elevator without a word from any of them.

Moments later I'm downstairs, waiting patiently on my ride. A few of the hotel staff give me curt nods as they pass while I pretend to look at the spa services near the front desk. Finally, Zara signals that Theo is in the meeting spot and I head out one of the entrances. Nearby is the frozen fountain where my shoe fell and it remains, halfway propped up beside the stone. I bend down and snatch it quickly as I make my way to Theo's SUV and hop inside before anyone from the hotel can say anything.

Once inside, Theo turns in the driver's seat, giving me a rueful smile. "Not exactly to plan?"

I open my robe, showing him the shredded dress. "Not exactly."

"Oh love," he says. "She isn't going to be happy about this."

"Tell me about it."

# Chapter Four

"I JUST DON'T SEE how you manage to shred a two-thousand-dollar dress," Zara says as I hand over the ruined garment. Theo is standing off to the side, leaning against the doorway with his trademark smirk and too much of a twinkle in his eye. He's a little too pleased with the chaos in front of him, which is just another reason why I don't fully trust him. But Zara is my best friend, and I remind myself I need to be supportive. She is head over heels for this guy, despite his shady background, and I can't forget he's handed us some of our biggest wins over the past six months.

"I did the best I could," I say, placing the high heels next to it. "At least I recovered the shoe."

Zara sighs. "How am I going to explain this to Hephner? I promised her we'd return it in pristine condition."

"Just tell her the truth. Shit happens in the field. It isn't like the FBI is hurting for money," Theo says nonchalantly.

My mind zaps back to all those budget meetings when I was trying out the job of SSA. Of how much emphasis was put on keeping the spending under control. Apparently, the new administration is a stickler about spending and wants to try and balance the budget before they leave office in a few years. Best of luck with that.

"I just hope it wasn't for nothing," Zara says, turning back to her computer. She's been working on decrypting the files since I came back, but just like she thought, it's going to take time. And it's not something she can do on her own.

"Trust me, it will be worth it," Theo says, heading over and rubbing her shoulders as she works.

"And why couldn't your contact just tell us what was on there?" I ask.

"Because they didn't know," he replies. "They just said you'd be interested."

I suppress the urge to confront him. But my face must say it all because he playfully cocks his head at me. "They've never let me down before. Whatever this is, it'll be worth it."

Considering I almost just died, it better be. "Uh-huh." Theo strikes me as the kind of person who always keeps something extra in his back pocket for emergencies. And given we're treating him as an independent contractor instead of a member of a fellow service overseas, I wouldn't blame him. He doesn't have the protection of the crown or anyone else. He's out on his own.

I grumble, heading out of the motel room to get something from the vending machine and pass by without looking at him. This whole relationship started at our homecoming, when he left that damn "present" on my countertop after my aunt had been captured. Little did I know that it would be the intro to half a dozen different operations together.

I didn't even think about opening it until days later, and when I did, all I found was a ring with a giant diamond inside. Despite how it looked, he wasn't proposing, not even close. The ring had come from a widower who had recently passed away, passed down to her son. But when the son went to sell it, it turned out the diamond had been a missing piece of evidence in a decade's old murder case: the murder of a young woman back in the seventies. It ended up being the crucial piece in the case that led back to the widower's husband, who had apparently been killing off young girls before and while he was married. Zara and I managed to connect four different murders to him by the time it was all said and done. And even though he was already dead, giving those grieving families relief was more than worth it.

Ever since then, it's like Theo has been a constant supply of new information. Some of it relevant, some of it worthless, and some of it what I would call suspicious. How he gets his information is somewhat questionable and we all know it. And normally I wouldn't keep my mouth shut about such things, but I won't do that to Zara. She has to be the one to confront him. Until then, I close my trap and try not to think about it.

"Bring me something good?" Theo asks as I return from the vending machine with a bag of chips in my hand.

"Sure," I say, holding up the bag in one hand. "These are for me, and these…" I hold up the other hand, empty. "Are for you."

"Aw, don't be like 'at," he says, his accent growing thicker. "Give a fella a break."

"Get it yourself, you know where the machine is." I head past him back into the room where Zara has set up.

"Em, this…I'm not going to be able to get through any of this before we make our report." She's still compiling the information. "We need to take it to Caruthers."

I open the bag of chips and pop one into my mouth, crunching loudly so Theo can hear. "At least there's some good news. I can't do heels for one more day. But let's make it tomorrow. I need to get back home and get some sleep."

She turns back to me, stealing a chip from the bag. "Right. Tomorrow."

∾

Before I even make it halfway up the driveway, I spot them. Staring at me, like a pair of assassins, their eyes glinting in the low light. They're watching my every move closely, each step as if it will be my last. I pause for a moment, returning the heavy stare and I see one of them flinch. That's all it takes. Both figures disappear from the upstairs window and moments later I hear the commotion behind the door. I slip my key in the lock, and before I can even get the door open, I am assaulted by two snouts, both of them vying to be the first to get to me.

"Hey there boys," I coo, setting my bag to the side and leaving the keys in the door as both dogs circle me, sniffing up and down as both their butts wiggle with excitement. Timber is practically shaking as he always does, but Rocky is a little more reserved. He's still extremely happy if his wagging tail is any indication, but he's not as fervent as Timber. Like Timber, he's something of a rescue.

Eight months ago, just as Liam and I had been toying with the possibility of another dog, we heard of the tragedy. A K-9 cop shot in the line of duty, leaving his "partner" without a handler. After some back and forth, we agreed to take Rocky in and retire him from any further police work. He's strictly a house dog now. And while his transition was a little rough in the beginning, he warmed to us eventually. I think Timber helped with that a lot. Thankfully they get along great.

"I missed you guys," I say to both of them as I pull myself inside, making sure to grab my keys before leaving them in the lock again. Liam has already caught me on more than one occasion; he says I'm slipping. But I just say that I'm getting comfortable.

On the counter sits a handwritten note.

*Both did great. Gave them an extra treat after dinner. -Tess.*

Liam must have had to work late and called Tess to come in and feed the boys for dinner.

"You got an extra treat?" I ask absently as I leave all my

stuff on the counter and head into the kitchen for some water. I haven't been home in three days, and I'm looking forward to getting into something comfortable and just lying on the couch for a few minutes. Both dogs follow me into the kitchen, no doubt hoping to wear down my resolve. And lucky for them, after the past few days, my willpower is just about shot. I'm just happy to see them both. "Where's your dad, huh?" I ask. Our job can be unpredictable, so it's not unusual for us to run long hours, which was one of the reasons we hired Tess to begin with. Just so we had someone on call in case we couldn't get home to feed them or take them out.

I check the time on the microwave. It's already ten, though it feels closer to midnight. The debrief with Zara and Theo took longer than usual, not to mention I had to fill out the last of my reports for the undercover job. I'll palaver with Caruthers in the morning and hopefully we'll get clearance to move on Fletch so I don't have to do any of this shit anymore. I forgot just how hard undercover work was, and I have no desire to do anymore if I can help it.

There's no text or call from Liam to let me know when to expect him home. Of course, I didn't text him; so he probably doesn't expect me back tonight either. Being out of the loop for a while, I have no idea what job he could be working right now. He might not have time to come back home at all. I type out a quick text to let him know I'm back home and to call when he can.

"C'mon, let's go out," I tell the boys. They follow me to the door and I let them out into the backyard. They're both anxious to get out of the house and spend a good five minutes just running the perimeter of the fence, despite the chill in the air. After they do their business, I get them back into the house and turn on the fake fire. Despite our schedules, Liam and I have spent the better part of half a year working to make this place a home. I never put this much effort into my apartment, and Matt and I were never together enough for us to do any actual homemaking. We would just pass in the day or night, barely ever home. Timber was the real head of that household.

But life with Liam has been completely different. We've both made an effort to be together as much as we can, and to make this house something of our own. I think everything we've been through has made us closer in many ways. They say shared trauma can do that. And after the near implosion at the FBI and then the debacle with my aunt, both of us were happy to settle into a routine. One which means going to antique stores or baseball games on the weekends, or meeting up with Zara and Theo, or even Elliott and Nadia for some social event or another. It's a far cry from the solitude I'd known for so long and probably what many people would consider the "perfect" life.

Still, I can't help but get a feeling that something is...off. I can't explain it and I haven't said anything to Liam about it. God knows that man has had more patience with me than I deserve, especially after I left to go after my aunt and didn't tell him or anyone else. I thought we might not have made it after that, but he never wavered. Anyone else in their right mind would have left me right there on the porch. Not Liam. It's like we're attached in some way.

I shake my head, knocking the thoughts from my head. I do that too often—look for drama that isn't really there. I'm trying to make up problems that don't exist. Why can't I just be happy with the way things are?

After another snack, Timber and Rocky settle together on the rug in front of the fake fire while I head upstairs to the bedroom to unpack, not that I have much. Zara took all my undercover clothes back, presumably to try and explain to the department head how we ruined some expensive FBI property. But I think given the outcome, the ends will justify the means. And Caruthers isn't a stickler for that kind of thing anyway. He's more results driven.

Just as I'm about settle down into a warm bath, anxious to wash the smell of perfume and concrete off me, I hear the door and the dogs' paws skittering across the wood floors downstairs.

"Hey," Liam yells up the stairs.

"Hey," I call back, already comforted by the sound of his voice. I didn't realize how much I'd missed it the past few days. There's only so much of Theo's cheeky attitude that I can take at once. Liam climbs the stairs with the pups close behind and I meet him in the hallway.

"You're home," he says, and I swear he's looking at me like he hasn't seen me in a month.

"We finished up this evening," I say. "I only had—" But before I can finish, I find myself in his arms with his lips on mine. I feel Timber pass by on one side and Rocky on the other as they head to the bedroom. They already know where this is going.

Guess I'm not getting a bath after all.

## Chapter Five

I WAKE up early with Liam sprawled out beside me and the dogs at the bottom of the bed. It was a good thing we upgraded to a king, otherwise there wouldn't be enough room for everyone. It was tight when it was just Timber. But with all four of us there was no way. So far it seems to have worked out well.

"Hey," Liam whispers when he feels me stirring. He turns over and brushes some of the hair out of my eyes.

"Hey," I reply. "I missed you."

"I could tell," he says. "You guys run into any trouble?"

I think back to me jumping a six-foot gap a hundred and fifty feet in the air. He probably doesn't need to know about that.

"Nothing I couldn't handle."

He smiles, not taking his eyes off me. I'm struck by how different the experience is to how Fletch looked at me. His eyes were lecherous, like I was a piece of meat to be devoured. But Liam has never been anything but kind. In every way imaginable.

"I need a shower," I say.

"You do have a distinct odor," he replies.

I scoff. "Let me guess. Stripper mixed with hot garbage."

"I didn't want to say anything." He grins.

I give him a playful smack. "Thanks." This causes the dogs to stir.

"You take a shower; I'll get breakfast started."

"Thank God," I groan with pleasure. Liam has always been an excellent cook and after subsisting on little more than fast food the past few days, I'm anxious for something substantial and not full of salt.

Liam takes the pups out, and by the time I'm out of the shower and halfway dressed, I can smell the waffles from downstairs. I hurry up and I'm down the stairs just in time to see him extract waffles as big as my head. Both dogs are watching him, drooling, and I must admit to feeling a similar sensation.

"Feel better?" he asks.

Let's see, I'm not in a slinky dress, or heels sharp enough to impale someone through the heart and I only have a bare amount of makeup on. "Yep. Much."

"How is the lecherous bastard?"

I grab a cup and start making coffee as he finishes up. "Handsy-er than I would have liked, but I took care of it."

"Let me guess, broke both his thumbs? Left him bleeding in the street?"

"If I only I'd had the clearance." Even though we're generally not supposed to talk about our cases, anyone who knows us knows Liam and I don't keep secrets from each other. That has been one of our big rules. He's known everything about the op from day one. "What about you? Late nights?"

He nods. "Yeah, I've been pulling surveillance shifts with Elliott. We're looking at what could be a counterfeiting operation. But mostly we're just sitting in the car, waiting to see if anyone pops their head out. I had to hire Tess for a few extra sessions, at least until I'm back on a regular schedule."

"No, that's what she's there for," I say, filling my mug. "I'd rather her come by than not."

He plates the waffles and throws a couple of small pieces to the pups before setting them on the table. Somehow, he's managed to make fresh preserves for toppings, along with thick slabs of butter. "This is going to put me on the treadmill for six hours."

He smiles. "There are other kinds of workouts."

I laugh. "Yeah, I've seen your handiwork. And I'd take you up on it again if I knew it wasn't going to make both of us late."

"I'm sure we can make up for it this weekend," he says.

I give him a smirk. He's not usually this frisky, but then again, I have been away for a while. "We'll see."

"Ouch," he replies, but there's a laugh in his voice. "Sidelined."

As I shovel the waffle in my mouth, I want to stop and savor it, but it's just so damn good I can't help myself. I feel like I haven't eaten real food in days. I'm not proud of it, but I manage to clean the plate in under two minutes. I'll regret that later, but that's a problem for future Emily. Present Emily is very much satisfied.

"Good?" he asks.

"Mm-hmm," I say, patting my stomach. "I'm going to tell Caruthers today I can't have any more long-term assignments. If I don't get breakfast like this every day from now on, I won't survive."

Liam chuckles. "I'm glad it was to your liking."

We finish and I help him clean up. And even though the food was amazing, my mind drifts and I find him tapping my hip. "What's up?"

"What? Nothing. Just thinking about that waffle some more."

"Right." The sarcasm in his voice is unmistakable. "What's *really* going on?"

I turn around and face him, defiant as ever. "Who says something has to be going on?"

"Because I know you," he says, wrapping his arms around my hips and pulling me close to him. "I know when you're distracted. And I don't think it's the case."

I have to fight to hide a smile. "How do you do that?"

"Do what?"

"Know what I'm thinking?"

He taps one temple with his finger. "I'm a keen student of observation. Now out with it."

"Really, it's nothing."

He levels his gaze at me, his face going serious. "If it was nothing, it wouldn't be occupying so much of your brain."

I let out a breath and work my way out of his grip, going to the end of the counter to grab my mug of coffee. "It's stupid. Champagne problem."

"Emily *Slate*. Out with it."

"*Fine*. I just feel...listless lately."

He screws up his face. "Listless?"

"I don't know how to describe it. It's like...I don't know which direction my life is going in anymore. Ever since I turned down the promotion." When I first joined the FBI, there had been a plan in place. A structured, yet difficult path ahead of me. Being suspended and almost losing my job put a crimp in that plan, but when Janice unexpectedly promoted me, I thought I was getting everything I wanted. Only to find out I hated it. And now that I'm back doing field work, I feel like I've let something slip through my fingers.

"That was almost nine months ago," Liam reminds me. "And you're just starting to feel this way now?"

"No," I admit. "It's just gotten worse, little by little. At first I thought it would go away. But I just feel like I've lost my purpose."

"Even though you hated the job." He joins me at the end

of the counter. "Why make yourself miserable just because you *think* it's the right thing to do?"

"Because maybe it would have led to something I *did* like to do, and now I've closed that door. If I can't advance in my career anymore, what am I even doing?"

"I think you're thinking about it too hard," he says, taking a sip from his own mug. "Being hard on yourself is one of your favorite past times."

"Ha, ha," I deadpan. "Thank you, Dr. Frost."

"Maybe you should talk with him about it," Liam suggests.

"I tried. But he wasn't very much help. Apparently, I'm the kind of person who is motivated by upward movement. And to get out of that mindset would require rewiring my brain."

"Seems kind of extreme," he replies.

"I just…I don't want to be wasting my time."

"Are you kidding me? Em…" Liam comes around and wraps me in a hug. "You have made a difference in so many people's lives. How could that ever be a waste of time?"

I know he means well, but Liam doesn't understand. He's never once talked about moving up in the organization. I don't think it plagues him like it plagues me. But he's trying to help, and that's what's important. "I guess. Thanks," I say.

"Listen, you can always talk to someone other than Frost."

"No, I'll be okay. Thanks, though. C'mon. We need to get moving. I have an appointment first thing with Caruthers on this Fletch case."

We finish cleaning up, make sure the dogs have chew bones and go outside one more time before heading back to the office. But the whole way, I can't quit thinking about why this is bothering me so much. I got exactly what I wanted.

So why don't I feel satisfied?

∽

"I WISH YOU HAD MORE."

Zara and I are sitting in Caruthers's—my former—office, as he reads over our reports from last night. She and I keep exchanging glances as he looks over the information. Caruthers isn't someone who I would describe as verbose. Whenever he finally does say something, you listen.

"We still believe the intel will be good," Zara says. "There's something there, we just need to crack the encryption."

Caruthers arches an eyebrow before going back to reading the reports. Like me, he shares a healthy skepticism about Zara's boyfriend, though he can be more transparent about it. "Mr. Arquenest has proven his value, there is no question about that. But this isn't what I'd call a slam-dunk."

"Fletch is a known information dealer, whatever the intel happens to be, I'm sure we can put it to good use," I say.

Caruthers slides his eyes from me to Zara, then returns to the reports, reading them in silence for another solid five minutes before finally stacking the papers on his desk and slipping them into a manilla folder. He puts the folder into the drawer and addresses us. "I was hesitant about this operation from the beginning, especially about sidelining two of my best so they could work on it. Still, even though I don't always understand them, I trust your instincts." Even sitting, Caruthers is a tall man. He towers over most of the people in the office, thin and lanky. He also sports a shock of white hair, combed neatly to the side. Before becoming our boss, he used to work in Intelligence with Zara, so he knows the seriousness of something like this. Out of all the bosses I've had, he's been the most even-keeled. He operates without the ego of Wallace or the impatience of Janice. But one thing he is not is soft in his delivery.

"Did Mr. Arquenest give up his source?"

Zara seems to be trying not to squirm in her chair. "No. He just said he was given the information from an old friend in MI6 intelligence. Someone who still knows all the players."

"Ah," Caruthers says, placing one hand on top of the other on his desk. "And he insists we can't know the identity of this person."

"Not without compromising their security," she says. Ever since Theo became a source of information for the Bureau, Caruthers has been decidedly wary about it. But for the time being, he's helping the Bureau. Which means we have no choice but to keep operating in good faith.

"Sorry to be the bearer of bad news," Zara says.

"Don't misunderstand me. This is excellent work," he replies. "It's a complex situation. In the meantime, I want you to refocus your efforts on breaking that encryption. I'll see if we can't spare you some help, but we're stretched thin at the moment."

Zara exchanges a look with me. "Sure, but Em has—"

He taps the top of his desk with his fingers. "I'll need Agent Slate for something else." The room descends into silence as Zara and I look at each other. Just as well. I'm crap with computer stuff anyway and would probably only slow her down. She gives me a pitying look that says "good luck" before heading back out. Ever since her own experience with undercover work, Zara has been splitting her time between field work and Intelligence. I think this case may have dredged up some bad memories for her, which is why she's probably happy to sit in a room with a computer all day long. But ever since Theo has become something of an informant for the FBI, she has been working harder than ever to make sure everything surrounding that relationship goes as smoothly as possible. I know she wants this to work, badly, and she's been putting in a lot of overtime to ensure that happens.

"What's going on?" I ask after Zara has closed the door.

Caruthers pulls a laptop out from another drawer and opens it up, tapping at a few keys before spinning the screen to face me. I'm met with the faces of three different women, all races and colors. As best I can tell, there isn't a common theme between them, other than two X chromosomes.

"Are you familiar with any of these women?"

"Should I be?"

"Vicki Tolluse, Marian Stamper and Amy Van Allen. They've all gone missing on the island of St. Solomon in the past ten days," he replies.

"Kidnapping?" I ask.

"Unknown. There has been no contact with the abductors —if that's what's happened. No ransom notes left. Nothing of any kind. They're just…gone."

"Okay," I say. "What does that have to do with us?"

"The local police don't seem to be working very hard to find these women. All three of them are US citizens, and one is a local on the island." He turns the computer back to him.

"Has the local government asked for help?" St. Solomon is right in the Caribbean chain and is one of the top tourist destinations for the East Coast, though I've never been before.

He eyes me. "No. But because it's still US soil, we have jurisdiction," he says. "And given your recent successes in undercover work and your penchant for cases like this, I thought it would be a good fit. You managed to get close to Mr. Fletch. I want to see if you can do it again."

"Wait, you want me to go in there, undercover?" I ask.

"Two of the three women have disappeared from some local gathering. One from a crowded open-air grocery store, and one from a hotel bar. The other was apparently abducted from her vacation home on the island. I want you down there to figure out what's happening before things get any worse and find these women." He pauses and I wait for him to continue. Clearly there is something else on the tip of his tongue. "There is a man on the island named Rafe Connor. He's a real estate mogul based out of Europe. One of the missing women, Vicki Tolluse, is an ex-employee of his, and I believe he will be the best source of information for you. Or at the very least, provide you with a starting point. However, as you know, the wealthy aren't always the most... forthcoming with law enforcement. I believe going in undercover would give you the best chance of success to gather intel from Mr. Connor. You're to present yourself as a socialite, much like you have been with Mr. Fletch. You can even use the same cover if you wish, considering it's established."

And here I thought I was done with all of that. "Is that really necessary? Wouldn't I have more luck going in to work with the local police?"

"All my attempts at professional inquiries have gone unanswered. Whether that's intentional or not I don't know, but it doesn't leave me with a lot of hope." He closes the laptop, tapping the top. "I was able to find the preliminary reports by concerned parties. Nothing else." I can think of a few reasons why the local police wouldn't want to shine a light on something like this. They wouldn't want a copycat coming in and muddling the investigation. And getting wind to the media could throw a wrench in things as well.

"Have you spoken with anyone there?" I ask. "Maybe they have a strategy." He crosses his brows, and for the second time, I see something else on the tip of his tongue. "What is it?"

He sighs and I see some of that hard façade melt away. "I admit, I have a personal stake in this. Vicki Tolluse is the ex-wife of a former colleague of mine. From my life before the FBI. He's been in constant contact with the island police and they've frozen him out. So, he reached out to see if I could help. It wasn't until I looked further that I found she wasn't the only one."

"None of this information is public?" I ask.

"No, but there are rumors circling. I want you to go down there and see if you can't get a handle on things. And for the time being, I think it's best if you keep the fact that you're an

FBI Agent a secret from everyone. If the police are intentionally trying to bury these cases, I need you to find out why."

"We could always send in a full contingent," I say. "Show them we mean business."

"And risk everything seizing up," he replies. "No. Going in under the radar is your best chance for success."

My heart sinks a little as I realize Liam and I won't get that weekend together after all. This isn't the kind of job I can wrap up in forty-eight hours, not unless I'm incredibly lucky. Though, there are worse places to end up. It will be a nice change of scenery, especially this time of year. Even though I'm not a big summer weather person, there's something about a tropical island that makes me want to change my mind. Maybe it's something we can do together.

"Should I bring some backup?" I ask. "Agent Coll—"

"—will stay here and continue working on his caseload," Caruthers says. "You can handle this one by yourself. This Connor person shouldn't be difficult to find. Get the lay of the land, find out what's happening, and then I can requisition additional resources. Miami has a field office and can have someone down there to you in an hour if you determine it's necessary."

While I wish Liam could join me, I understand his position. Flying down to a tropical island for a few days with my boyfriend would be downright magical, but I refrain from vocalizing my protestations. He's right, this is something that I need to take care of on my own, which would be difficult if Liam was there. I'd be too distracted all the time. Though I don't revel in the thought of going undercover again. At least I won't need to craft a brand-new persona.

I stand, straightening my jacket. "I can be on a plane first thing in the morning."

He nods. "Good. Best of luck down there."

## Chapter Six

THE OCEAN SPARKLES with the brilliance of a million diamonds as the plane banks and lines itself up with the airstrip in the distance. I get a perfect view of the lush island as we descend in the clear blue sky. It was thirty-four degrees when I left Washington, DC. this morning. When we land, it should be closer to eighty. I'm looking forward to a little bit of summer climate during the dead of winter.

The island of St. Solomon is an oasis in an endless sea of blue, with a few other smaller islands off to the east. Most of the island is a national park and thus hasn't been developed in any way. As far as I know, the other islands are privately owned, so they will maybe have one or two residences on them, but otherwise remain untouched. The point is this place is *remote*. There are no big box stores here, no corner convenience pharmacies. I had to make sure I had doubles of everything I might need because I can't just run to the nearest market and pick something up if I forgot it.

But I think that's the allure of a place like this. As the wheels touch down, I spot a smattering of small, white buildings just outside the airport. They pop up out of the lush green of the hills like mushrooms growing in a field of grass.

Ten minutes later, I'm walking on the tarmac with my bag, feeling the sun on my face and the breeze in my hair. It's almost too easy to forget why I'm here. And while I would normally be wearing my suit, since I'm undercover, I've had to opt for more casual wear which is basically just a tank top and jeans, though I think I'll probably have to change at the hotel. It's a little too warm for long pants.

Words can't describe just how pissed Zara was that she wouldn't be able to accompany me. She would be in her element here, but Caruthers was adamant she stay and work on the Fletch case. Given Caruthers and Zara have a good working history, I'm surprised she didn't try to ply him to get him to change his mind. Then again, maybe she did and it just didn't work. Caruthers isn't the kind of boss who can be swayed easily.

I stop, close my eyes and breathe in, relishing the salty air. I can't help but feel some of my stress melt away. Maybe there is something ingrained in humans that responds to this kind of climate, something that just makes us relax and want to kick back. Then again, maybe it's because it's been so long since I've had anything resembling a real vacation. Maybe my body is just starved for something other than the East Coast weather.

The airport is small with only five gates, one of which is outside. It's a stark contrast to the bustling atmosphere of Dulles. It's like even the airport is on vacation here. As I glance up to the departures and arrivals board, I see there's only five flights today. Looking around, I spot crispy families who have taken advantage of the sun before heading back to winter or people who are just arriving, ready to soak up some of the beautiful weather. I think this is the first airport where I haven't experienced at least some form of anxiety.

Though, as I make my way through the breezeway and past the security checkpoint, I feel eyes on me. Not wanting to draw attention to myself, I check my peripherals, then pretend to stop and get something out of my bag as I check behind me. But there's no one there. No one paying me any attention, at least.

Unfortunately, my experiences with being surveilled has made me somewhat jumpy. Sometimes I'll still feel Camille looking over my shoulder, or my aunt keeping an eye on me from afar. But I have to remind my stupid brain that those days are behind me. Camille is dead. The Organization is dismantled. And my aunt is in jail. Even though it's not why I'm here, I need to take this opportunity to relax a little.

At least, that's what Dr. Frost would say.

On the other side of the airport is a parking area and a place where I can hail a cab. It doesn't look like rideshares exist here, which isn't surprising. I hail one down and slip in the back. The driver gives me a nod but doesn't ask my destination, instead waiting for instruction from me.

"Grand Solomon Hotel, please," I say. He nods again and flips the meter as he pulls out. The drive winds around to the main road and he pulls on the street after barely looking, because there is no traffic to speak of. Unlike back home, the roads aren't clogged with cars trying to get in and out of the airport. Instead, it's just open road as he heads around the bends of the island until we begin to climb in elevation.

"First time?" the driver finally asks as we crest a hill, giving us a gorgeous view of the Atlantic Ocean as far as I can see. I also catch sight of Queen's Bay ahead, the only city on the island.

I have to keep myself from audibly gasping as it is nothing short of stunning. But I think he can probably tell from the look on my face. "I've been meaning to visit for years. Just never had the chance."

"Here for business or pleasure?" he asks.

"Both," I say. "Hopefully the business part goes quickly."

I'm keeping my undercover persona of Emily Agostini, a business executive with Thompson Intermodal who is visiting the island on vacation—a nice getaway from the stress of the big city.

But really I'm here for one reason only. And that is to intercept my "target" and hopefully squeeze him for some information. Rafe Connor is not a full-time resident of the island, but he has been staying here for the past two months, at the Grand Solomon. Before I left, I did a full background on him. He was born in Boston, but he moved to Spain in the early 2000's with his family. From there he built a thriving real estate empire that he's been aggressively expanding for the past five years. He was married, but his wife passed away about eight months ago, which could make things complicated. Then again, it might just make my job easier. Though I'm getting really sick of needing to use my looks to ply men.

My plan is to locate him, draw him in, and then start working him and his inner circle. As an employee of *Thompson Intermodal*, I have a compelling reason to be hobnobbing with these people: my "company" helps businesses expand into global conglomerates. And if there's one thing rich people love, it's the opportunity to get richer.

While I would normally ask the cab driver about the missing women—cab drivers hear everything—it wouldn't fit my character, so I stay silent. Ms. Agostini has no idea about any missing women, nor would it interest her. And the last thing I need to do is sabotage myself before I get started.

We descend the hill again and start to come into town, the houses becoming more and more frequent as we go. Eventually there's no space between them at all and they begin to stack on top of one another, like building blocks set up by a giant child. What few yards I see either have dogs, chickens, or a mix of both.

When we arrive at the hotel, I'm struck by its grandeur. The entire building is white, with peach accents along the roof. It's about seven stories tall, by far the largest building I've seen so far, and sits on a large parcel of property, big enough that the cabbie pulls around to the back where a large turn-around is full of other cars dropping off guests. The front of the hotel faces the water, and it looks to feature a large recreation area complete with pools and bars that sit right on the beach.

The cabbie pulls to a stop, and I get out and grab my bag before he can. Still, I tip him well before heading into the open-air lobby, which is accessible by large wooden doors with slats all the way down. The doors have to be fifteen or twenty feet tall, leading into an absolutely massive atrium inside. The entire place is filled with light, and there are plants everywhere. In the middle of the sunken lobby is a freshwater pond, full of fish and surrounded by plants and flowers. A light breeze blows through the lobby, and large fans overhead spin at a lazy pace.

It would be easy for anyone to lose themselves here. I imagine that is part of the idea—for people to forget all their troubles when they arrive. Everything about this place is designed to make you forget the outside world exists. Which is why they never put prices on the menus. Money doesn't exist again until you get home.

I spot the check-in desk and head over, trying to get a sense of the clientele here. Most are wearing breezy clothes, or coverups of beachwear. Gone are the stuffy suits of DC. Men have on straw hats and women wear long, flowy dresses that nearly reach the floor. And *everyone* is smiling.

"Good afternoon, miss," the man at the counter says. "Checking in?"

"Yes, Agostini," I tell him, slipping him my manufactured ID.

"Ms. Agostini, yes, of course. Your room is ready for you, and I see we have a card here on file for incidentals, is that right?"

"Yes," I say, though I don't plan on using any *incidentals*. This place is already costing the FBI enough as it is.

"As a thank you for staying with us, we've left a gift in your room," the clerk says, smiling. "And we'd also like to let you know our concierge is available at your service, twenty-four seven."

"Thank you," I say. "That's very generous."

He hands my ID back to me. "We like to treat our special clients well. Is there anything else you need?"

"That'll be all, thank you." This place certainly is high class. *Z...what have you gotten me into here?*

"Your room number is 612. Here is your key." He hands me a metal card, which is much sturdier than the "keys" I'm used to in regular hotels. "Do you need baggage service?"

"Thanks, but I packed light," I say, slipping the key into my pocket.

"Very good. We hope you enjoy your stay with us." He smiles as I thank him and head to the elevators, which are directly across from the check-in desk. I do another quick sweep of the lobby for my target, but he's nowhere to be found. As I take the elevator up, I can't help but anticipate what might be awaiting me in room six-twelve. Emily Agostini is a wealthy world-traveler. I can only assume Zara set up my hotel room to reflect that.

But when I reach the room and open the door with the metal key, even I could not be prepared for what's inside. It has to be the largest hotel room I've ever stayed in, including Fletch's. There is a living room, which attaches to an adjacent bedroom. Both are accented to the nines with ornate and opulent décor. The unobstructed views of the ocean put Fletch's room to shame.

"Guess it's time to join the ranks of the rich and famous," I say, setting my stuff in the hallway.

In the middle of the table in the living room is a large bouquet of flowers, as well as a large welcome basket full of local fruits, snacks, wine and even some cheese. The card says it is all from the hotel, hoping I'll enjoy my stay.

With amenities like this, how could I not?

I just can't wait to see how Zara explains this one to the budget committee.

# Chapter Seven

IT DOESN'T TAKE LONG to get unpacked. I told the clerk at the check-in the truth. All I brought were a couple of changes of clothes and anything I would need to maintain my cover. At the same time, I'm not about to be sloppy. It takes me a minute, but I find one of the vents that supplies the suite with cool air. Using a tool from my wash kit, I unscrew one side and tilt it up, placing my badge, phone, and my real ID inside. I wanted to bring my gun, but that would have meant clearing it with the FAA, and Caruthers was adamant I keep a low profile coming down here. You never know who is watching. Plus, if things get hairy, I can always check out a firearm from the local police precinct.

Once my real ID is stowed away and the grate is replaced, I put my fake documents in the room safe, on the assumption if someone comes looking, all they will find is Ms. Agostini's documentation. As part of my cover, I also brought a stack of cash to help sell it, which I store inside as well. It's five thousand dollars that I can't afford to lose. But I have to hope that anyone smart enough to get into my room and my safe isn't concerned about such a "small" amount and will leave it. It's there for show and little else.

As soon as I'm satisfied everything is properly stowed and concealed, I grab my second cell phone—the one loaded with all of Ms. Agostini's pictures, contact info, et cetera, don a wide-brimmed straw hat, and head back down to the lobby. There is no time to waste.

Thankfully, pretending to be Ms. Agostini for the past few weeks has acclimated me back to undercover work, otherwise this would be a lot harder. I can't even remember the last time I wore shorts, but it would look strange if I were in anything else here. Except maybe a dress, and I'm not going back down that route again—not until it's absolutely necessary. But with my hat, large glasses, and warm-weather designer clothes I look every bit the part: a wealthy businesswoman from DC, here on her first vacation in ages. Except for the wealthy part, it's about as close to the truth as I can get.

The Grand Solomon Hotel is the largest and most expensive hotel on the island, and thus boasts the most premium clientele. But unlike DC, these people aren't all senators and politicians. Instead, they are businesspeople from all over the world, here for a variety of reasons and I'm sure not all of them venerable.

I head over to the bar attached to the lobby, keeping a sharp eye out for Connor. Odds are he won't be at the hotel in the middle of the day, but I figure there is no better way to start than by playing the part. But I don't spot him anywhere, so instead head out to the pool.

The pool deck is large and spacious, extending far out on both sides of the hotel. Two different bars are situated around the deck, and chairs lined in rows close to the pool hold guests sipping colorful drinks. Palm trees sway overhead, shielding sunbathers from the harshest rays. The people out here are either asleep or reading in the roomy lounge chairs, or gathered around the bars, laughing and drinking. Tropical music filters in from somewhere and birds call out overhead. Even though this isn't my usual scene, I have to admit it's pretty nice. The truest essence of paradise. Zara would absolutely dissolve into this place; a perfect natural. Since she can't be here with me, I'll just have to experience it for both of us.

But I can't get lost in the feeling. I still have a job to do, despite the fact it may not seem like it.

I decide to do what Zara would in this situation, so I can give her a full report. I head over to the closest tiki bar and order a *Bahama Mama*. I then take it over to one of the deck chairs and take a seat, only drawing a small sip from the straw. From here, I have a hundred and eighty-degree view of the pool deck and surrounding area. If Connor shows up here, I should be able to pick him out of the crowd easily enough.

Sitting here with a cold drink in my hand and the warm sun on my face while three women are missing feels like an absolute farce. I want nothing more than to head down to the local police station and start an official investigation, but I need to be more calculated. If I'm going to find out anything helpful, I'll have to plug myself into Connor's social pipeline. The easiest way to do that is, unfortunately, to appeal to the carnal nature of humans...especially men. However, it took weeks to infiltrate Fletch's inner circle, and Caruthers expects me to do this in a matter of days, if not less.

I know if it was up to Zara, she would have me out here in the smallest bikini possible, going for the shotgun approach. But I think I can be a bit more targeted. Not to mention all I have with me is a one-piece bathing suit, and that's only for laps if I decide I need the exercise. The shorts and tank top will have to do.

Still, I know what she would say. Grumbling as I put my drink on a table next to one of the deck chairs, I take a seat and make a big show about extending my legs as I lie on the chair. I feel stupid as hell, but she swears this works, so I try to strike as alluring a pose as I can while still maintaining a modicum of dignity. Thankfully I've chosen a seat that is mostly in shade, so I don't have to worry about the sun just yet. But in another hour, I'll have to find some sunblock. I can already hear her in my head that I can use it as another opportunity to draw more attention.

Then again, maybe I'll just abandon this whole plan.

After about fifteen minutes I no longer feel as exposed, and I begin to relax as the warmth of the air seeps deep into my bones. Am I really here working, or is this just an excuse for some down time? I take a couple of sips of the drink, and for a short second allow myself the pleasure of the moment, just taking it all in. It isn't often I get to do something like this, I need to enjoy it while I can. Zara would be proud.

In fact, I feel so good for a short moment I quit thinking about my recent discussion with Liam and instead just let my mind go. It's surprisingly easy.

Part of me can't help but crave this all this time. I know everyone on vacation says that they should just quit their jobs and move. I think a vacation is supposed to make you want to do something like that—it's part of the fun. And even though I know I would be bored out of my mind if I just came to a place like this and sat around the pool all day, it's still an alluring prospect. Part of my problem is I don't know *what* I want to do. It's like I told Liam, things just feel...*off track* lately. And I think deep down that's why I agreed to go undercover in the first place. I needed something different, something that would challenge me in a new way. I think if I had to sit in on one more stakeout, I might have gone insane.

But as I'm thinking, I spot someone out of the corner of my eye. Turning my head slightly, I catch sight of my target making his way across the pool deck. He's in swim trunks, a light shirt, and a Boston ball cap and he looks like he's come out for a swim. Maybe this was the right call after all.

He's walking with purpose, but he's also scanning the crowd. I lower my glasses to get a better look and lock my gaze on him until he finally notices. He does a double take, as if he's pretending he didn't see me the first time and already I know I have him nibbling on the line. I smile, but don't take my focus off him and finally he slows before reaching the pool. He smiles back and heads in my direction.

God, sometimes it is almost *too* easy.

"Hi there. Enjoying the view?" he says, his voice rich and even. He's got something of a northern Boston accent, but it's very subtle. Like he's worked hard to rid himself of it. I can't get a good handle on all his features because he's backlit, but just like his pictures online, he has a fair complexion and short, dark hair. "I don't mean to be that guy, but I would be kicking myself if I didn't come over and at least introduce myself."

I arch an eyebrow, which should just barely be visible beyond the frame of my large sunglasses, waiting for him to continue. He holds out his hand. "Rafe Connor."

*Yeah, I know.* I reach up and take his hand, careful not to squeeze too hard. "Emily Agostini. Pleasure."

"Do you mind if I join you?" he asks. I motion for him to take a seat on the chair next to me, but I don't sit up or change positions at all. Now I have to play a little hard to get...hook him as it were. When he sits, I get a better look at him. He's in his early forties though he looks younger, clean shaven with good features. He no doubt does well with members of the opposite sex, and I catch the glint of a wedding ring on his finger. He still wears it. Interesting.

"What are you drinking?" he asks.

"Mr. Connor," I say. "If you're going to engage me in conversation, I'd hope you could come up with a more interesting subject than my choice of beverage."

This seems to amuse him as he grins, then leans back on his chair, matching my posture. "Okay then, tell my why you're here."

For a brief second my heart thumps as the fleeting thought flashes across my brain that he somehow knows I'm an FBI agent and has figured me out. It was something I had to learn to ignore when I first started undercover work years ago, and something I haven't been practicing. I do everything I can to look as relaxed as possible. "I'm taking a well-deserved break after a busy year."

"Obviously you must be doing something right, to be staying in a place like this," he says. His voice has a tone of playfulness to it, and it's not lost on me he's probably looking for a hookup. But that's not about to happen. What I did with Fletch is as far as I'm willing to go, and even that has to be an extreme situation.

"What about you, why are you here?" I shoot back.

"Research," he says, grinning at me.

"For?"

"Real estate," he replies. "I maintain a healthy portfolio of properties across the globe and St. Solomon has been on my radar for a while now. It's a beautiful place and should be accessible to everyone."

I decide to turn things up a notch. "You're the Rafe Connor of Connor Investments International."

His eyes go wide, and I can tell he isn't often recognized. I worry for a moment I may have overplayed my hand before he breaks out a smile. "Impressive. Who are you again?"

"Me? I'm just here for the international espionage. It pays very well." He screws up his features for a second before he realizes I'm kidding. "Have you heard of Thompson Intermodal?"

"I can't say that I have," he says.

"We've expanded a lot in the past few years, but we're still relatively new to the scene. I work for the export division of the company. We're certainly not on the same level of CII, but we're making a mark. The world has gotten so much smaller in the past ten years; we like to think we've been a big part of that." I sigh. "Of course, the whole reason I do any of it is for the free drinks."

A bevy of emotions fly across his face, from pleasure to

amusement to even a hint of desire. "You're an interesting woman, Ms. Agostini," he says.

"Emily, please," I say.

"May I get you another drink, Emily?"

*There is no way in hell.* "Actually, I was just about to take a walk on the beach. Care to join me?" Now that I've hooked him, I need to know what he knows. Find out more about his former employee that went missing here on the island, Vicki Tolluse. What does Rafe know about her? According to my information she's been gone for almost a week. And this man may be my only clue to her whereabouts. And does he know about any of the other women?

"I would be delighted," he says.

"Good," I say, swinging my legs off the chair and slipping them into my sandals. "Maybe we can talk about more than just the view. My company is looking to expand, so perhaps this chance meeting is something that can pay off for the both of us."

"My favorite types of collaborations are the ones that happen by accident." He stands, his eyes never leaving me. Just like Fletch, all I have to do is reel him in.

As we head down to the beach, I can't help but notice my apprehensive feelings about the future have completely disappeared.

## Chapter Eight

"YOU DON'T STRIKE me as the kind of person who likes to vacation," Connor says, strolling beside me as the waves wash up and over our feet. The Grand Solomon features a "private" beach for the frontage that's directly in front of the hotel. But on either side is public access that extends for roughly a half mile in both directions before eventually fading away into the trees. We made it about halfway down the beach before running out of "safe" topics to discuss. Since then, things have become more...personal.

"Why is that?"

"Because you're trying so hard to work," he replies. "And while I appreciate meeting a fellow hustler, there's a time and a place for everything."

"That's easy for you to say, you're already at the top of your game," I reply, though I don't like that he's hit at something deep. "For those of us who are still up and coming, we can't afford to sit back and wait for the opportunities to come to us."

"And yet, that's exactly what happened." He grins when I turn to look at him. "There you were, sitting back and enjoying your vacation, and an opportunity—me—just happened by."

"Oh yes, I'm sure your interest was purely business," I reply. "You didn't even know who I was."

Our discussion had mostly revolved around what I do at Thompson Intermodal, until it began to veer off into *what is a beautiful young woman doing on the island by herself* territory. Which makes me grateful that I had those weeks of practice with Fletch. He was never this interested, but Rafe wants to know all about Emily Agostini, where she grew up, her family, even her favorite flavor of ice cream. I'll admit, he's putting me through my paces, but somehow I'm managing to hold the cover. I had hoped to keep him distracted with professional topics, but it's clear to me he's got more than business on his mind. I try to turn the conversation back to him, but at every opportunity, he flips it back again. He must *really* want to get laid.

"You know, to have accomplished as much as you have, you really must be a hustler. I remember being your age, having that desire. So don't think I've forgotten what it feels like. But something else I learned young is there has to be a balance. If you're always trying to hustle the panda, you're going to miss the important conversations."

*Great, now he wants to be my mentor?* "Hustle the panda?"

"Industry term," he says. "What I'm saying is don't be so focused on the big sell that you're missing the more important conversations."

"You are just a wealth of information," I say. "So where would one get to be a part of these conversations?"

"Damn, you are ambitious, aren't you?"

"Hey, I'm walking on the beach next to a multi-millionaire," I reply. Anything not to talk about my so-called personal life anymore. "Do you blame me?" I tilt my head up so he can just see my eyeline under the hat.

"I guess not. Well, I might as well bite the bullet. I was

going to invite you anyway, but I'm afraid if I don't get this out now you might find a way in by yourself. There's an event tonight, a kind of…gala. I was hoping you'd accompany me."

"As your date?" I ask. "Aren't you, I mean…" I nod to the ring on his finger, knowing full well what it means.

"Oh." He grimaces. "My wife passed away about eight months ago. It was…there was an accident." There's real pain in his voice. Maybe I'm wrong about him, maybe he's not looking for a hookup. This could just be his way of coping, but the odds aren't on his side.

"I'm very sorry to hear that," I say.

He squeezes his features together before resetting himself. "Sometimes all the money in the world…well, no matter. Let's just say I had a hard time letting go. I haven't been able to take it off yet. But as for tonight, I was hoping you'd come as my business associate, nothing more."

"I could do that," I say, softening my voice. Maybe this "gala" will give me the opportunity to speak to some of his colleagues. Someone on this island *has* to know something.

"It's being held by Jeremy Breckenridge, have you heard of him?"

I shake my head. The name seems familiar, but I can't immediately place it.

"He's a big benefactor for St. Solomon. Donates to every charity on the island, works with the local population to maintain the quality of the schools, of the parks, etc. He's always raising money for some cause or another. I'm sure I can secure you an invitation. I'll even cover the donation minimum."

"That's very generous, but you don't have to do that," I say, thinking back to that five grand I have in the room.

"I don't mind, $10K per plate is expensive, even by my standards."

*Ten thousand?* Caruthers would kill me if I spent that much just to get into an event. Not that I could cover it anyway. It's already costing the Bureau enough to make it *look* like I'm rich. "I don't know what to say. Thank you."

"It's my pleasure," he says, holding his head high like he's just saved a drowning puppy. I'm sure in his eyes, I'm nothing more than a little fish in a big ocean, and he's throwing me a bone because I've got nice legs.

But whatever he thinks, Mr. Rafe Connor is of no more interest to me than the access he can provide. Someone is sure to know something at this party, it's a prime opportunity for information gathering.

As for what happens after, I'm afraid I'm going to have to disappoint my *gracious* host.

# Chapter Nine

I CAN'T BELIEVE I'm right back here. *Again.* Except this time instead of walking up a series of stairs in an evening gown, I'm walking down them to a black car waiting outside the hotel. A man in an immaculate suit stands beside the back door of the car, waiting to open it for me. As soon as we got back from the beach, I had to scramble to find a dress. Thankfully, the concierge at the hotel was able to point me to a store in town that apparently deals with this kind of thing all the time. And thanks to Zara's guidance with Fletch, I knew exactly what to look for and what would look good. Thankfully, I skipped the Louboutin's and went with a standard pair of more maneuverable heels. After making my initial report to Caruthers and getting five minutes on the phone with Liam, I barely had enough time to get ready before I received a call on the hotel room phone informing me the car was here.

All of this just feels so…unnatural. I almost want to crawl out of my own skin. I should be out there, banging on doors and interrogating people about these missing women. Instead, I'm all dressed up and heading to a fancy party with the one percent. What's even worse is this is becoming a regular occurrence.

The doorman opens the car for me, and I carefully slip into the back seat. These dresses don't leave a lot of room for error. Rafe sits beside me, smiling as I tuck my legs in. The car has to have one of the most comfortable seats I've ever relaxed into. I don't miss how his eyes travel down my legs quickly before snapping back up.

"Good evening," he says. "You look stunning." He's dressed in a black tuxedo, his tie completely perfect. I notice the face of a Bvlgari on his wrist and solid platinum cufflinks decorating his sleeves.

"You don't look so bad yourself," I say. "Thank you again for this, Rafe. It really isn't necessary."

He waves me off. "It's no problem. Usually, these things are a bore. At least with you there it will be a lot more interesting. Care for something to drink on the way over?"

Zara would be losing her mind if she could see me right now. "No, thank you. Alcohol and moving vehicles don't mix for me. I'll wait until we arrive."

"Fair enough," he says, though he grabs a bottle of five-hundred-dollar champagne and pours himself a glass as the driver pulls away from the hotel, headed up into the mountains. Is this how people like this really live? I find it hard to wrap my head around.

Being in the FBI is a lot like being a soldier. We see terrible things all the time—the worst of what humanity can to do each other. So, when I'm presented with situations like this, I can't take them seriously. These people live in their little bubbles and have no idea how bad things can get. They don't understand how *hard* life can be. And they never will.

Still, I plaster a smile on my face and continue to answer Rafe's questions as we drive. He can be charming in his own way, and I could see how he might think a show like this could wow a woman. I just play the part, keeping my goal in focus until finally we pull up to an expensive pair of metal gates set into a high wall. A man stands outside the gates, though they are already open. The driver hands over a small card and the man waves us through.

As we pass through, I notice a car sitting just inside the gate itself, though it's too dark to see who is inside. My guess is there's a security detail in there, keeping an eye out in case something looks or goes wrong. We head down the short driveway and reach the roundabout in front of the house in short order. A smattering of expensive-looking cars sit out front, all colors of the rainbow. Rafe must see me staring at them because he pipes up again.

"You wouldn't believe what it costs to get them here," he says.

"Sorry?"

"The McLaren and the Bugatti. I know for a fact they were both on the same ship that came over last week. Their owners wanted them here so they could drive them around the island, except the idiots didn't realize half the island is dirt roads and would tear those cars up. They're used to driving around Monaco or Miami. But here there are few roads flat enough to not rip the transmissions right out of those things. Which means they're limited to driving around town and to a few, select houses."

"And you hope to change that," I say, turning back to him.

"A reliable road system is the backbone of a thriving economy," he replies. "I just have to convince the local government to loosen the restrictions a little."

Personally, I think the last thing this island needs is more development. The entire allure of this place is because it's remote, hard to get to and still mostly wild. If Connor ends up developing even a small portion of the island, it will fundamentally change everything.

I think back to what Caruthers told me about the missing women. For the first time, I consider that Connor's business may have more to do with the disappearances than we thought. Any time a lot of money is on the line people will go to extreme lengths to protect their interests. Which might include abduction. I wonder what Vicki Tolluse knew about his operation?

When the car pulls to a stop, I forget myself again and open my own door before the doorman can get there. But I use the extra time to get out of the car without tearing or messing up the dress. He seems embarrassed that he couldn't get to the door in time, but I just smile and thank him anyway. Rafe comes around the other side of the car and holds out his arm for me. Maybe anyone else would think he's just being a gentleman, but I know men like this. I'd be naïve to believe he wasn't working me, either personally or professionally. No one spends ten grand and doesn't expect to get something for it. And yet, that's exactly what he's going to end up with, one way or another.

I take his arm and he leads me down the long sidewalk which turns into a walkway over a large water feature. Small fountains on either side of the sidewalk bubble and lights under the water change color as we cross the bridge to the house awaiting us.

It's large and expansive, but only one story, like a spread-out ranch. Uplighting makes the house glow in the evening light, and it's built in a modern style so that the windows run from the floor to the ceiling, allowing us to see the people milling about inside. When we reach the front door, two doormen pull the doors towards us, and we're met by a lively and animated crowd inside.

"Wow, this place looks...ostentatious," I say as we enter. Finally, Rafe drops my arm, for which I say a silent prayer of thanks.

"Mr. Breckenridge is not known for his subtlety. He may enjoy his charity work, but he enjoys showing off his money even more."

As we pass through the vestibule there's a coat check, but only a few light jackets hang behind the attendant. It seems like an unnecessary expense to staff something like that here, but it only goes to prove Rafe's point. Breckenridge pulls out all the stops. Now I'm *really* glad I'm not paying for this.

Inside, the house opens up to a large living area, filled with people talking and milling about. Rafe leads me through the house to an indoor pool, along with an indoor/outdoor bar that sits just outside large picture windows which have been pushed to the side along a track, allowing the room to flow from inside to out. I also notice the pool itself feeds into the outdoor pool, allowing anyone swimming to move seamlessly between the two. But the two pools are empty of humans. Instead, small lily pads with LED lights float harmlessly on the surface. But the real star of the show is the view. Beyond the edge of the infinity pool, the ocean stretches out forever. The full moon reflects off the surface, creating a beam of light that runs all the way to the horizon and shines so much light that it could almost be mistaken for daylight. Small lights dot the rest of the dark island before it melts into the ocean beyond.

"The man made one hell of an investment," Rafe says, coming up beside me. I think I feel his arm reaching around me, but it never materializes and I'm not sure if I imagined it or not. This must be something he does all the time, try to impress women by bringing them into a place like this. Fortunately, he doesn't know anything about me. And I know for a fact as beautiful as places like this are, they are always built on the backs of the poor, and usually house more than a few dark secrets. It's all surface level. And I'm not about to be fooled by the gilding.

"Fifteen years ago, he bought this plot of land and spent the better part of a decade building this house. Lucky bastard. If I'd had the funds back then..." Rafe trails off.

"How did Mr. Breckenridge make his money?" I ask, my curiosity getting the better of me.

"He's involved in a couple of offshore operations," Rafe replies. "Things that might seem...controversial to some." I turn to him, imploring him to continue. "He owns a few diamond mines in Africa. But don't worry, they are completely humane. Not the blood diamond mines you've heard of. I've worked with Breckenridge in the past. He's on the up and up."

*Sure he is.* Just another suspect to add to my list. I don't care if it takes a month, I'll investigate every person on this island if necessary.

The party is in full swing and Rafe leaves to procure some drinks. I take the opportunity to eavesdrop nearby conversations before he can return. Breckenridge's guests don't seem to be shy about their conversations. They think they're safe here, that they're among their own kind. Which is something I can use to my advantage.

Unfortunately, I'm still not a hundred percent confident in shoes like this and must take it slow. My feet are already yelling at me, but I push past the pain as I pass nearby groups of people, listening for anything that might be helpful. Most of the conversations are surface level, and I find myself heading deeper and deeper into the party hoping to hear something of consequence.

*"You know it's where he keeps all the bodies, don't you?"*

The words stop me dead in my tracks. A small group of people to my right are talking in lowered voices, but we're far enough from the majority of the guests that I manage to hear the conversation.

"I just can't believe he would do something like that," a woman a little older than me replies to the man whose words caught my attention. The woman looks like she's swallowed something sour before spotting me out of the corner of her eye. I smile apologetically.

"I'm sorry, do you know where the restroom is?" I ask. "I've never been here before."

The first woman, who is probably about twenty years my senior, snickers. "Better show her Barry, or she'll end up in the dungeon with the others."

"Shut up, Marie, it's not a joke," the man replies. He's probably in his mid-fifties as well, sporting a handlebar moustache and a widow's peak. He's holding a glass of brown liquid while the two women are clutching wine glasses, though I notice Marie's is nearing empty.

"Why does everything with you have to be a conspiracy?" she asks before turning to me. The other woman is watching the two of them with interest but hasn't spoken up yet. Marie points to me with her empty glass. "Would you believe a man like Breckenridge would have built an underground bunker in this house?"

"Sure," I say. "Plenty of people build them for storage, emergencies, all sorts of things. Though I'm not sure I've ever heard of one on an island like this before."

"See?" Marie says, turning back to Barry. "Why would Breckenridge go to the trouble when he could just helicopter out of here?"

"Because it's not for emergencies," Barry insists, his glass sloshing a bit. "He's doing something down there. Everyone knows about it; they just pretend not to."

"There you are." The strong voice startles me and I turn to see Rafe, having come back with two glasses full of clear liquid. I have no idea what could be in mine and I have no intention of drinking it, but I take it from him. Everyone else seems to stiffen at Rafe's appearance.

"Barry, Marie," he says. "I see you've met Emily."

"Not formally," Barry says, holding out a stiff hand. "Barry Wirt. Berringer & Berringer. This is my wife, Marie."

I shake his hand before taking Marie's. "Emily Agostini. I'm with Thompson Intermodal. Is that a law firm?"

Barry nods. "One of the many that handle Mr. Breckenridge's affairs, I'm afraid."

"And this is Claire Taylor," Rafe says, turning to the young woman next to me. She smiles but it doesn't quite reach her eyes. "Claire is lead coordinator for Pyron Elite, a subsidiary of Connor Investments International."

That's interesting. I thought Rafe was representing CII on the island by himself. And even though it's a subsidiary, Ms. Taylor is obviously an employee. She might know something about Vicki Tolluse.

"Pleasure," I say, taking Claire's hand for a quick moment.

"This is Claire's first visit to St. Solomon," Rafe says. "We brought her down to help us coordinate some of the negotiations with the local government."

"Enjoying the island?" I ask.

"Sure," she replies before taking a sip of her wine. I recognize that body language. She doesn't want to say too much in front of Rafe. Whether that's because she feels like she'd be putting her career at risk or because there is something more personal going on, I can't say, but I know something about this meeting is off. Instead, she keeps to herself, her free hand playing absently with a ruby necklace around her neck. From the looks of it, the ruby is genuine.

"So, what are we talking about?" Rafe asks.

Marie opens her mouth, but before she can say anything there is a loud gong that turns everyone's head. At the far end of the pool, beside what looks to be an eight-foot-high cymbal hanging from a makeshift pagoda, stands a man dressed all in white, complete with bushy white eyebrows. He holds his hands out to both sides with a giant smile on his face.

"Welcome, everyone, to the most exciting night of your lives!"

# Chapter Ten

A QUIET CHUCKLE runs through the crowd as the man at the pool lowers his hands. On either side of him are two men in their early thirties, both dressed completely in black. Immediately my hackles are up. What have I stumbled into here? I glance over at Rafe, but he's just looking back at me, a curious grin on his face and I realize he's watching my expressions. Watching for what? At any rate, I have to be extremely careful. I can't let him see anything other than what I want him to see.

"That's right," the man in white says again. "I promise you an adventure so amazing that you will forever look back on this evening and wish you could experience it for the first time all over again."

The men beside who I assume can only be Jeremy Breckenridge, retrieve silver platters from behind them and begin making their way through the crowd. "Tonight's dinner will be confronted on the fly, in other words, the food will come to you. It has all been specifically engineered to compliment not only the local flora, but the sea air and the exact altitude of this *abode*."

One of the men in black comes to our group and removes

the platter's top. Underneath are six small plates, each with a small piece of round food that is probably no larger than my thumb. It is coated with two different colored sauces and seems to come on a kind of cracker, along with a single blade of grass on top.

"What is it?" Barry asks.

"*Rais en tours*," the maitre'd replies. "It has been specifically prepared—"

"I heard the spiel," Barry replies and takes the cracker from one of the plates, popping it into his mouth in one bite. His eyes widen in surprise before he takes another sip of his drink.

The rest of us take a cracker each, and while Marie attempts to nibble on it, Claire eats hers in one full bite as well. Rafe and I follow suit. I'm not expecting much, but an explosion of flavors hit my tongue all at once and for a brief moment I'm struck by a quick buzzing sensation in the back of my throat as I swallow.

"What was that?" I ask.

"Probably Acmella oleracea," Claire replies. Everyone turns to her. "It's a plant native to Asia, used in culinary dishes. It has a temporary numbing effect when used in large quantities, I expect there is a small amount in whatever this is to give it that punch at the end."

"Did I mention Claire is a trained chemist?" Rafe says before wrapping his arm around her and pulling her closer in a side hug. It's not hard to see how Claire tenses until he lets go. "She's one of the smartest people on our team and we're lucky to have her."

"Cheers to that," Barry says, raising his glass and taking another sip.

"Chemistry, that is so interesting," Marie replies. "I could never do something so cerebral. Is that what you do at your company?"

"Something along those lines," Claire replies, looking

away. Something very odd is going on here, but I'm not exactly sure what.

The gong rings again, pulling all our attention. "Time for the second course!" Breckenridge calls out, and more men with more silver platters descend upon the crowd.

Rafe chuckles. "He certainly isn't boring. Excuse me a moment, I need to speak to our host." He leaves before the second platters arrive and I notice Claire's shoulders drop. I close the gap left by him so it's just the four of us again.

"Have you known him long?" I ask Claire, hoping to find out more about Rafe from someone who clearly knows him better.

"A few years," she says, then takes a sip of her wine.

"Is this a regular thing?" I ask, motioning to the people gathered for the event.

Barry scoffs. "You mean Rafe showing up with some pretty young thing on his arm? Yes. Absolutely." Marie smacks his shoulder, offering me a sympathetic look.

"Stop being an asshole," Marie tells Barry, smacking him again for good measure before turning to me. "You'll have to excuse him. He gets like this when he has a few drinks. The rudeness surfaces and the conspiracy theories start coming out."

"I'm not just talking out of my ass here, Marie. *Everyone* knows about the rooms," Barry says, though the words begin to slur. "They're *real*, whether you decide to believe it or not."

"What are real?" I ask.

Barry leans in. "A secret underground facility in the house. Not just some concrete bunker. It's like another wing of the house. Full plumbing and electrical, but with six rooms, each with their own doors. Now you tell me that doesn't sound just a little suspicious."

I furrow my brow. Six rooms? Each completely cut off from the house in an underground concrete bunker. I've had experience with things like this in the past, and they never lead to anything good. "You don't know what he uses them for?"

"I can take a wild guess," Barry replies.

"*Barry*," Marie shushes. "Stop being rude. This is not appropriate conversation for this venue."

"No, Marie, this is the perfect conversation, especially for these two." That causes both me and Claire to look up before sharing a glance between us. "You've heard about the disappearances."

"What disappearances?" Claire asks.

"Young women, being abducted from the island," he replies. "Been going on a few weeks now."

I glance over at Rafe and Breckenridge, who are deep in conversation as the kitchen crew prepares the next round of the meal before returning my attention to the group. "Is that common knowledge?"

"People here don't like to talk about it," he says.

Marie interrupts, tossing what remains of her cracker in the nearby bush. "It's nothing but unsubstantiated rumor. And don't you say another word. This evening is going to be long enough without your wild conspiracy theories flitting about."

"Fine. But when someone else goes missing, don't come crying to me." He drains the rest of his drink and heads off for the bar.

Marie gives the two of us a placating glance. "Don't mind him. Just another reminder that I should have married John Wilcox in high school instead." She sighs and heads off after her husband.

"Have you heard anything about any disappearances?" I ask.

"I just arrived a few days ago," Claire replies. I notice Rafe seems to be wrapping up his conversation with Breckenridge.

"I still need to use the restroom. I don't guess you know where it is?" She shrugs at me. I can't get a read on Claire other than she is very guarded. She doesn't want to let people in, which I can completely understand. Still, Barry's little "theory" has me curious.

I excuse myself before Rafe begins heading back to what remains of our group. As I leave Claire, I notice her wrap her arms around herself as she stares out at the endless, dark ocean, despite the fact it's quite warm out. There's barely even a breeze.

The gong sounds a third time as I walk back inside and pass a couple of waiters heading in the opposite direction with more trays, obviously bringing more and more courses to Breckenridge's guests. But honestly, ten thousand for a few bits of finger food? These people really must have money to burn. I guess it is for charity, after all.

I head back through the house and pass the obviously marked bathrooms, keeping a close eye out for anyone who might try to stop me, but it seems everyone is focused on the party. I check the next door I find, discovering it only leads to a boardroom with a long mahogany table surrounded by eight chairs. I guess Breckenridge needs a place to conduct business.

Finally, I reach a door with a small window inset in the upper portion. Peering inside, a staircase heads down to a lower level. So far, I haven't seen any bedrooms; I wonder if that's the private wing of the house. If Barry wasn't just mouthing off and these rooms are real, then they could be my first major clue to finding the missing women.

Before I can figure out how to open the door, a shadow on the wall along the staircase dances in my periphery. Making my way back in the opposite direction, I duck into an open alcove as the door opens. A check around the corner reveals a security guard heading away from me. He's broad-shouldered, looking like he could probably take down a linebacker. But he's moving quickly in the opposite direction.

I rush forward and just happen to catch the door to the stairs, slipping inside before it closes behind me. Immediately,

I'm bathed in silence. There must be soundproofing on this side of the house, sealing it off from the rest. I descend the stairs slowly, careful of my steps, only to find yet another long hallway at the bottom, walls lined with doors. Taking a quick glance inside the doors, I see I was right that the house's bedrooms are down here. Two of the rooms on my left are open, showcasing opulent guest rooms.

But as I make my way further down the corridor, I realize the rooms on the right, built into the side of the hill, can't have any windows. The first is nothing more than a powder room. But a little further down, I encounter a locked door with what I'd have to describe as a very substantial lock. The door itself is metal, meaning there is no way I could shoulder my way inside. Whatever is in there, Breckenridge wants it kept out of sight.

Further down, there is another, similar door. Could this be what Barry was talking about? But there are only two, and not six. This door, much like the first is made of metal and requires a large key to unlock. I try the door anyway, but as I do, some kind of alarm goes off, sending a high-pitched wail through the hallway.

"*Shit*," I say and rush back the way I came, though the heels are slowing me down. But before I can reach the stairs again, a large form descends quickly. It's the security guard I noticed earlier.

"You! Stop right there," he yells.

*Not good.* I turn and begin running back the other way, but my ankle buckles under the lack of support from the heel, and I go down. I'm sure I've sprained it. Despite the sharp pain, I yank the shoes off and scramble up, doing my best not to put any more weight on it as the man begins running in my direction. "I've got her. South wing, lower floor. She's in a maroon dress, dark hair—"

The rest of his report is lost to me as I turn the only corner to the left and find myself in a home office. Awards of all kinds cover the walls, and pictures of Breckenridge shaking the hands of different officials fill the shelves. There's also a computer, but I don't have time to inspect it. The back wall is all glass, looking out on a lower-level pool that must not be visible from the main pool. It's smaller and more private, but it does tell me the foundation of this building definitely goes lower than this floor. I slide the door open just as the goon behind me reaches the door.

"Hey, stop, you're trespassing. No one is allowed down here." I continue to hobble forward but he's gaining on me and I've reached the edge of the concrete pad. There's no fence, and beyond the pool is nothing but a steep slope that descends three hundred feet down to the Atlantic Ocean. There's nowhere else to go.

Before I can contemplate going back, a strong hand wraps itself around my arm and jerks me back. Instinctually, I grab the man's wrist and twist it off my arm, causing him to cry out. He goes to his knees and I pull his arm behind him, putting pressure right on the elbow so he pitches forward.

"Freeze!"

I look over and see another man with an actual gun pointed at me. Breckenridge isn't screwing around with his security. I release the man and hold up both hands. He grunts as he gets up, pulling my arms behind me. "You're in big trouble, little girl."

"Call me a little girl again and you'll be eating through a straw for a month," I growl.

"Yeah?" he asks as soon as he has my arms tight so I can't wiggle out. "Let's see how tough you are when the police arrive."

## Chapter Eleven

THE FLASH of the camera causes me to flinch.

"Turn to your left."

I turn, still holding the small placard, and the camera goes off again.

"This way," the officer says, taking the placard with my fake name on it. She leads me by the arm over to another station where I'm fingerprinted. The bright lights of the police station cast everything in a harsh glow. The place is stark and lifeless. I can relate; I feel the same inside.

Amazingly, the police were very quick in their response to the Breckenridge property. So quick, in fact, that I was hauled out of the lower floor, up the stairs, out the side entrance and to the awaiting police car where I was shoved into the back while the officers discussed what had happened with the security personnel. As far as I can tell, no one at the party even knew what happened. Though I'm sure Rafe is trying to figure out where I went missing.

After less than five minutes, I was informed I was being arrested for trespassing and assault and that I would be driven to the local police station where I would be processed.

The entire time, I said nothing. Keeping my cover intact is

still the top priority and hopefully, if not a lot of people witnessed what happened, I may be able to get out of this unscathed. Of course, I'll have to call Caruthers as soon as they allow me my call. Not only that, but my ankle is still sore from rolling it earlier. I did ask for an ice pack, but so far I haven't seen one.

After the officer finishes fingerprinting me, she takes me into another room where I'm sat at a table and left alone. They have my wallet, ID, and the second phone I've been using, along with, presumably, my shoes. But as best I can tell, this oven of a room has no air conditioning and I begin sweating as soon as I sit down.

"I'd like my phone call," I tell the officer as she leaves the room. She just scoffs at me before pulling the door closed and locking it behind her. On either side of the door are caged windows where I can see into the hallway. She heads off to the left but is stopped by another officer, this one with captain's stripes. He's also wearing a hat denoting his rank. He speaks a few words to the officer while I watch, then nods a couple of times. He's also got something in his hand, but I can't tell what it is. Finally, the officer heads off as the captain opens the door, regards me for a brief second, and then closes the door behind him.

"I'd like my phone call," I repeat to him. "And I need some ice for my swollen ankle."

He holds a folder in his hand and sets it down on the table in front of us before taking the seat across from me. "Emily Agostini. From Dallas, Texas. Born, November 13, 1993. Attended public school for four years before transferring to the Millennium Academy, a prestigious private business school where you excelled in logistics. Graduated from Brown with a degree in Management before being hired by Thompson Intermodal. That about cover it?"

His nametag says *Montenegro*, and his skin is almost a tawny color, like worn leather. It's clear he's spent most of his life outside and the sun has taken its toll. His eyes are bright blue though, like mine, and they are sharp. He regards me with an intensity reserved for people who don't take any bullshit.

"If you want to reduce me down to my hometown and my schools, sure," I reply.

"What were you doing trespassing on Mr. Breckenridge's property?" he asks, barely allowing me to finish.

"I got lost, I was looking for the restroom. It's a big house."

"Bullshit," he replies. "You and I both know you're not stupid enough to get lost."

I furrow my brow. "I'm sorry, do we know each other?"

He pushes the folder towards me, opening it. Inside is my official FBI file. "No, but I know an FBI agent isn't dumb enough to just happen to find herself lost in someone else's house. So I'll ask again. What were you doing in Mr. Brecken-ridge's home?"

It takes me a second to register that I'm looking at my own file. There's nothing compromising on there, but obviously Montenegro has some friends at the FBI, otherwise he never would have been able to get his hands on this. I narrow my gaze at him.

"Surprised?" he asks. "We may not be on the mainland, but that doesn't mean we don't have good detectives here."

"You've been on me since the airport," I say.

"I don't appreciate the federal government sticking their nose where it doesn't belong," he says. "Here's the deal. Go home, or I expose this little operation of yours. Whatever you hoped to get out of being undercover just evaporated."

I'm simultaneously furious and relieved. Relieved that I don't have to act the part anymore, but furious that everything I've done up until now just went down the toilet. I was just starting to make some progress on this case. But if Montenegro wants to try and bully me, then he's going up against the wrong person. "Good," I say, and I mean it. "I'm tired of playing nanny to a bunch of overprivileged children. You have a problem and it's not me. I'm not leaving here until I find out why you seem to have misplaced three women. Unless you want to fill me in."

If he's surprised from the accusation he doesn't show it. "We're conducting appropriate investigations," he says. "When and *if* the federal government needs to be involved, we'll let you know."

"These aren't just some locals who decided to go camping for a few days," I say. "You're missing three US citizens, two from the mainland. It's no longer just an island issue. You want to expose me, fine. But I'm not going anywhere. And you can bet I'm getting to the bottom of this."

He sits back and runs his tongue over his teeth. It has the effect of making me want to turn away in disgust, though I'm not sure it was even meant that way. I can tell Montenegro is trying to decide how far he can push me and get away with it. At least one good thing will come out of all of this: I won't have to deal with Rafe any longer. "Fine. Have it your way. Enjoy your night in jail, Ms. Slate."

"*Agent*," I remind him. "And you can't just keep me here because you're throwing a tantrum."

"Actually, I can," he says, taking the folder back. "It turns out we won't figure out you're with the FBI until the morning, and Ms. Agostini is facing a trespassing and an assault charge."

"You know that won't hold up when I speak to my superiors," I say, attempting to stand, but my ankle seizes and I'm forced to sit back down.

"Looks like you're not going anywhere no matter what. I'll make sure to get you something more appropriate to wear during your stay with us." I practically bore into his head with my gaze but it only seems to egg him on. He gives me a shit-eating grin then heads back out, the door locking closed behind him.

Son of a *bitch*. Blew the cover and got arrested all in one. So much for my stellar return to undercover work. Oh well, I wasn't really suited for it anyway. I'm much better when I can be direct with someone. I'm just not looking forward to explaining this to Caruthers.

Still, I can't discount the fact that Breckenridge may have some kind of underground bunker under his house. I'll need to get access to make sure he's not pulling a *Douglass Kraus*— keeping women underground against their wills. I rub my ankle absently. What I really need is some ice, but based on Montenegro's response, I'm unlikely to get it anytime soon.

As I'm rolling around what I'm going to tell Caruthers as soon as I'm allowed anywhere near a phone, I catch elevated voices from down the hall. I swear one of them is Montenegro. But just as I'm leaning forward, I see Rafe storming his way in front of the windows. He catches sight of me in the holding room and turns to Montenegro, shouting back. Rafe points at the door, and though his voice is still too muffled for me to hear exactly what he's saying, I get the gist. Rafe is practically red in the face as Montenegro yells back at him.

But then Rafe's face changes abruptly, falling. He turns to look at me and I realize Montenegro has just told him my true identity. Well, he wasn't bluffing at least. Rafe seems to regain some of his resolve and says something else, pointing at the door again.

Montenegro sighs, pulls out a key, and opens the door. He and Rafe stand in the doorway and in Rafe's hand is the ice pack I asked for. My heart softens just a bit at that little act, but I don't think Rafe and I are going to be sharing any more walks on the beach after this.

"Is it true?" he asks, the light casting him in total shadow. "You're with the FBI?"

I don't even bother trying to hide it. "Yes."

"You lied to me," he says, taking a step into the room.

"I was undercover," I reply. "I lied to everyone." He tosses the icepack on the table. It lands with a thud. "Look, I don't know what you thought our relationship would be like, but I came here to do a job, undercover or not. And I'm not looking for anything. I have a boyfriend back home."

He doesn't move. "Guess I shouldn't be surprised." He turns to Montenegro. "So, what happens to her now? You're not going to leave a federal agent locked up, are you?"

Montenegro sighs. "No. We're just sorting through some of the paperwork. This caught us off guard."

"Surely you can do that without keeping her here."

Montenegro does that teeth thing again. "Of course." He motions to the door.

I huff, standing more carefully this time, and I take the ice pack, limping my way out into the hallway on bare feet. It's cold and dirty, but I don't have any other choice. As I walk past Rafe, I give him a nod of thanks he doesn't return.

Back out in the main processing area, an officer hands me my purse along with all of my effects. I double check to make sure everything is inside, which they appear to be. I feel all eyes on me as I head for the exit. But then Rafe comes up beside me, not looking at me, not even acknowledging me. Though he does hold the door, which is a big help.

"Do you need a ride back to the hotel?" he asks once we're outside.

"I can just call a cab," I say. "Thank you for that back there. I fully believe he was going to keep me in lockup all night."

Rafe grunts in response before walking down the few steps to the parking lot where his car is waiting, complete with the same driver as before. He gets halfway there before turning around and coming back. I brace myself.

"I expect to be compensated," he says, finally, a new harshness in his voice.

"Excuse me?"

"Ten thousand dollars," he replies. "Your entry fee for the dinner. I'll make sure to send the bill to the State Department."

I scowl at him. "Whatever you want."

"Good," he says. "I'm not a charity. And I'm certainly not about to use my resources to further the interests of the United States government."

"And here I just thought you wanted to get into my pants," I shoot back.

"Don't flatter yourself," he replies. "I saw a business opportunity and I took it. Enjoy the rest of your time on the island, *Agent*." He turns and heads back to his car without another word. I wait until he's out of view before I take a seat on the steps and place the ice pack against my ankle.

Well, that's one bridge burned. Here's hoping I can still conduct an investigation without the man's connections. Either way, I need to get out of this dress. I'm tired of being dolled up. It's time for me to get down to business, and I'm not about to do it in six-inch heels anymore.

I pull out my phone and call myself a cab.

# Chapter Twelve

"So what are you going to do?" Liam asks as I flop down on the bed. I'm back in my hotel room, ice pack strapped to my leg with a scrunchie and a fluffy robe in place of the evening-wear. It's close to one in the morning, and I've decided to wait until tomorrow to make my report to Caruthers. But I needed to talk to someone. And Liam has never not been there for me.

"I don't know," I reply. "I can't just leave knowing the local police isn't working very hard to find these women. At the same time, without my cover, I'm not sure how effective I can be."

"You've never needed to be undercover before to make a difference, not since I've known you," he says softly.

"That's true." I think I'd been so focused on keeping my cover because I thought I needed to prove something to myself, that I hadn't lost my touch. But I've been getting the job done without the need for a cover for almost two years now. And those have been some of my most successful cases. "I'll talk to Caruthers in the morning. Montenegro obviously doesn't want me here, but that's nothing new. In fact, he made it clear he couldn't wait to be rid of me."

"You think he's dirty?" Liam asks.

"He's something," I say, sitting up and adjusting the ice pack. "An asshole for one. But I don't know much else about the man. One thing is for sure, if I stay, I'm on my own. He's not about to assign me any help." I sigh. "How's it going up there? I wish you could come down here. The weather is about as perfect as it gets."

"Wish I could, but Elliott and I are closing in on our counterfeiter. Maybe once you get back, we can have a weekend away. I'll go ahead and schedule some time off."

"That sounds like a wonderful idea," I say. "After dealing with this and the case up in DC, I'm more than ready for some alone time with you."

"Yeah?" he teases. "You sure I'm not too boring?"

"Oh, no you absolutely are. The most boring person I know. But you're a good cook. That's the only reason I stick around." I smile. Liam and I have settled into the closest thing resembling a routine that two FBI agents can hope to have.

"I'm just glad I don't have to play the wide-eyed innocent Ms. Agostini anymore. All the attention is uncomfortable."

"Let me guess, too many guys hitting on you? Do I need to come down there and start roughing up collars?"

I hold back a laugh. Not that Liam couldn't do it, physically. He absolutely could. "Oh yes, I need my big man to come and save me."

"Booking a flight right now. Should I bring the brass knuckles or the bag of oranges?"

"Oranges," I say, definitively. "Brass knuckles are outlawed. You don't want the police involved, do you?"

"Sounds like it might be something they'd sanction." We fall into silence again for a moment. I've grown to appreciate these silences with him. They're small spaces where I feel like I can just relax and be myself without needing to say or do anything. But eventually, my curiosity gets the better of me.

"How are the pups holding up?"

"Good as ever. Tess was here again today because I had to work late. But she must have really run them because they are both sound asleep in front of the fireplace." The thought of the dogs lying on the rug in the living room while Liam cooks dinner, the smells wafting through the house, are such a disparate concept to me here. The door to my balcony is slightly open and I can still hear tropical music drifting up from the tiki bar and beyond that, the sounds of the ocean breaking against the shore. It's two very different atmospheres that I'm trying to rationalize in my brain. And I want to be in both at the same time.

"I should let you get some sleep," I finally say after a few seconds of silence. "I know it's late."

"Never too late for you. I'm always here."

My mouth turns into a wistful smile. Liam is holding down the fort while I'm here doing what? Parading around in fancy dresses going to expensive parties? Well, not any longer. "I'll let you know what Caruthers says in the morning. Who knows, maybe I'll be on a plane back tomorrow."

"Somehow I doubt that," he says. "You're too stubborn."

I purse my lips despite myself. The man knows me too well. "I love you. Sleep well."

"I love you back," he says. "Goodnight."

I hang up and set the phone on my nightstand. I test my ankle, thankful some of the swelling has already abated. I try putting a little pressure on it and find it's not as bad as I originally thought. Taking a few ginger steps, I head out to the balcony where I lean over the railing, looking out into the dark ocean. The moon has dipped below the horizon, and it's a lot darker than it had been earlier this evening.

Somewhere out there are three women who just want to get home to their families. I don't care what Caruthers says tomorrow, I'm not giving up, undercover or not.

∾

THE FOLLOWING MORNING, I'M ON THE PHONE WITH MY BOSS for the better part of half an hour while I explain the situation. While he agrees the arrest was excessive, he's not sure about leaving me down here given I no longer have the protection of anonymity. But I must be pretty insistent because he finally relents, though he's not sure how much he can help given Montenegro's antagonistic attitude.

That's okay. I've dealt with men like him before. He's not about to get in my way.

Now that I know I'm not going anywhere until this is taken care of, I retrieve my actual ID from the vent in the room, and don my normal work clothes, though I layer carefully. It can get warm out there and I've only got one suit. I don't want to sweat right through it on day one.

And that's what this is. A brand-new day one to start over and begin this investigation in earnest. No more subterfuge. My first order of business is to return to the police station and determine how much they've managed to accomplish with the investigation so far. Then I can decide the best course of action. Montenegro won't be happy, no matter what I come in with.

One of Caruthers's conditions for me staying was to move somewhere more affordable, so after I'm dressed, I pack everything up and head down to check out before taking a cab to a smaller, more budget-friendly motel further inland. As the cab pulls up, I get a better look at the place. It's not terrible, but it's much more in the vein I'm used to. I have no business staying in a five-star resort. Looking at the faded blue wooden awnings and peeling paint from the concrete walls, this already feels more like home.

Twenty minutes later, I'm set up with a room for the week at less than a third of the cost of one night at the Grand Solomon and I'm in another cab to the police station. I need to think about getting my own set of wheels if I'm going to be running an investigation here. Something with four-wheel drive because it's like Rafe said, half the island's roads are little more than dirt.

The cab drops me off, and I head back up the front stairs of the station, still careful with my ankle, though a good night's rest seems to have helped things a lot. I can put weight on it without too much soreness, and I'm hopeful I'll be good as new in another day or two. But what I'm most thankful for is my closed-toe shoes with proper support. If I'd been wearing these last night, instead of those god-forsaken sticks, I could have gotten away from those two goons.

This time when I enter the station, no one looks up or even seems to notice me. *Better*, I think. The last thing I want is a bunch of gawkers. But it means I have to tap on the glass at the sergeant's desk to make her look up. She scrunches her features when she sees me, like she recognizes me but doesn't. I show her my badge. "I need to see Montenegro."

"You're the FBI agent from last night," she says.

"In the flesh."

She quirks her mouth, though I'm not sure why. "Yeah, sure. I'll buzz you through." She hits the button and the door beside the partition opens. "Know where his office is?"

"No, I—" But before I can finish the sentence, the man is already in my field of vision. He sees me as soon as I begin to come through the doorway.

"What are you doing here?" he demands, dropping the folder he was wagging at one of the other officers.

"I'm here to finish my investigation," I say, approaching him. "Remember our discussion from last night?"

Montenegro shoots a quick glance around the room. The activity has dulled; eyes are definitely on me now. But it's different than last night. Where that had been disdain and maybe even pity, this atmosphere feels charged with something, though I don't know how to describe it.

"I don't have time for this," he says. "Your services are not needed or required." I notice a couple of the other officers leaning down and whispering to each other, shooting glances our way. It looks like we're going to have our standoff here in the middle of the station.

"Considering you tried to arrest me, I don't think I'll be relying on your judgement of whether or not you need me here," I say. "You have three missing women. I would think you'd appreciate any help to find them."

"Four," the officer at the desk beside us says.

"*Carson*," Montenegro warns.

"Four?" I ask. "What do you mean?"

Montenegro grimaces, then picks up the folder again, handing it over. "She's been missing since last night. Never returned to her hotel. You were there, maybe you know something about it."

I take the folder, confused, but when I open it, I have to steel myself. A picture of Claire Taylor is staring back at me, along with a missing person's report. As I continue to read, I realize it was filed late last night by Rafe Connor.

"Rafe called this in?" I ask.

"Mr. Connor made the initial report," Montenegro says. "Apparently no one has seen her since the party."

I check the time of the report and see it was called in at one sixteen a.m. exactly. "Have you spoken to Rafe?"

Montenegro's posture changes ever so slightly. I push past the man and head to the back of the building where he was holding me last night. Beyond the holding rooms where I was, there are a series of interview rooms, each with a small window on the doors. I check each until I find Rafe sitting in one, sipping from a Styrofoam cup as he checks his phone. There's no one else in the room with him.

I take a deep breath and open the door.

## Chapter Thirteen

RAFE GLANCES up but does a double take when he sees it's me. "Emily?" he asks, sliding his phone into his pocket. "What are you doing here?"

"Claire is missing?" I ask. "What happened to her?"

"That's what I want to know," he says. "When I got back to the party, she was already gone. I assumed she had just gone back to the hotel, but when I went to check on her, there wasn't anyone in her room."

"Wait a second, back up," I say, taking a seat across from him. "What time did you get back to the party?"

His face falls, and a few strands of his dark hair come loose, requiring him to push them back into place. "Around eleven. After...well." He sighs. "I want to apologize for my behavior last night. I was angry. I didn't mean what I said."

"I don't care about that," I say, not wanting to get into it again. "Tell me about Claire."

He blinks, not used to someone so blunt, but he recovers. "It's like I said, I went back to the party, spoke to some of the guests, but I didn't see her anywhere. I thought she'd left so I didn't think to ask anyone if they'd seen her. When the party was over around one, I went back to the hotel. I stopped by her room to check on her, but she wasn't there."

"How did you get in her room?" I ask.

"I have a key," he says. "After all, I'm the one who paid for it."

I sit back. "And you don't consider that an invasion of privacy?"

"Not really, no. I have keys for any room I reserve under my company's name. Doesn't matter who they are."

I tuck that little nugget into my back pocket for later. It's certainly disturbing; I wonder if Claire knew he had a key. "So, you went into her room?"

He nods. "I knocked first, of course. But when she didn't answer, I used the key to open the door. I then called out for her. I didn't want to startle her if she was in the shower or something. But the room was dead quiet. I looked around, but didn't see anything. It didn't look like she'd been back."

"Why do you say that?" I ask.

"Because the bed was still made and nothing looked disturbed." How he could determine that from never being in the room, I don't know. Maybe that wasn't the first time.

"How long were you in there?"

"About five minutes," he says. "I checked everywhere. The bathroom, the closets. Nothing."

"And how do you know Claire just didn't head out for a night on the town after the party? Maybe she went to a club."

"She wasn't answering her phone. Besides, Claire isn't that kind of person. She's a bookworm. I've never known her to go out unless someone forces her to."

"Did you force her to go to that party?" I ask.

"Not so much force as strongly encouraged," he says. "It's important for all aspects of Connor Investments International to put in some face time, especially with the number of deals I have in the works on this island. I need everyone at top form."

"How many employees do you have on this island? Right now."

"Only a few, why?"

"What about former employees?" I ask. I want to gauge his reaction, but there is none. He just looks at me quizzically.

"What?"

"Vicki Tolluse," I say. "You weren't aware she was on the island? She worked for you, didn't she?"

"I have no idea," he says. "My company employees a thousand people. I can't keep track of them all."

"And you don't find it suspicious she is missing as well?"

"She is?" There is the briefest hint of something on his face, but I could have imagined it. Then again, he could be lying through his teeth to me right now. The problem is I don't know how well he knew Vicki Tolluse, if at all.

He's about to open his mouth to say something else when the door swings open to reveal Montenegro. "Just what the hell do you think you're doing?"

"I'm gathering information," I say. "About your missing person."

"We have already done that," the man says. "We know how to run an investigation here, Agent Slate."

I glance at Rafe, who is exchanging glances between Montenegro and me. His shoulders are hunched, more withdrawn than he was only a moment ago. I get the sense there's something he's not telling me about Montenegro.

"Do you have anyone at the Breckenridge residence right now?" I ask. "Apparently that was the last place Claire was seen."

"Mr. Breckenridge is a very important philanthropist on the island," Montenegro says. "We aren't about to just drive up to his—"

I hold out a frustrated hand for him to stop talking and get up. "Clearly you have your priorities in order." I push past the man for the second time in under five minutes.

"*Agent Slate,*" he shouts as I head back down the hallway. "You do not have my permission to conduct this investigation!"

"Good! I don't need it," I shoot back. "We're on the clock here, Captain. If we want any chance of finding Ms. Taylor, time is of the essence. I don't care how much money the man gives away, if that's where she was last seen, that's where I'm going to start."

I hear him mutter something else under his breath before storming off in the opposite direction. I'm halfway back to the main floor when I hear footsteps behind me. Rafe comes trotting up, looking the most flustered I've ever seen him. "Emily, wait."

"What?" I ask, turning.

"I...I hoped we could start over after last night. I don't want you to have a bad opinion of me. I'm not that kind of guy—the kind who tries to get women in bed with him by, well, paying for everything."

*No, you're just the kind of guy who has unfettered access to his employees, especially the vulnerable ones.* "It doesn't matter," I tell him. "We were both just using each other for our own purposes. Now we're not. What else is there to say?"

He winces and I can tell I have struck a nerve with him. But I'm not here to make friends. I'm here to solve a crime. And I don't really care what Rafe Connor thinks of me. "Don't leave the island, Mr. Connor," I add.

"Why?" he asks, taken aback. "You can't possibly think I had something to do with this. Claire is my employee. *I'm* the one who called in the report."

"I'm not ruling anything out at this point," I tell him. "Have you notified her family?"

"Well, no, I didn't want—"

"You would do best to provide Montenegro with all the information you have on her," I say. "And make sure you're thorough."

"Emily, seriously?" he asks.

I grimace. "That's Agent Slate. Excuse me, I have an investigation." It's like Rafe's trying to play the nice guy on the outside, but I keep seeing all these gigantic red flags all over the place. And this makes *two* missing women in connection to Rafe Connor.

Still, this feels better. Now we're on even footing, and we each know each other's motives. At least now I can conduct a proper investigation.

But the fact that Claire went missing from under my nose is troubling. Something seemed wrong last night, though maybe it's like Rafe said and she's just not used to parties. Not everyone is a social butterfly. But at the same time, it seemed like something else was going on, something she wasn't about to talk about with a bunch of strangers.

Which reminds me, I'll need to track down and locate Barry and Marie Wirt to see if they spotted her at any point last night after I left the group. But the first order of business is speaking with Mr. Breckenridge. Presumably, Claire went missing from his property, which isn't looking good for him, given these rumors of an underground bunker. A bunker I feel I was close to cracking. But this isn't going to be easy. His security detail won't be happy to see me again so soon.

I head back outside determined to call a cab to the nearest car rental facility, only to find myself staring at a rusty sedan that looks like it barely survived the eighties parked right in front of the door to the station. All four windows are down and a woman with dark hair and sunglasses sits in the driver's seat, smoking a cigarette. She spots me and steps out of the car, the cigarette still hanging from her mouth. Her hair is pulled into a low ponytail, and she looks like she's probably in her mid to late forties.

"So you're the FBI Agent," she says, removing her shades. An old scar runs from just above her left eyebrow, barely missing her eye and down her cheek.

Immediately I'm on the defensive. That's two people who've ID'd me in two days. She reaches in her back pocket and I stiffen, unsure if she's going to pull a weapon on me while I'm unarmed. But it turns out to be a black wallet, which she tosses to me. I open it to find I'm staring at a police badge.

"You're with the unit?" I ask.

She nods. Her ID reads *Detective Alysssa Peregrine*, Queen's Bay Police. I toss the badge back to her. "How'd you know who I was?"

"News travels fast in a place like this," she says, leaning on the hood of her car as she takes a few more puffs of her cigarette. "Can't keep a secret here for long."

Great. There goes any chance of salvaging my cover, not that there was much there to begin with. If she's right about secrets, I should have no trouble finding out what Breckenridge is doing up there in his house. I'm not above using any avenue of information that's presented to me. "What do you know about Jeremy Breckenridge?"

Her posture doesn't change. "You're looking into the missing women," she says. "I should have figured. That's why you're here, isn't it?"

I can't tell if the deflection is because she's out here fishing for Montenegro or if she has some other agenda. But whatever is going on, I don't have time for it. "Listen," I say. "I'd love to chat, but I have an investigation to conduct."

She drops the cigarette, putting it out under her foot as she circles her car to come face to face with me. She's got a few inches on me, but I don't feel like she is trying to be threatening. "Let me guess, Montenegro tried to send you back home, didn't he?"

I eye her carefully.

"Doesn't surprise me. That man will do anything he can to undermine real police work."

"What does that mean?" I ask.

"It means I had to take on this case in my personal time because it was obvious to me that no one here gave a damn," she says, pulling out another cigarette as she leans up against this side of her car's hood. "Three missing women in two weeks. If it were anywhere but here, it would be front-page national news."

"You're working the case?"

"Trying to," she says, covering her hand so she can light against the breeze. "Montenegro keeps freezing me out, so I've only been able to conduct a rudimentary investigation. It's been slow to say the least. And I have a bad feeling that the longer this takes, the worse it's going to end up."

"If you have a problem with your boss, why not go up the chain?" I'm not sure I buy this bit about not being in league with Montenegro. As far as I can tell, he's got all his people on a pretty short chain, if last night was any indication.

"Tried. But guess what? The people who hired him, know exactly the kind of person he is. And they don't want this story getting out any more than he does."

"Why not?" I ask.

"It's bad for business. Bad for the island. Would you come to a remote island if you found out people were disappearing at random? Anything that hurts the tourist industry here is summarily swept under the rug." There is real disgust in her voice, real anger. If she's putting on a show, it's a good one. Still, I'm not sure I'm ready to trust her just yet.

"So you've been operating on your own? Looking into the missing women?"

"I've been trying," she says. "But I know Montenegro is keeping information locked away. He claims he doesn't have anything else and that the disappearances are just low on evidence, but I know better. He's hiding something."

That's intriguing, and it matches up with Caruthers's suspicions. "Like what?"

"If I knew, I'd tell you, trust me. I just hope now that

you're here, things will finally start moving in the right direction."

If this is a trap by Montenegro, I don't see how it would help him. By pooling my resources with a local cop, I can be that much more effective in my investigation and find these women faster. "There are *four* missing women. Not three."

"Four?" she asks, the cigarette drooping.

"Claire Taylor went missing from Breckenridge's party last night. No one has seen her since. And your boss doesn't seem willing to look into the matter for fear of upsetting Mr. Breckenridge."

"Son of a *bitch*," she spits and winces, looking like she wants to kick something. Only, the nearest object is a fire hydrant, which she wisely avoids.

"If you'd be willing to share what you've gathered so far, it would go a long way to helping my investigation," I say.

"Be happy to," she replies. "Not that I think it will help much." She walks around to the backseat of her car and pulls out a file folder from a small box behind her front seat then hands it over. Inside are the original missing person's reports for the three women, along with transcripts of interviews Peregrine has done with anyone who might have witnessed something. She's done some footwork on this, and it's solid.

"Unfortunately, the women who went missing from the public places, Tolluse and Van Allen, didn't leave much behind. Somehow, no one saw *anything.* Which is suspicious in itself. Stamper is another story. I tried to get access to her property but got repeatedly stonewalled."

I close the file, having made my decision. "That's the good thing about being a federal officer. I can requisition resources from your local department as I see fit. *Without* Montenegro's authorization if need be." It will take some convincing calls to Caruthers, but I think I can swing that, especially with Peregrine's insistence that Montenegro is actively impeding this investigation.

"Damn, really?" she says. "I wish you'd been here the whole time."

"I'm here now," I say. "And it just so happens I need a car. Mind driving me up to Breckenridge's house?"

"Need a second pair of eyes up there?" she asks.

I smile. "Couldn't hurt."

# Chapter Fourteen

THE DRIVE UP the mountain doesn't take very long. And it's a very different experience from last night in the hired car. Apparently, the windows in Peregrine's car don't work, so the wind blows my hair back the whole way. I eventually have to clip it back to keep it from medusa-ing all over the place.

We go over the basics of my experience from the night before, including the rooms I was able to find under the house, which are news to her. It seems like some secrets on the island manage to pass under the radar after all. I'm still not a hundred percent sure I trust her. But we have the same goal, and that's enough for now.

The lush greenery of the island recedes as we continue to climb until it reveals the beautiful blue of the ocean in the distance. Last night all I could see was darkness, but today the world is alive with color. As we get higher, the lushness drops away completely before turning into what I could only describe as sticklike prickly bushes that line the side of the winding road, taking up residence and ready to put up a fight to anyone who would cut them out.

But as we approach the Breckenridge estate, that's exactly what happens. All the natural flora disappears and is instead replaced by artificial barriers with cascading flowers. Peregrine pulls up to the main gate, which sits just off the road. Where it was open with a security guard last night, today things look locked up tight.

"It's always like this," she says. "Except on the nights when he opens it up for a fundraiser."

I take quick stock of the area as I get out of the car; the place is dead quiet. When I glance up, a small camera mounted over the gate tells me they already know we're here.

There's a keypad next to the gate, and I cross over and press it.

"Yes?" a voice over the intercom says.

"FBI. Open the gates."

"Do you have an appointment?" the voice asks.

"We're investigating a missing woman who was last seen at this address last night. We'd like to ask a few questions and find out if anyone knows where she might have gone."

"You'll need to schedule an appointment with our house coordinator," the voice says. "She can be reached—"

Peregrine is beside me in an instant and presses the button three times in succession. "Are you saying Mr. Breckenridge is not willing to aid the FBI in finding a missing woman? A woman who witnesses last place here only twelve hours ago?"

"Hold please," the voice says.

I have to admit I'm impressed. Peregrine doesn't take any shit. I can appreciate that.

"Our team will meet you at the front of the house," the voice says, and the gate automatically begins to open.

"Thanks," I say.

"These guys are all the same," she says before heading back to the car. "And Breckenridge is skittish about bad press."

"He hasn't come up in your investigation yet?" I ask as we get back in. The gates in front of us open slowly towards the car.

"No, but I can't say I'm surprised he could be involved. I don't trust rich people."

That makes two of us.

Today the house looks much less impressive than it did last night with all the water and light effects. While still huge and embedded in the side of a mountain, it's much less ethereal in the daylight.

"How do you want to handle it?" she asks.

"Handle what?"

"The obstruction?"

I take a breath. "Let's...not go full bore right out of the gate. If we push too hard, they'll just kick us out and then we really *will* have to approve a warrant from a judge. Let's just take it easy at first, see what they know. I doubt Breckenridge is here anyway."

"Think he skipped town?" she asks, pulling up to the same area where the driver dropped us off last night. Gone are the expensive cars.

"Who knows. Someone with this much money probably takes three jet trips per day," I say before getting out. A man in a black suit stands at the front doors to the house. I notice it's my friend from last night. The one whose arm I almost broke. "Maybe you should take the lead on this one."

She gives me a frown, but it doesn't last as she leads the charge across the bridge to the front door. As soon as the man spots me, his nostrils flare. "What the hell?"

I pull out my badge. "I'm Special Agent Emily Slate with the FBI. Last night I was here undercover."

"Wait, what's going on here?" he asks.

"Are you head of security?" Peregrine asks, showing him her own badge.

"Yes, and *she* almost broke my arm last night," he says, glaring at me over her shoulder.

"Which is why you shouldn't touch people without their permission," I say.

"How's the ankle," he asks, his eyes boring into me.

"Just fine."

Peregrine clears her throat to break the tension. "We need to ask you some questions about the party last night. Are you familiar with a guest named Claire Taylor?"

Finally, he breaks eye contact with me before addressing her. "I don't believe so."

"She had on a dark purple dress, blonde hair, about five-seven," I say. "She works for Rafe Connor."

"I don't keep track of everyone," he says. "There were over a hundred guests here."

That's going to slow things down. I hadn't realized there were so many, probably because I was sticking to my little group. But given the size of the house, I absolutely believe it.

"We're going to need to speak to your entire security team. I also want to see any security footage from last night." I turn back to the gate. "Are all the cameras exterior?"

"No," he replies. "Mr. Breckenridge invests in only the best technology," the man says. "The types of cameras he uses inside are strategically placed not to be noticed."

"Is that so?" Peregrine asks. "So there could be cameras in rooms considered private? Such as restrooms?"

The man bristles. "Perhaps you should go get that warrant. I'm not sure I should be speaking to you without some kind of representation."

"All we want to know is what happened to Claire Taylor after I left the party," I say, trying to diffuse the situation. "If we could see the footage, we'll be out of your hair."

He hesitates.

"Or we can go speak to my friends down at the St. Solomon Source and let them know a woman disappeared from this property and the owner is refusing access," Peregrine says.

The man pinches his features. "Ten minutes."

"Great, thank you," I say.

The man turns and opens the door to the property, allowing us to enter. I ask for his ID and credentials, which he hands over. His name is Henry Roberts, and from the information he provides, he's been head of the property's security team for three years, ever since the house was finished. Once we're inside, he heads back through the coat check room I saw last night. We can hear him on the radio with someone while we stand there.

"I'm going to take a look out by the pool," I tell her. "When he comes back, have him show you the footage from last night."

"How will I recognize her?" Peregrine asks.

"Do you know Rafe Connor?" She nods. "She'll be the one who looks like she's trying to crawl out of her skin to get away from him." Peregrine gives me an appraising nod as I head back through the house out to the pool area. While I would love to go back downstairs and get into those locked rooms, there's no way that's happening without a warrant. Best we can hope for now is seeing the cab company that picked up Claire Taylor after the party was over.

As I reach the pool deck, I find myself facing off with two men dressed in black. I recognize one from last night as the man who spoke to the police while I was in the back of the car. I pull out my badge and hold it up. "Just here looking for a missing woman," I say.

"Missing woman?" one of them asks, stepping forward. "Did Roberts clear this?"

"Mr. Roberts is helping my colleague look at your security footage last night," I say, putting my badge away. "I'm just making sure there couldn't have been an accident."

"An accident?" his voice is rough and harsh.

"This house sits on the side of a mountain. If someone falls over the edge, it would be impossible for them to climb back up."

He scoffs. "No one has ever fallen over the edge."

"That you're aware of." I sidestep him and proceed to the edge of the deck. Upon closer inspection, there appears to be a clear glass barrier that would prevent someone from going over, but last night it was almost invisible. The only place the barrier isn't present is along the edge of the infinity pool, which flows over an edge to a reservoir a few feet down on the other side, kind of like a gutter that recycles the water back up into the pool. Beyond that it's just dirt and more of those sticker bushes all the way down the face of the hill.

I lean over the barrier as best I can, but there's no indication of any disturbed soil or anything that would lead me to believe someone fell over the edge and tumbled down. I should be seeing some indentations, disturbed dirt or displaced bushes, but there's nothing. However, out of the corner of my eye, I can see the lower pool on the next level down, just peeking out from the edge of the landing up here.

"What about that pool?" I ask. "Is there a barrier down there as well?"

"You were the only guest down in that area last night," the man says. "No one else went down there."

Of course, I have no way of verifying that until we inspect the footage. But I can see the lower deck level is almost completely obscured from the upper. It's as if it was designed to be the owner's private deck, while this is the one used for all the socializing.

Still, I continue to inspect the entire area, the man following me like a shadow. On the far side of the "main" pool, I see a pathway that winds off into what looks like a garden.

"What's that over there?" I ask.

"It's where Mr. Breckenridge keeps some of his more prized flowers," he says. "It's generally off-limits to guests due to the delicate nature of the herbology."

And the perfect place for someone to get lost if they just happened to wander off. Or if they were lured away.

"Have you taken a look at it today?" I ask.

"It is part of my rounds first thing in the morning," the man replies. "Didn't see anything out of the ordinary."

"Do you remember Claire Taylor from last night?" I give the man her full description.

"I remember when she arrived. Five minutes after the appointed event start time."

"How did she get here?"

"White cab," he says. "Dropped her off. I was at the door as it was still early. I checked her name off the list and let her in."

"And you never saw her again after that?"

"Not that I recall."

"Slate!" Peregrine calls out, waving me towards the house. I nod to the two men and trot over to her.

"What's going on?"

"Here, come look at this," she says, and I follow her through the house, back past the coat rack and into a security office. Roberts is sitting down at a terminal showing a variety of feeds from all over the house. Some of which show the two men I was just speaking with outside by the pool.

"What?" I ask.

"Show her," Peregrine says.

The man grimaces and goes into the security files. "All the security files are recorded and stored here, hour by hour." He points to the list of files on the monitor. I see them marked out with time stamps starting with the year, then month, day and hour. "But the last recording here is from six last night. The next file isn't until six am this morning."

"Someone erased the files?" I ask.

"It looks that way," he says. "I don't understand this."

"Who would have the clearance to erase files?" I ask.

"Just me and Mr. Breckenridge," he replies, looking at me sheepishly.

I glower at him. "Find your boss. Immediately."

# Chapter Fifteen

I TRUDGE BACK OUTSIDE, the morning sun beating down on me. There's no breeze today and even though the climate on the island is usually near perfect, up here in the mountains it's less forgiving. And without any natural shade, I'm sweating before I can get halfway across the grounds back to the round-about where our car is parked. In this harsh daylight, the house has lost any of its remaining luster from the night before. I'd rather see it as it really is anyway.

After learning about the missing footage, I believed we had enough for a warrant. And after speaking with Caruthers and a local judge on the island using Peregrine's connections, it was approved. Even Roberts agreed that a full investigation was warranted and seems as disturbed by the missing footage as we are, though he's proclaiming innocence on his part. It's not hard to tell he takes pride in his job, and losing an entire night's worth of footage isn't something he's used to. Conveniently, no one seems to be able to contact Mr. Breckenridge, who left the island early this morning in his private helicopter.

As I reach the roundabout, I'm met by two St. Solomon police vehicles pulling up. Two officers get out of each, and I hold up my badge. "I'm Special Agent Slate," I say.

One of the other officers nods and hands over a warrant issued by the judge. It isn't as comprehensive as I had hoped, but it at least allows us to visually search the entire property, which will include the rooms in the restricted part of the house.

I turn to address all four of them. "The property is large. Coordinate and go floor by floor. I also want to get a drone overhead. The grounds around the property are expansive, and if she's out there somewhere, she'll be easier to spot from the air."

"I've got one in the trunk," an officer says, popping the back.

"Good. Check in with me or Detective Peregrine every fifteen minutes. And if you find anything that looks even the slightest bit suspicious, come get us immediately."

I leave the officers to get to work as they begin planning out how they're going to divide up the house. So far Peregrine has turned out to be an ally, but I still need to be careful. I'm operating on my own here and can't trust anyone to keep an eye on my back. At least she seems as determined as I am to find these women, which is a nice change of pace from Montenegro.

As I return to the house, I hear the whine of the drone's engines as it takes off. I'm thinking specifically about the gardens off to the west of the house. Even though the security team checks them, there's a possibility Claire might have wandered that direction. And without any footage to back it up, we need to be thorough. As far as I can tell, the gardens back up to some heavy brush where she might have veered off the paths.

Then again, she may just be locked up in the basement.

"Look, I don't know what else to tell you," Roberts says as I walk back into the main living area. He's sitting on one of the couches while Peregrine stands in front of him, her arms crossed. The same man from before stands close; he's identified himself as Daniels, the nighttime security manager. "Only two people have that authority. And I wasn't the one who erased them."

"Then your boss did," Peregrine says.

"No, he left this morning," Roberts replies. "He never would have had the chance. After the party was over, he was never alone until we drove him to the heliport."

"Then either you have a security leak, or you're lying," I say, approaching him. He doesn't seem to like either option.

The door down the hall opens and two of the officers come in. The man behind Roberts stiffens. "Calm down," I tell them both. "They're here with the warrant."

"We're just not used to having security problems," Roberts says, turning back to us. "Usually things are quiet."

"How often does Mr. Breckenridge have these... fundraisers?"

"About once a quarter," he says as two of the officers head through the house, visually inspecting everything.

"And how often does he entertain when he's *not* raising money?" I ask.

He purses his lips. "If Mr. Breckenridge is here, there are usually guests."

"How many and how often?" Peregrine asks.

"Could be just a few to dozens," he says. "He's here more often in the winter. He'll stay for a few weeks at a time. But he's got another house down in Antigua. Mr. Breckenridge... he likes to entertain. As you can see, he built the house for it."

"And these...*guests*...he brings with him. Do you vet them in any way?"

He grimaces again. "You have to understand, Mr. Breck-enridge, he wants his guests to feel...free to express themselves when they're here."

"What the hell does that mean?" Peregrine asks.

Roberts breaks eye contact for the first time. He gets paid to keep his boss's secrets, so I'm not surprised he's not willing to answer the question. "So you could have security leaks and not even know it," I say. "How do you know he hasn't invited someone in his house who will rob him blind?"

"These aren't those kinds of people," he replies. "They don't need money."

I nod, working my jaw. "How do you know that? If you don't do any background checks on them?"

"I've been given specific instructions…" He trails off.

This is getting us nowhere. Breckenridge has dozens of people coming in and out of this house every month. Someone could have gotten close to him, infiltrated their way into his inner circle and found a way to pressure him. We could be dealing with a professional job here. How else would they know how to erase the footage? But was it specifically to cover up what happened to Claire, or just a coincidence?

I motion for Peregrine to join me out of earshot of Roberts and the other guy. "He's not going to risk his career, missing woman or not. Are any of the other women in Breckenridge's circle at all? Did he interact with them in any way?"

"Like I said, I hadn't found anything to implicate him from what little I've gathered," she replies. "Doesn't mean he doesn't have a hand in it, though."

"I think it's worth investigating," I say. "We need to find out if any of the women had any connection at all to Breckenridge."

"I'll get started on that as soon as we leave."

I turn back to Roberts. "Okay. Here's the deal. By your own admission either you or Breckenridge erased that footage. Since he's gone, that leaves you, which means a woman is missing on your watch and you are potentially the only person who could have covered up her disappearance. That makes you a suspect."

"What?" he says. "I'm being cooperative."

"You want to be cooperative? Show me what's in those rooms I was checking last night."

He grits his teeth. "Mr. Breckenridge won't be happy about that."

"I don't care what he's happy with. We have a warrant, signed by a judge. Either show us, or I take you into custody and I get him to show us." I nod to Daniels.

His face begins to go red and he grimaces, looking back and forth between us. "Get the keys."

Daniels steps forward. "But——"

"Get the fucking keys," Roberts shouts. His anger is palpable as he turns back to us. "You want to see what's in there so bad? Fine. But I'm telling you, this wasn't Breckenridge. Or anyone on my team."

"Your loyalty will pay off when you're in the clink," Peregrine says. "It'll help when you need to join one of the gangs to keep from having your ass kicked on a daily basis."

Daniels returns with a set of keys. They catch the light at an odd angle, practically gleaming. There's no mistaking the fact they are at least plated in solid gold. Daniels hands over the keys to Roberts as he stands. "Follow me."

Peregrine whistles and gets one of the cops from the other room to come trotting in. "Stay with him until we get back," she orders, pointing at Daniels.

We follow Roberts back through the labyrinth of the house I explored the night before, finally leading to the hidden staircase. We take the stairs slow, with Roberts at front as we descend to the lower level of the house. As we pass through the hallway, I feel a distinct twinge as we pass over the spot where I tweaked my ankle. It's still sore and I'll need to ice it again. But at least I'm not limping anymore.

We reach the first door and Roberts slides the key in, mumbling something under his breath.

"What was that?" I ask.

"I said I'm going to have to start looking for a new job after this."

"Better than looking at the inside of a cell," Peregrine

replies. It doesn't surprise me she has the experience to deal with something like this. Maybe she just needed some backup, like I did. It would have been hard to do this alone.

As Roberts opens the door, the light in the room immediately flickers on.

We're greeted by what looks like some kind of museum. Glass cases fill the expansive room, all of them cluttered with different objects. The backs of the cabinets are mirrored, giving the whole room a polished, upscale feel. Cool LED lights illuminate everything in the cases, each of which has small placards describing the items.

"What the hell?" If someone were to ask me to identify anything in these cases, I'd have a hard time doing it. One thing I can say is everything looks *old*. It all looks like something out of a history museum.

"Mr. Breckenridge's collection," he replies. "Most of these items are from St. Solomon and the surrounding area. Archeological treasures found when the island was developed."

I take a closer look at the cabinets, noting they all have pinpoint laser lights across them, which, if interrupted by something, say a hand, would probably sound an alarm. Each item is labeled, and it is all catalogued.

"What's the point of keeping this all behind locked doors?" I ask. "You'd think he'd want to show this off. Billionaires love showing off their money."

Roberts shuffles. "There may be some...issues with a few of the items. Legally speaking."

"He stole them," Peregrine says.

"They are contested." He's doing his best to remain composed, but the man is sweating. And I doubt it's because of a couple archeological trinkets that may or may not be stolen relics from native peoples. This isn't what we're looking for.

"Okay," I say. "Next door."

He lets out a long breath as we leave and locks the room

behind us. I doubt it's worth my time to even investigate this avenue of potentially stolen goods. I can't see how that would connect to Claire or any of the other missing women. But it does give me some more insight into Breckenridge himself.

Roberts hesitantly moves to the next door and slips the key inside. His rigid stance and non-averting eyes tell me he's nervous about this one. Much more than the last one.

As he opens it, he stops for a split second, as if he's questioning whether he should be doing this or not. I'm about to encourage him along but he proceeds on his own and is the first one to pass through the door as soon as it's opened.

Peregrine and I exchange glances before following him in.

Inside, the room is decorated in dark velvet, moodier than the rest of the house. Candelabras are attached to the walls down a long hallway that ends in a staircase. It's like stepping into a glass of red wine. There's also the faint smell of lilacs and rosewood.

Roberts is ahead of us, nearing the staircase. He looks back with a miserable face. "This way."

If there are cameras down here, I can't spot them. But just like upstairs, that doesn't mean they don't exist.

We descend the stairs, and I think back to my conversation with Barry the night before. This place would definitely fit the description of what he was talking about. There are no windows anywhere; I believe I was right last night. This has to be embedded within the side of the hill itself.

"What's down here?" I ask Roberts, not liking the feeling creeping up the back of my spine. Nothing good can come from a place like this.

"It's a sex thing; it has to be," Peregrine says. "Why else would you put velvet on the walls?"

Roberts lets out a long sigh and opens the first door at the bottom of the stairs. I notice a "1" on the front. But there is no lock on the handle. He steps aside as the door swings inward.

In the middle of the room is a large, four poster bed. But this is no ordinary bed, all along the posters are metal ring hooks. The bed is plush and covered in more dark red, but there is a mirror on the ceiling above it, though it's smoky and aged. The walls are covered in...*tools*, for lack of a better word. Whips, floggers, a cat-o-nine-tails, and everything in between. There are long bamboo sticks lined up like pool cues and a big chest in the middle of the wall. Behind the bed is a large wooden X, also with ring hooks at each of the four ends.

"What did I tell you?" Peregrine says.

"BDSM?" I turn back to Roberts. He drops his gaze. "This is why Breckenridge entertains so many people. They come here for not only the privacy, but the selection." I head over to the chest, opening drawer after drawer. It's full of everything a loving couple, or throuple could want. Lubes; cleaners; phalluses of all shapes, sizes, and colors. The selection is virtually endless.

"The other rooms?" I ask.

"All the same. More or less," Roberts replies.

While I don't have a problem with what people do in their spare time, my issue is the secrecy surrounding all of it. But none of the doors have locks, and as far as I can tell there isn't anything here to indicate any of this wouldn't be consensual. I pull out my phone to check the notifications. No service. "Do you have some kind of interference down here?"

"It's too deep for a signal to get through," he replies. "But that's what people seem to want."

I inspect the room further. There is a bathroom attached, accessible by an almost hidden door along one of the walls. It has a shower, tub, and even a hose in the event someone needs spraying off. It's taking all my willpower not to imagine all the things that have happened down here.

"Did Mr. Breckenridge use any of these rooms last night?"

"No, not on a fundraiser night. He was too busy," he replies.

"Would anyone else have used them?" Peregrine asks. "Who else knows about them?"

"They are a well-kept secret in his circles."

"Great, so hundreds of people," she mutters under her breath.

"Let's see the other rooms. Have you checked down here since Claire Taylor went missing?"

He clears his throat. "We didn't have the chance before you showed up this morning."

I motion for him to continue opening the rest of the doors for us. As far as I can tell, this room looks unused from last night. Unless housekeeping was in here early to clean up.

"I'm telling you," Roberts says as he goes through the next five doors, two more on this side and three on the other. Some are bigger with different equipment than the others. "No one would have been using these rooms during the fundraiser. They're off-limits. That was the whole reason the alarm went off when you tried to get in."

Peregrine gives me an appraising look with the hint of a smirk on her lips.

"Uh-huh," I say. I just want to make sure I check every square inch of this house.

Roberts goes through the rest of the rooms, all of which seem unused, like he says. When we reach the final door, he hesitates again. It's that same hesitation I saw at the main entrance.

I motion to Peregrine to make sure she picks up on it, which she does. Finally, though, he opens the last door. Half of me fully expects to see Claire Taylor's body splayed out on the bed, but it's just like the others. Empty.

A quick check of the room confirms it is like the others, and after checking the en suite, I have to accept that she's not down here. This is it. It's a large, completely inaccessible part of the house, but as far as I can tell, there wasn't any foul play involved.

Still, I'm not about to let go so easily. "Don't bother locking anything up down here," I tell Roberts. "I want to dust for any prints." That is going to be an absolute *nightmare*, but if Claire was down here at any point last night, I need to know it.

"Prints? You can't be serious," he says.

"I am," I say and even Peregrine returns a skeptical look.

We leave him in the hallway and head back up. As soon as we're back in the main hall with the two doors, Peregrine's phone buzzes.

She glances at it, then her eyes go wide. "Back upstairs," she says. "They've found something."

## Chapter Sixteen

"WHAT DID YOU FIND?" Peregrine asks as we get back to the top of the stairs where one of the officers is waiting. Daniels is still where we left him near the couch.

"Picked something up with the drone," he says. "Come look." We follow him outside where his partner has a remote control in his hand. On the remote is a monitor that shows the view of the camera mounted on the drone. It's above the property, high in the sky.

"What am I looking at?" I ask, looking up to shield my eyes from the sun. Just above us, in the blue, I spot the black drone as it hovers.

"Check this out," the man operating the remote says. The drone zips off to the east, in the direction of the gardens. The drone descends until it's about a hundred feet in the air. As the gardens end and the brush begins, a clear trail of worn dirt can be seen from above. It might not be readily noticeable from the ground, but with a bird's eye view, it's unmistakable.

"Where does that lead?" I ask.

"We're not a hundred percent sure," he says. "Off to the east." The drone continues following the path for a good minute or two, the operator taking it slow enough that we can tell where he's going. But as the path curves around the slope of the hill, the brush itself grows thicker and dirt changes to worn grass that's harder to discern. Finally, the path disappears into the tropical tree line.

"That's as far as we've gone," the operator says. "I didn't want to lose the drone in the trees."

Great. I guess that means we're headed into the woods. I turn to Peregrine who—from the look on her face—has come to the same conclusion.

"Keep that above the gardens so we can see to reach the path," I tell the operator. He nods before Peregrine and I head back to the house.

"Think the security team knows?" she asks.

"It's well-hidden, but I would hope they had some idea it was there," I say. "Then again, maybe we're looking at another underground room situation. Maybe no one is 'supposed' to know it's there."

"Daniels," I call out as soon as we're back in the house. He stands and follows as Peregrine and I head over to the gardens.

"Those are off-limits," he says, trotting behind us. We plow forward into the gardens regardless. The flowers on both sides tower above us, almost like a hedge maze, but I don't need to see over them to know which direction we're going. Breckenridge must employ a small army of landscape employees to keep this area looking this good. A white pebble stone that I'm sure isn't native to this island makes up most of the path, and it crunches under my feet as we walk. The garden itself is full of lush, tropical plants of all colors, some of which I'm sure are toxic to the touch, though there is no signage to indicate as such. Still, I keep my hands to myself as we navigate the path, eventually coming to the eastern border where the path curves back towards the house.

"I must insist," Daniels continues to protest. "Mr. Breckenridge doesn't allow anyone—"

Above us, the drone flies towards the extreme edge of the gardens. It takes us a few minutes to reach it.

"I don't see it," I say, looking around. We're almost right under the drone.

"See what?" Daniels asks.

"It must be...*here*," Peregrine says, stepping off the path between two bushes. At first, it looks like she's just walked into the middle of the brush, but when I follow, I can clearly see the worn dirt from many trips. Above us, the drone whirrs as if to indicate we're on the right track.

"You can't do that!" Daniels says. I turn around and push back through the brush onto the rocky route of the garden again.

"Did you know about this?"

"About what?" he asks.

I motion for him to go ahead. "See for yourself." He gives me a tentative glance before swallowing and stepping through the brush. I follow, and all three of us find ourselves looking at a strip of dirt, cutting through the grass as it winds away from the Breckenridge estate.

"This is impossible," he says.

"Looks to me like someone has access to your boss's property without your knowledge," I say.

He looks a bit lost. Between him and Roberts, there seems to be a massive security breach within Breckenridge's ranks. "Where does it lead?"

"That's what we're going to find out," I say. "But first, we're going to all go back and answer some questions."

The three of us head back through the garden and reach the house again. I gather the other four officers and make sure we're all on the same page, going over the location and accessibility of the path before taking time to sit down and interview each of Breckenridge's employees.

An hour later and with no new information, I catch Peregrine shooting glances at the garden. I admit, I'm anxious to get down there as well. But we have to make sure we don't let anything else slip under the radar first.

As we're working, the CSI team arrives, though one of the team warns Peregrine that Montenegro caught wind of what we were doing and is on his way up to the house. I guess I shouldn't be surprised; we could only operate under the radar for so long. And if he shows up, so what? I'm not about to let him bully me off this case.

"C'mon," I tell Peregrine, pulling her to the side. "We need to check that path out before your boss gets here."

"What about the rest of the statements?" she asks.

"Let your colleagues handle those," I say. "We're running out of time."

"Right."

We head back out to the garden again, this time finding the path much more easily now that we know where to look. In less than five minutes, we've lost all trace of the Breckenridge mansion as the path winds its way around the hillside, the grass knee-high on either side of us.

We continue to make our way down the hill with treacherous footing in places. I keep thinking about how grateful I am that I'm not wearing heels anymore. There is no way someone could have navigated this path in them, and Claire was wearing them when I last saw her. Doesn't mean she couldn't have come this way at some point, but still, I'm skeptical she would have made it this far on her own.

I'm also worried about the security risk this path poses to Breckenridge and his guests. The front of his house is like a fortress—no one is getting in without going through a rigorous process. But anyone with a good pair of hiking boots and some determination could make this easily.

It feels like an hour has gone by when we finally reach the tree line, but when I check my phone, it's only been about fifteen minutes. Still, I'm sweating through my blouse and thinking I probably should have brought some water with me.

As soon as the canopy envelops us, it cools off a little and isn't as difficult to manage. Peregrine doesn't seem fazed, I suspect she's used to it living on the island.

Once in the trees the path opens up a little, though it's still barely there. I pay close attention to not lose it. At this rate, we're going to end up all the way down the mountain and I have no idea what I expect to find.

"Agent, look."

I glance up, having been keeping my eyes on my feet so I don't trip on anything. Ahead of us is a large clearing, though it's still under the tree canopy. And in the middle of the clearing are five standing stones arranged in a circle probably fifty feet in diameter. Each stone is nine or ten feet tall at least.

"What the hell is that?" I ask.

"I know what it is," she says. "There's another one on the far end of the island. Those are the *Killing Stones.*"

"I'm sorry, the *what?*"

"Ancient stones left by the native people to this island. Most believe they were used for human sacrifices back before the island was colonized."

If someone was looking to make a statement, they could have brought Claire down here for some kind of ritual. I'm apprehensive about what we might find. "And that's what people call them?"

"People call them all sorts of things, but yeah. It's how they're known."

Looking at the path, it leads directly to the stones. "Do you really think Breckenridge's people didn't know this was here?"

"It's possible," she says. "The stones on the north side of the island, they're a tourist destination. I knew there were other monuments somewhere on the island, but I've never seen them in person. I guess a lot of people just forget they're here."

"Someone hasn't forgotten," I say, pointing down at the path. Well-worn or not, someone knew this was here. And they came down here enough to wear a path all the way to Breckenridge's property.

"How do you want to proceed?" she asks.

No doubt Montenegro has reached the Breckenridge house by now. And since we're already out here, a cursory investigation of the area couldn't hurt. But we need to be on guard. There's no telling who could be out here watching and waiting. "I think it's worth investigating. But let's take it slow."

She nods. We approach the site gently. The jungle is alive with the sounds of insects and tropical birds. Some even fly overhead as we approach. I don't see any evidence of footprints, or anything else that immediately stands out. And when I stop to listen, I don't hear the sounds of anything larger than a mongoose moving in the distance. That doesn't mean someone isn't out there. Still, I allow myself to relax a little and inspect the rocks more closely. For indigenous people to have moved these here and stood them up like this must have taken some extreme ingenuity on their part. They have to weigh hundreds of tons each.

As I'm looking at the base of one of them, trying to figure out how deep they might go, something catches my eye. It's subtle, but I bend down to take a closer look. "Detective," I say, pulling out my phone to take a picture.

She comes over, looking over my shoulder. "What is that?"

I snap a few pictures, then remove a clear evidence bag from my jacket pocket. I also pull on a glove before reaching down and picking it up. As I do, the ruby at the end of the chain sparkles in the pinpricks of sunlight that reach the clearing.

"It's Claire Taylor's necklace," I say. "The one she had on last night."

# Chapter Seventeen

A YELL from somewhere on the other side of the clearing catches our attention. My hand goes for my weapon, realizing too late it isn't there. I never checked one out from the police station, despite it being on my to-do list this morning. After Montenegro's combativeness, I didn't think he'd be receptive to loaning me a firearm.

And as if the thought of the man has summoned him from the ether, he emerges from the trees, followed by another officer from the house with a reproachful look on his face. Montenegro, however, looks ready to spit fire, though I notice he's limping. Still, knowing it's him and not some wild animal or would-be kidnapper allows me to relax my shoulders a little.

"You," Montenegro says as soon as he sees me.

"Me," I say as he makes his way into the circle.

This only seems to piss him off more. I expect steam to start billowing from his ears any second. "Do you have any idea what you've started here? I just got off the phone with Mr. Breckenridge demanding to know why a warrant has been served at his residence."

"Did you speak with the officers on the site?" I ask.

"Of course I did," he spits. "That doesn't change the fact I told you not to look into this matter here and you did it anyway."

"Captain, whether you want to believe it or not, I don't work for you. You have a royal mess on your hands here and your attitude isn't helping matters any."

"My...*attitude*," he yells. Birds above us scatter. But before he can go off any further, I hold up the evidence bag with the necklace. "What is that?"

"Claire Taylor's necklace from last night," I say. "She had it on during the party."

He narrows his eyes. "Where did you find that?"

I point to the stone nearest to me. "Right there. At the base." He glances over, only now seeming to realize where he's standing. He takes a cursory look around the clearing, soaking in the fact he's at an ancient monument.

"Still think we shouldn't be looking at Breckenridge?" I ask.

"That's...he's..." Montenegro sputters before turning to Peregrine. "What the hell are you doing here?"

"Working the case," she says. "Just like I told you I would."

I can tell he wants to go off on her, but he glances at me and wisely keeps his mouth shut. "This is enough for me to *officially* take over this investigation. I'll need you to keep your resources available in case they're needed."

"I'm sorry," he says, stiffening. "But all our officers are busy on other matters."

"That's okay," I say, not missing a beat. "I'll just call in a contingent from Miami. I can have ten agents down here in an hour or two. We'll need to use your station as a staging area, and everyone will need vehicles. Not to mention—"

He holds up his hands. "Okay, okay. What do you need?"

"I need your CSI team down here," I say. "They need to check this area for any other evidence, then I want them working on the Breckenridge house, specifically the basement."

"The…basement?"

Peregrine steps forward and gives him a quick rundown of what we found down there. Montenegro's face turns sour at the thought. "There could be hundreds of prints down there."

"I know," I say. "But if Claire was in any of those rooms, we need to know. I want to find out if Breckenridge had a hand in this or not."

Some of the air goes out of Montenegro. "You don't understand. We can't just…he's a…and the mayor won't…"

"Listen, I know billionaires operate on their own set of rules, so we need to keep it quiet for now. He knows about the warrant; he doesn't need to know anything else. Though I would like to interview him."

"I believe he'll be back in a few days. He has a meeting with the mayor and Mr. Connor."

I perk up. "A meeting?"

"Something about a land deal," he says. I shoot Peregrine a look, but it seems this is news to her too. "I can request some time on his schedule, but unless you have hard evidence to charge him, I wouldn't expect to see him in an interview room anytime soon."

I have to agree with him there. And the necklace isn't strong enough to connect him to Claire's disappearance. It's still plausible she could have wandered off out here and gotten lost.

"We'll also need to perform a grid search," Peregrine says. At least she and I are on the same page. A grid search will take the rest of the day, if not longer. But we have to eliminate the possibility.

Montenegro looks around, his hands on his hips. Now that he's calmed down, he seems more lucid. "Yeah, yeah. I'll get a couple more guys out here."

"Thank you," I say, genuinely meaning it for the first time.

He turns to the officer behind him. "Get back to the house and call in Eduardo's unit. Tell them to get up here as soon as possible." The officer nods and heads back the way we came. Montenegro turns back to us. "I'm not an unreasonable person, Agent. But you have to remember, this is a small island with a small community. Rumors get around easily." I send Peregrine a quick look. "And the last thing we need is to be accusing our biggest benefactor without a mountain of evidence."

"I understand," I say. "But you see how this looks."

"I do."

Somehow, I think we've managed to reach an agreement. It's a miracle. Montenegro stays to help us set up the parameters of the grid search before the other set of officers arrive. Once they do, he directs them and us, using his knowledge of the island, to build the most efficient search pattern possible. I find myself grateful for his help, but also suspicious of his sudden heel-turn. He came in here all blustery and combative, and now he's willing to help? Of course, finding the necklace is a game-changer. Maybe now that he realizes he's being watched by the feds, he's willing to put in a little more effort.

WE SPEND THE REST OF THE DAY WITH THE TEAM AROUND THE site, performing the grid search until the sun finally begins to set and we lose the light. By the time we're done, I'm hot, dirty, thirsty and my stomach is just about to tear itself in two. I have to give it to them; the police here are very efficient with their work. If Montenegro had given them full permission from the beginning, I believe at least one of these women would have been found. Or at the very least we'd have more evidence. I don't know what his endgame is, but he's playing for something. I just need to figure out what.

Unfortunately, there are no more signs of Claire Taylor or

anyone else beyond the necklace. No footprints to cast, no usable fingerprints on any of the rocks, nothing. The natural environment is not the easiest place to gather evidence. We've covered almost a thousand square feet, but that is little more than a drop in the bucket. I think to really search this wilderness we're going to need ten times as many people.

Peregrine isn't the talkative type, though as the light wanes, she offers to drive me back. She must hear my stomach rumbling over the blast of the wind because she offers to treat me to some local cuisine before dropping me off at my new hotel. I gladly accept, though I have to admit I'm missing all the amenities of the Grand Solomon right about now. My feet are going to be sore as hell tomorrow.

"So what's your story?" Peregrine asks as she takes a seat across from me. We've stopped at a food truck by the side of the main road. It's in a pull-off area complete with string lights and picnic tables. Bug zappers surround the edges of the eating area, but given the enormity of the bugs out here, I doubt they're very effective. It's like trying to use a .22 to stop a bear. I swat a couple away before I unwrap the burrito before me.

"Sorry?"

Peregrine finishes chewing her own bite. "How'd you get into the FBI?"

"Oh," I say. "I always wanted to be in some kind of law enforcement and I'm kind of an over-achiever, so there wasn't really another option." She nods, almost like she expected me to say something like that. "What about you? Why a cop?"

"In the family. Dad was a cop," she says. "Grew up around it. People think this place is a safe little bubble, that nothing bad can happen here. Unfortunately, bad things happen everywhere."

"You ever think about leaving? Transferring somewhere else?"

She shakes her head. "It's my home. I don't have much

family left, but I wouldn't leave anyway." She grins for the first time. "I don't like the cold."

"Then you wouldn't like DC," I say. "I think it was thirty-three there this morning."

She makes a sound of disgust before tucking back into her food. We sit in silence as we finish our meal, only one other table near us occupied. It's a family of four, and given their beachwear, I have to assume they're tourists.

"How much do you know about Breckenridge?" I ask, watching the family out of the corner of my eye. One of the kids is struggling to eat the local food, and from the looks of it, on the verge of throwing a fit. The father, face red from sunburn and eyes sunken in, doesn't seem like he has the patience to put up with it. But to his credit, he helps the kid out, picking out all the "yucky" stuff from his plate.

"As much as anyone," she replies. "Though it doesn't surprise me to learn he's got that basement set up. Rich people, am I right?"

"What about Rafe Connor?" I ask, continuing to watch the family. "Ever had any interactions with him?"

"I can't say that I have," she says. "But I know he's been a big mainstay on the island the past few months. Montenegro has had a couple of meetings with him. And I know he's been talking to the city council and the mayor. I assume it has something to do with his business."

"He and Montenegro know each other?" I ask, perking up.

"I wouldn't say they're friends, but I've seen them together a few times, either at the station or out in the wild. Why?"

I furrow my brow. "It was just...nothing. It's not important." I'm thinking back to when I was in that interview room and Rafe came in, ice pack in hand. How had he known I'd twisted my ankle? Did Montenegro tell him? Unlikely, as he would have taken the opportunity to inform him of my true identity then, rather than waiting until Rafe arrived at the station. And I doubt he just carries ice packs around with him on a regular basis.

"I want to take a closer look at Rafe Connor," I say as I finish my plate.

"To what end?"

"I want to know what Claire Taylor knew about his business and further, how he might be connected to the other missing women. You said yourself you haven't investigated him, right?"

"Not seriously, no. Montenegro has been dragging his feet on this one, so we don't have a lot of information on the women yet."

"I think I can help with that," I tell her. "Sometimes the resources of the federal government can come in handy."

"What about the search?" she asks. "I had planned on starting bright an early in the morning. We still have a lot of ground to cover."

"What more can you tell me about those Killing Stones? What are they?"

She lets out a sigh. "That's how most of us refer to them because of the sacrifice thing. In school we learned that they were probably used for some kind of ritual, though it may or may not have been sacrifices."

I shuffle in my seat. "What do you believe?"

She levels her gaze at me. "I've been on this island most of my life. Tales of the 'savage' activities of native peoples is always exaggerated if you ask me. Were there probably some animal sacrifices? More than likely. Human though? I doubt it."

I'm not about to sit here and challenge a woman who knows this island and culture much better than I do. She obviously has a connection to this place that I can't understand. "In my experience, it's not always about what really happened, but what people want to believe happened. Why else would they start calling them the Killing Stones if not to scare people?"

"Exactly," she says as she gathers what's left of her plate and dumps it into the nearest receptacle. "People don't know what they're talking about."

"Do you think Breckenridge has any connection to the island's history?" I ask. "He obviously likes collecting it. And given how much he seems to enjoy it here and—at least on the surface—helps the local population, he shows more than a passing interest."

"You're thinking he might know about the stones," she says. "And has decided to use them as part of whatever strange things he gets up to?"

"It wouldn't surprise me," I say.

She gets up, pulling out another cigarette and lighting it. "Me neither. But until he returns, there's not much we can do. In the meantime, we have to go with what we have." She heads back to the car as I toss my trash. She's right. We need to work what's in front of us, though I'm tempted to bring in some extra help. Not just to piss Montenegro off, but because I feel like I might need some backup on this after all.

# Chapter Eighteen

"EM, I feel like I'm working two jobs here," Zara says. I'm sitting back in my motel room, my laptop on one side of me and copies of the files for the missing women on the other. I've spread everything out so I can try and assimilate it all at once, look for patterns in the data, anything that I can possibly use. My phone is propped across from me with Zara's face on the screen. Well, most of her face. She's obviously placed the phone on her desk while she continues to work. I have a great view of her chin.

I had to call Zara to start doing a deep dive into some of these women, as these files are light. Peregrine decided to head back out to the stones this morning with the team from the station. They're continuing the search.

"I know, I promise I won't keep you much longer. I just need a little more help with this."

"Do I need to come down there?" she asks. I've had her on the phone for the better part of an hour as she gathers as much information about each of the women as possible using the FBI's database. I even had her pull Caruthers in for a few minutes to provide any supplemental information on Stamper.

"Nice try. Caruthers was very clear in his orders," I say. "And as your former boss, I happen to agree with him."

"Yeah, well maybe I'll pull an Emily Slate of my own and disobey a direct order. You don't know how badly I could use a tan right now. Seriously. I'm turning transparent."

I chuckle as I read over the file for Marian Stamper, who went missing from her vacation home two weeks ago. A search was done of the property, but no forced entry was found. And there's a large swath of time where she's unaccounted for, meaning she could have been abducted any time within a twelve-hour period. But that's not what has piqued my interest. "All these women except for Stamper disappeared from crowded areas. Including Claire Taylor. That has to mean something."

"Why does that have to mean something?" she asks.

"Because I say it does," I reply, detecting the snark in her voice. But she's right, coincidence doesn't mean correlation. Still, it's odd.

"Didn't you say Claire was there with this Connor guy?" Zara asks.

"If they were together, it wasn't amicable. She didn't look like she wanted to be there, and he wasn't paying her any attention."

"That's right, because he only had eyes for you," she coos.

"Get it out of your system now," I say. "Because you won't get the chance when I get back."

"Emily Rachel Slate," she says, her voice lithe and dreamy as she bats her eyes at me. "Out there breaking the hearts of men all over the world. Fletch has been doing everything he can to get in contact with you since you left him in his hotel that night. The email box is filling up quickly, and the voice-mail—well, let's just say he's eager. *Very* eager."

I sigh. "I'm going to suggest to Caruthers that he pull me from that case," I say. "I don't think returning to undercover work was the best idea. I'm clearly not suited for it."

"That's just your low self-esteem talking." I can hear the condescension in her voice. "If you weren't good at it, you wouldn't have made it this far with Fletch."

"I don't like not being myself around people. It feels... wrong."

"I know," she says. "It was weird for me too. To become this other person, which is completely not you...it's hard. Especially when things go bad."

I think back to her brush with death while she was undercover. Zara has completely sworn it off, so why can't I do the same thing? "I might have just gotten lucky with the Fletch case. They sniffed me out within a day down here."

There's no response on the other end and I can hear her thinking. "Let me check something."

"Wait, hang on," I say but she's disappeared from the screen before I can stop her. I turn back to the file on Stamper. She'll come back when she's ready, I suppose.

Looking through the information we have on the woman, I can't find anything that would connect her to anyone on the island. I suppose her kidnapping could be a coincidence, as it's the only one that doesn't fit the pattern. But I'm not sure I'm ready to believe that yet. As I'm looking at her official picture on her website, I notice she's wearing a wedding ring. In the picture in the file, it's only a headshot, but if she's married, why is she using her maiden name? From what I've found, she was born Marian Stamper, in Columbus, Ohio, 1974.

"Hey," Zara says, popping back into the screen. "I think I have something. I pulled the records requests for a few nights ago, and found out Morgan—you know Morgan, over in IT? The guy with the socks?"

"The socks and the sandals, yeah, you've mentioned him," I say, grinning.

"It's a travesty, trust me," she says. "I wanted to check with him to make sure there hadn't been an official request on any field agents working in the Virgin Islands."

"And?" I ask.

"Nothing. At least, nothing in the past two months. Sorry, Em, I thought maybe someone had just made an error somewhere."

"That's okay," I say. "Somehow Montenegro got that info, but right now I don't care. The cover is gone. I need to focus on the case in front of me."

"You *should* care. We can't have our agents' covers exposed like that. You know, the more I work on this info you retrieved from Fletch, the more it leaves a sour feeling in my stomach. I haven't uncovered a lot, but given how encrypted everything is, I suspect this might be government-level info. Maybe even something to do with the Bureau."

"Seriously?" I ask.

"Like I said, I need to get into it. I'm still working on the decryption. But this is some serious shit here, Em. Whoever took this info went to great lengths to protect it."

That can't be good. We've already had to deal with the Organization infiltrating the FBI. I'm not sure the Bureau could withstand another hit.

"Thanks anyway for checking," I say. "I appreciate it."

"I'll keep looking once I finish getting through this mess. Just watch your back down there. I don't like you working without any backup."

I return my attention to Ms. Stamper. "You'll be the first person I call if I get into trouble," I say. "But look at this. The Stamper woman. She's married."

"No, she's not," Zara says, glancing away from my screen to another I'm sure she has pulled up. "Oh, wait a second. Maybe she is." I hear her keys clacking in rapid succession. "Shit, I didn't think to look. She was married to a Henry Avecido back in 2000. But she kept her maiden name."

"Okay, why?" I ask.

"Who knows, probably so she wouldn't have to begin her law career under another name." She scans a few more lines on her screens. "This is interesting. Wanna know who Mr. Avecido works for?"

"Let me guess, Jeremy Breckenridge?" I ask.

"Close. The very eligible and single Mr. Rafe Connor, of Connor Investments International."

# Chapter Nineteen

INSTEAD OF TAKING the taxi over to the Grand Solomon Hotel, I have them take me to the nearest Jeep rental location. It's a tiny two-story building smashed between a restaurant and an insurance office and looks nothing like a vehicle rental business. But there are two Jeeps sitting out front in the only two parking spaces in front of the entire building. Ten minutes later I'm driving the red Jeep back toward the Grand Solomon. I'm tired of relying on other people to get around this island. I also need to have a very serious discussion with Rafe. Not only did Ms. Stamper's husband work for him, but two of the other women, one of whom is Claire, have some ancillary connection to his businesses. I'm not willing to accept that as coincidence.

The truth is Rafe is an accomplished liar. He tried to play me, and I suspect he's still doing so with his wide-eyed deer bit. The reason he knew Claire Taylor was missing is because he orchestrated it. How else better to cover your own tracks?

I pull up to the Grand Solomon and opt for a parking space around the side of the hotel rather than valet. But when I get inside, I'm informed that Mr. Connor is out for the day.

Convenient. Just like Breckenridge, he's managed to disappear when things get squirrely.

"Wait a moment," the concierge says as I'm shooting frustrated glances around the room, trying to figure out my next move. "You were here with us the other night, weren't you?"

"I was," I say. I'm about to tell him I'm with the FBI, but Zara's voice pops into my head and I hold back. "I...was with Mr. Connor, attending the gala at the Breckenridge mansion."

"Ah, yes. I heard that was quite the party. I hope you found it enjoyable."

"I did," I say, dropping the hard edge in my voice. "That's actually why I'm here. I can't seem to find my phone and I think I might have accidentally left it in Mr. Connor's room." I lean closer to the concierge. "We came back together after the party."

"I would be happy to leave Mr. Connor a note. How can we get in touch with you if he finds it?"

"That's the problem. I have to catch a flight in about an hour. And I really need that phone. It has all my business contacts on it." I lower my voice again. "As well as some... sensitive pictures that I'd rather not get out into the public. Is there any way I could just go look for it?" I see the hesitation on the concierge's face. "Please. I wouldn't be asking if it weren't an emergency. You don't know when Rafe will be back?"

"I'm afraid not, Miss..."

"Agostini," I say. "Emily Agostini. I represent Thompson Intermodal and believe me, they are not going to be happy if I come back and tell them all my work information is still in St. Solomon."

"And you don't have any way of contacting Mr. Connor?" he asks.

I hold my hands out. "I've looked everywhere for him." It sickens my stomach to act so helpless, but it's working. His eyes are softening and I can tell he pities the young woman who was stupid enough to leave her phone in the man's room during a night of "passion."

He snaps his fingers and a bellhop comes trotting up. "Please escort Ms. Agostini up to room 1162. Help her find her phone and return back here immediately." He turns back to me. "I'll leave a message here with Mr. Connor informing him of the situation. Please, be brief. We take guest privacy very seriously at the Grand Solomon. But I can understand mistakes happen."

"Thank you," I tell him, pure relief coloring my words. "You've probably saved my job." He nods at the bellhop who escorts me to the elevator.

"What kind of phone?" he asks as the doors close on us.

"Samsung," I say. "The newest model. It's got one of those cases covered by rhinestones. It should be easy enough to spot. It's probably behind the bed somewhere." I glance at him under hooded eyes. The bellhop can't be older than nineteen. He swallows hard and avoids my gaze, which is perfect.

When the elevator doors open on eleven, he leads me down the hallway, though I should technically be leading him. When we reach the door, he uses his master keycard to open the door. "I'll, uh, just leave this open here," he says, using the doorstop to keep the door itself from closing again.

"Great, thank you." As soon as I enter the room, I hear distinct guttural sounds coming from what has to be one of the bedrooms. That and what sounds like someone crying.

I rush forward, all thought of the investigation gone. I've heard that sound before, and I know what it means. It's a sound embedded in my head from months of working a dozen different cases, of finding nefarious men abusing women in their control and being too late to do anything about it. But not today. This stops now.

I erupt into the bedroom to find Rafe and a woman who is probably my age or younger in what some would call the "throes of passion." Both of them nude as the day they were born and glistening with sweat, Rafe has positioned himself at the foot of the bed and the woman is facing the headboard, but they jump as soon as I throw the door open.

"What the fuck!" Rafe yells, grabbing a nearby sheet as the woman screams, trying to tuck herself under the covers.

"FBI!" I say, holding out my badge. "No one panic. Ma'am," I say, holding out one hand. "Are you all right?"

"What is this, Benny? What's going on?" the woman asks, pulling the covers up to cover her chest.

"Oh my god," the bellhop says, and I realize he's followed me in.

"Benny?" I ask, looking at Rafe who is standing near the plate glass windows, nothing but a small towel covering him. Suddenly I'm not so confident about what I heard.

"Emily?" he asks, incredulous.

"Wait, you know her?" the woman in the bed asks. "I told you; I don't do groups." She jumps out of bed, still holding the covers and walks into the bathroom, slamming the door behind her.

"You need to leave," Rafe demands. "I don't know what you think you're doing here." He grabs some clothes from the nearby chair to cover himself more.

"I'm here because no one seems to be able to find you." I glance at the closed bathroom door. "I'm assuming everything that was happening in here was consensual?"

"Of course it was. What kind of monster do you think I am?" He glances over my shoulder. "Get the hell out of here!"

The bellhop jumps and races from the room. I'm sure this will be all he talks about for a solid month.

"And that goes for you too," Rafe demands. "I should sue you and the entire FBI for breach of privacy."

"I'm sorry for interrupting," I say. "Really, I am. But it sounded like someone was in trouble."

The door to the bathroom opens again and the young woman appears, fully dressed. She flips her blonde hair behind her as she leaves, brushing past me. I'm not sure any apologies will help now. "But I'm not leaving. You and I need to have a talk," I tell Rafe. "I'll wait for you in the living area."

"You can't be serious."

"Trust me. It's better you talk to me now rather than later."

"Fine," he says, his posture relaxing somewhat.

Ten minutes later, after I've explored most of the suite, Rafe joins me in the living room. He's back in a finely-pressed suit, no longer sweaty and smells of expensive cologne. "My lawyers are going to love this," he spits as he crosses the room to the small bar that sits beside the kitchen.

"That's...you know what, I wouldn't blame you," I say, taking a seat on one of the two couches facing each other. "I blatantly violated your privacy. I'm sorry."

He grunts.

"I hope I didn't ruin your...relationship."

He pours himself a bourbon and knocks it back, grimacing as the liquid goes down. He then refills the glass with water and takes a seat on the second couch across from me. "I think we both know that was no relationship."

"Still, I'm sorry," I say. "I didn't mean to embarrass you."

He glances out the large windows that look out on the Caribbean. "Forget it. Why are you here?"

"We need to talk about Claire," I say. "And Marian."

"Marian?" he asks, taking a sip of the water.

I nod. "Marian Stamper. Wife of Henry Avecido." I wait for the recognition, but Rafe doesn't give me anything. "He works for CII."

"Okay," Rafe shrugs. "So do a thousand other people."

"Marian Stamper is one of the women missing from this island. Along with Claire Taylor. And Vicki Tolluse. In fact, three of the four missing women have some connection to your company. Either directly or indirectly."

Rafe's brow forms a deep V. He leans forward and sets his

glass on the table. "Are you suggesting I had something to do with their disappearance?"

"Did you know?" I ask. "About Stamper and Tolluse?"

"No," he says without breaking eye contact. I watch for any tells that might indicate he's lying. But he's either a practiced liar, or he believes what he's saying. "If I remember correctly, I was the one who informed the police Claire was missing."

"Let's talk about that," I say. "What was Claire doing here, exactly?"

"She was here to help promote her arm of the company," he says. "Network. Schmooze. That's what these things are about."

"So you paid for her to come down here to basically have a good time on the company's dime."

He sits back and quirks his mouth, like he's trying to get an errant piece of food out of his teeth.

"When did she arrive on the island?"

"Four days ago," he says.

"And how many interactions did you have with her between her arrival and the party?"

"I don't see what this has to do with anything," he says, standing back up and heading for the bar again. He pours himself a fresh glass. "I saw potential in Claire; I thought this would be good for her. Is that a crime?"

"Is that the only reason you brought her down here?" I think back to how she shied away from him that night, like she didn't want to get too close. Or even make it *appear* like they were close.

"Of course," he says taking a sip. "Why else would she be here?"

He's stiff, almost withdrawn. Setting aside the fact I just caught him with his pants off, there's a tension about him that is sending up red flags. He may be an accomplished liar, but there are some things you can't control. Like the fact he's tapping the counter with his index finger and not even realizing it.

"I think she was here as your date," I say, standing and rounding the couch. "Maybe what you're saying is true. Maybe you did see some potential in her. But I don't think that's the only reason you brought her down here. Is it?"

He drains the rest of his glass, then pours himself a third. "Fine. You want me to say I thought she was pretty? Of course. She's gorgeous. You want me to say I thought there was something between us? I admit it. Yes, I thought we had some chemistry. I suggested the trip to her back in December, because I knew it would be freezing in New York and she's always been ambitious. I thought she would enjoy some time on the island, and at the time she seemed enthusiastic."

"So what happened?"

He drains the third bourbon before leaving the glass and plopping down on the couch again. "When she got here, she was…different. Closed off. I tried taking her out, but it was like she was a different person. It was pretty obvious from that first night that she wasn't interested. So I just left her alone."

"And she didn't say anything?" I ask. "Didn't explain why she wasn't feeling good?"

He runs his hand through his dark hair. "I've never seen Claire like that. She's usually a very warm person."

"So when she didn't reciprocate your feelings, you went out looking for someone else," I say.

He huffs. "You make it sound like I was out trolling for anything with two legs and a heartbeat. What I told you was true. I noticed you and I was, for lack of a better word, stunned. I thought maybe we could have a nice night together. I didn't realize you'd go off and try to break into Breckenridge's secure facility."

"Do you know what's in that 'secure' facility?" I ask, ignoring the rest of his words because I really don't want to think about Rafe's *feelings* right now.

"I've heard rumors," he says. "But I've never seen it for myself."

"Then you knew Breckenridge has a certified sex dungeon under his house."

His eyes go wide. "A certified *what?*" I can't tell if his reaction is genuine or practiced. Which means I need to be careful going forward. Rafe knows how to lie convincingly.

"Did Claire know anyone else at the party? Anyone who might have had access to Breckenridge's property? Someone he knew well enough to allow down there?"

He sits up straighter. "Why? What's happened? Did you find her?"

"Not yet," I say. "But we can't rule out the fact she might have been in there."

"Listen to me. I only know Breckenridge through our business dealings," he says. "That's it. I don't know anything about any sex dungeons. That's not—" He glances in the direction of the bedroom and clamps his mouth shut.

I cross my arms. "You and Breckenridge seemed pretty chummy the night of the party."

"That was a business deal," he says, the octave of his voice going up slightly. "I was confirming with him our meeting with the mayor tomorrow. Breckenridge has been instrumental in coordinating with the local government for me. If not for him, I would have been held up in red tape for months to just get a proposal on the table."

That's the same meeting Montenegro was referring to. "When's the meeting?"

"Tomorrow, at noon," he says. "Why?"

"And Breckenridge is planning on being there? Personally?"

"That's the plan," Rafe says. "Why?"

"Nothing to worry about," I say. "So, you didn't feel any animosity towards Claire for rejecting you?"

"No," he emphasizes. "Honestly, she was acting so strange I didn't think it was worth the trouble."

And there it is. Just when I start to think Rafe may not be such a bad guy after all he goes and says something like that. "Yeah? Not worth the time to try and help her out? Or was her emotional state standing in the way of you getting your dick hard?"

His face hardens. "I think you should leave."

"I think that's a good idea," I say.

"And you can bet the FBI will hear about this little...*invasion of privacy*," he calls as I head to the door. I don't turn to look at him again, instead letting myself out. If he does decide to complain, it's going to be a heap of trouble for me. And I'm still no closer to finding out if he had anything to do with Claire or not. The man is frustratingly nebulous.

As I head back down and pass the concierge, his face is twisted like he swallowed something sour as I pass. No doubt thanks to the bellhop. I wave my phone at him. "Found it, thanks." As I reach my car it buzzes in my hand. I don't recognize the number. "Slate."

"It's Peregrine," she says. "We've got a problem."

## Chapter Twenty

THE JEEP HITS A POTHOLE, and I nearly slam my head on the roof. Although since it's little more than heavy cloth, it wouldn't have hurt much. But the seatbelt is doing precious little to keep me in my seat as I tear down the dirt road ten miles per hour faster than I probably should, as this road wouldn't be drivable in anything with a low wheelbase. I've already crossed one small creek and have driven over rocks that would have ripped the transmission out of those cars I saw back at the Breckenridge mansion.

Peregrine offered to come pick me up, but I declined. It would have taken longer, and now that I finally have a vehicle, I don't need anyone else driving me around. But even as I hurry to the site as fast as I can, I keep going over my conversation with Rafe. He knows nothing, yet he still lured Claire to the island under false pretenses. It's hard not to notice how quickly he turned his sights on me once she rejected him. Was he that afraid of going to that party without a woman on his arm? And was that purely pride, or something else?

Then again, I could be way off. Rich people are different. They live by a different set of rules, and strangely, are governed by a different set of emotions. I don't know what it is, but it's like once all their hierarchical or survival needs are met, they change. It probably explains why so many celebrities are batshit.

The road winds down through an open valley towards the water.

And then I catch sight of the ocean through the trees. They fall away, and I'm left with a gorgeous view as the road continues to descend to the shoreline. A couple of pickup trucks sit off the side of the road, their wheel wells rusting from the salt air. As the road levels, I see the police cars parked ahead. Another island patrol car and Peregrine's old beater. The sun is still high in the sky, and when I step out of the vehicle, an acrid smell assaults my senses.

"Ugh, what is that?" I ask.

"Sargassum," Peregrine says as she approaches, her long-sleeve shirt fluttering in the wind off the water. She's rolled up her sleeves and she's got nitrile gloves on. "It comes up from South America every few years. Sits in some of the bays. Smells awful. Any trouble finding the place?" she calls out.

"No, just followed your directions," I say, wrinkling my nose. "Who found her?"

"Fisherman," she says as I join her. She points to one of the trucks I passed on the way down. "Out for the daily catch. A lot of the restaurants on the island rely on locals to provide them with their menus for this evening. It's hell on the local wildlife; the governor had to institute fishing regulation programs to keep us from losing some species entirely."

"And Rafe Connor wants even more people to start coming here," I say, following her as we leave the road and trudge through the tall grass down to the small beach that sits on the cove.

"Money will destroy this place," she says.

Where the cove meets the beach, two other officers are standing, one taking pictures with his cell phone. As soon as my feet hit sand I see her, bobbing ever so slightly in a small pool that formed inside a group of rocks as the tide went out. The rocks aren't unlike smaller versions of the killing stones we saw before.

The body is white and bloated and she's facing up, her eyes milky and lips purple. But as far as I can tell, she's intact. "Marian Stamper," I say.

"Number two to disappear," Peregrine adds.

"Did you inform Montenegro?" I ask.

She nods. "He's pulling the CSI team from the Breckenridge house. They're supposed to be on their way now."

Damn. Though I can't blame him. Pulling a fingerprint from Breckenridge's property was a long shot at best. And probably frustrating for the CSI team. Who knows how many hundreds of people have been in those rooms under that house.

"What time did they find her?" I ask.

"A little after one this afternoon, when the tide first went out. They came back in from the morning's catch and found her. But it's a twenty-minute drive out of the dead zone down here to get a phone signal."

Given they had to notify the police, the police had to get here, and Peregrine had to be notified, it makes sense it took a few hours before I knew. But was this recent? Or has she been here for weeks?

"What's...how long do you think she's been in the water?" I ask.

"Well," Peregrine says. "I'm not a medical examiner. But I've pulled my fair share of bodies off the shore. I'd say with this amount of bloating, maybe a few hours? Certainly not days."

That means she was fine up until this morning, which means she was probably being held against her will. "Any injuries that you can see?"

"Nothing obvious," Peregrine says. "She might have drowned."

I look around the cove. It's completely empty of any kind of artificial structure. The cove itself isn't very large, but there are no houses down here, no docks. "Where's the closest settlement?"

"About two miles up the hill," she says. I glance up, noting the sheer rock face that starts about twenty feet above the water line. If someone jumped from up there, it's very possible they could have misjudged the angle and hit their head underwater. Or worse, hit the side of the cliff on the way down.

"Think she jumped?"

"Maybe," Peregrine says.

"How high is that?"

"A hundred, hundred and fifty feet or so," she replies.

A jump from that high could very well be deadly. At the very least she likely broke something when she hit the water, assuming she didn't strike anything else on the way down. "And she wasn't here this morning?"

"None of the fishermen saw her when they first went out." Peregrine pulls off her glove and retrieves her cigarettes from her inside pocket. "According to them, they were out on the boats for about five hours and came back to find her."

I look up at the cliff face again. "We need to get up there and investigate."

"Agreed," Peregrine says, lighting up. "We'll have to take some back trails though. There's no direct way to reach that area up there. Unless you're adept at rock climbing."

"Not really." I head back to my Jeep with Peregrine sticking close. "Don't you want to stay with the others? At least until the medical examiner arrives?"

"You're going to need some help getting up there," she replies. "It's easy to get lost in all this if you don't know where you're going."

I give her a nod of thanks. She relays instructions to the officers who are working on pulling Ms. Stamper out of the water. When she catches back up with me, her cigarette is still hanging from her mouth.

"Can you put that out?" I ask.

"Hmm? Oh, right," she says and drops the cigarette, extinguishing it under her boot. "It's a bad habit. Never should have started." She gets in the passenger side of the Jeep. It takes me a minute to turn around on the small dirt road and I take it a bit slower heading back out. I don't need to test this vehicle's suspension any more than I already have.

We end up heading all the way back out to the main road before Peregrine directs me to another, smaller path that's barely more than a trail. I pull off but can only get so far in the Jeep as we encounter more dense jungle about a hundred feet in.

"This?" I ask.

"It'll get us there," she says. "It'll be about a half mile hike back in."

For a brief moment I can start to see Rafe's point about wanting to make the island more accessible. "Any homes around here?"

"No, this is all protected land," she says. "Part of the park reservation. No one other than the government is allowed to build anything out here, and even then it has to go through a number of committees."

"What about rangers?" I ask. "Obviously there are trails for people to hike. What happens when someone gets lost or hurt?" I pull out my phone, noting my signal is spotty at best.

"The best thing you can do is notify someone where you will be and for how long. There are rules on the island stating as much and any tourist guide will tell you the same thing." She forges ahead, pushing through the dense brush into the jungle. As we head deeper in, I'm struck at just how familiar this is to the jungle near Breckenridge's property. In fact, it's almost indistinguishable.

We walk in silence for a good thirty minutes, me following

Peregrine while I try to keep my mental map of where we are about me. It's easy to get turned around in here; if Peregrine wasn't leading, I probably would have lost my way already, though I do have a compass app on my phone. I pull it out and sure enough, we're headed due west, back in the direction of the cove.

I check for any signs of human activity, but there's not much to see. There's no trash along the trails. Occasionally I'll see a footprint, but they look old.

"Okay," Peregrine says, "we're close." As we trudge forward, the jungle starts to thin. Part of the path is disturbed in one small place and I slow, bending down for a closer look.

"I think this is blood."

Peregrine turns as I pull on a glove and dab at the dark stain on the ground. It's almost indistinguishable from the jungle floor, but it's in the center of what looks like disturbed dirt.

"How did you even see that?"

My glove comes away with a small speckle of dark crimson. "This couldn't be Marian's," I say, rubbing it between my fingers. "It's still wet."

"The humidity can do that," Peregrine says. "If it's only been a few hours, it's possible that it could still be damp."

I pull the glove off and place it in an evidence bag, stuffing them both in my back pocket. Searching around, I find a nearby long stick that I drive into the ground near the disturbance to mark the area. "We'll come back."

She nods and we continue. But it doesn't take long before the trees fall away and we're looking down at the cove. Far below us, the officers are still working with Marian's body. Peregrine calls out to them, and they wave back to her. As I look over the cliff, I can't imagine what Marian might have been thinking. The drop is much too far for someone to survive, or at least survive without breaking something.

"Jumped or pushed?" Peregrine asks.

"I don't know," I reply. "That blood back there wasn't enough to make me think she was in a fight for her life. More like an injury she may have sustained."

"So she gets out to this cliff and...what? Misjudges the distance?"

"Maybe," I say. "And maybe she was cornered. Didn't have a choice."

"You think someone else was here." Peregrine's brow is furrowed.

"I do, and I think they may still be close."

## Chapter Twenty-One

We spend the remainder of the day searching through yet *another* jungle and coming up with nothing. And honestly, I'm not surprised. Given how vast the areas of wilderness on this island are, and the fact that we only have so many people at our disposal, it's no wonder we can't find anything. In fact, I have to believe that's part of the kidnapper's plan: to stretch us so thin that we have no chance of finding these missing women. I return to the site of the "blood" and try to take a sample for analysis, but who knows if it will come back with anything? It's nebulous at best.

But the question remains: did Marian Stamper escape or was she allowed to leave on her own? After conferring with the medical examiner, we discovered she died from a blunt force trauma impact, most likely when her body slammed into the water at close to seventy miles per hour. An experienced diver may have been able to make that jump with only minimal injuries, but the examiner also found Marian was heavily malnourished and dehydrated. She also has a rather large cut on her leg that was fresh when she died. Most likely, she snagged it on something in the woods. All of it points to someone who was probably in a state of delirium. I can't prove that she jumped, but my gut tells me that's what happened. She was scared, disoriented, and thought maybe she could make it.

The question is, who was she running from? And where are they now?

I had hoped a search of the jungle would have produced at least some evidence of someone else being out there, especially since we couldn't have been that far behind them. The medical examiner confirmed Peregrine's suspicion that Marian died somewhere between eleven and one in the afternoon, given how much water her body had absorbed by the time they pulled her out of the cove. Which means at worst we were only four hours behind whoever was chasing her.

Peregrine, however, isn't so enthusiastic about my theory. She isn't willing to discount the possibility Marian got lost and had been wandering the jungle for the better part of two weeks. While I have to entertain the possibility, the pattern of missing women doesn't fit. Marian went missing from her vacation home almost three miles from the cove, which doesn't seem like a lot. But the more I get to know this place, the more I realize that three miles could very well seem like twenty given all the elevation changes, the rough terrain, and the lack of road access.

Still, I have to believe if she was out there, wandering the wilderness, she would have found the coastline eventually. And she could have followed that back to civilization.

No, something about this is all wrong. I'm convinced Marian was captured, taken against her will, and was held somewhere. I think the others were too. How she got free, I can't yet say. But where she was found is far enough from Breckenridge's property that he's starting to look less and less like a suspect.

By the time I get back to my motel room, I'm completely

spent. The sun has taken it out of me, not to mention I've been drenched in my own sweat all day. I may have to wear something a little lighter tomorrow.

"Hey," Liam says as I flop back on the bed. He's in his sweats and I can just barely see Timber's head at the bottom of the screen. "You look tired."

"I am the personification of tired," I reply, my muscles too heavy to move. It's all I can do to hold this phone up.

"Going that well, huh?"

"It's barely going at all," I say, explaining about finding Marian today. "We're no closer to finding the other women and now I have a body on my hands."

"But it could have been an accident, right?"

"Maybe. Or maybe someone forced her to jump. I just don't have enough information." I can see the wheels in his mind turning. "What?"

"Hmm?"

"I can see you thinking. What's going on?"

"Nothing," he says.

"You know, one of the reasons I like talking to you is you're smart," I say. "And on occasion, you're even smarter than me. So spit it out."

He laughs. "I think on many occasions I'm smarter than you, but we'll save that argument for another day."

"Oh, will we now?" I somehow find the strength to sit up.

"It's not my case," he says. "But what if it was all an accident?"

"What was all an accident?"

"Her escape, and fall." Timber lifts his head up and must catch sight of me on the phone because he puts his nose flat up against the screen blocking out my view of Liam for a brief moment. Seconds later, Rocky appears on the screen and follows suit, both of the noses sniffing at the same time. I swear, those dogs are attached at the hip.

"Why do you think that?" I announce over the sniffing.

"Guys," Liam says, and gently moves them out of the way so I can see him again. "Sorry. They miss you. I'm just wondering because you said Marian wasn't the first woman to be captured, right?"

"No, that was another woman named Vicki."

"Wouldn't it make sense, if they were going to start pushing people off cliffs, to go with the first woman who was captured?"

"Not if she's already dead," I say.

"Okay, consider that she is. Why not leave her on the side of the road somewhere as a warning. Or a sign."

"A sign of what?" I ask. "There has been no communication with the kidnappers. Hell, some people here still aren't even sure that's what's going on. All we have are *disappearances*. And now a body."

"I'm just saying that whoever is doing this, they must have a reason. Otherwise, why aren't *more* women disappearing? And because you don't have four bodies on your hands right now, those reasons might not be as nefarious as you assume. What if the women are being held somewhere, and Marian just happened to get away? She's scared, running through the jungle, trips and falls to her death. It doesn't mean the kidnappers wanted her dead."

"I might believe that if not for the condition Marian was in," I say. "They're not giving them food or water. Or at least, not enough."

"Still, it might not be their ultimate goal to kill them."

I want to argue with him, because my gut tells me whoever is taking these women do not have altruistic motives. But I need to consider all the angles, look at things from the sides I may not want to consider. I can't allow myself to get bogged down in one train of thought so much that I miss what is right in front of me. "I'll keep it in mind."

"Good. Getting enough sleep?"

"It's not the sleep. It's being out in the sun all day long, traipsing through the jungle. I've been out there two days in a row with little more than a necklace and a splash of blood to show for it."

"I worry about you out there all by yourself," he says. "I'd feel better if Zara was there to back you up. Or anyone, really."

"I'll be okay," I reassure him. "Peregrine isn't too bad. Smokes like a chimney though."

"Just make sure you watch yourself," he reiterates. "I have half a mind to go to Caruthers and demand he send me down there with you."

"You know he'll just refuse," I say. "He's not the sentimental type. He believes I can do this on my own. And I think I can too."

"Yeah? So all those feelings you were talking about a few days ago—"

"Oh, they're still there," I say, lying back on the bed again. "I just buried them. The last thing I want is to be distracted while I'm trying to find these women."

He just smiles and I can tell it's killing him to hold back.

"Go ahead, say it. That it's not healthy to bury all this."

"Did I say anything?"

"You were thinking it."

He grins despite himself. "Maybe I was. But you don't need me telling you what you already know. And you don't need me to be your guardian. I'm here to help."

I roll over, still looking into those beautiful hazel eyes of his. "I know. And thank you. Hey, I walked in on a sex act today. So if you thought your day was bad, mine was probably worse."

"You walked in on a what?" he says, sitting up straighter.

I give him the rundown of what I "accidentally" fell into back at the hotel, though I leave out some of the more graphic details.

"Sounds like this Rafe is quite the character."

"He's proving to be more of a pain in my ass than I want to admit," I say. "But I know he's connected to this somehow. I just need to find the evidence to prove it. And to do that, I need to find those women."

"Do you have any more leads?"

"Nothing concrete. But Breckenridge is also coming back to the island in the morning, according to Rafe anyway. I'd like to get some face time with him if I can find my way in."

"Then you need to get some rest," he says.

"Yeah." I draw the word out because I don't want to get off the phone with him. He seems so far away here. Everything about my life does. I guess that's the point of a place like this. It's supposed to make all of that seem like a bad dream for the time you're here, so you can just relax into this fantasy. People take their vacations very seriously, and the businesses of this island do everything they can to indulge them. Because when everything is a fantasy, normal life becomes trivial.

"Hey," he says, his voice softening. "When you break this thing, and I know you're going to break it, maybe don't come back home so quickly."

"What, why?" I ask, an ounce of hurt leaking into my voice.

"Because I'm going to come down there to you. Caruthers or not. I've accumulated some more days. I just need to know when to use them."

"Mmm, that sounds nice." I allow myself to go back to the dream of having some time off with him. And having it down here would be amazing. We couldn't afford the Grand Solomon, but then again, we wouldn't have to. This motel would be just fine for us.

"Just keep it in the back of your mind," he says. He hesitates a moment longer. "Be careful, Em. I love you."

"I love you back," I say. "Goodnight." As the screen goes black, I catch my own reflection for a brief second. My eyes are sunken in, and I see the face of Marian Stamper again.

Maybe Liam is right. Her death might have been nothing more than a bad accident. But I'm not so sure. This island is very good at keeping its secrets, and I need to find a way to blow the lid off what's going on here, otherwise women are just going to keep disappearing without a trace.

And I don't want to fish any more bodies out of the ocean.

# Chapter Twenty-Two

"THERE IT IS," Peregrine says, shielding her eyes against the sun. I'm standing close by, watching as the helicopter comes into view. It's one of the largest helicopters I've ever seen and looks like it has some range. As best we can tell, Mr. Breckenridge retreated to Venezuela after his party the other night. I'm sure his people have informed him that we were searching his property for Claire Taylor, though they have been tight-lipped about any response. But I'm not worried, given we had a warrant.

Rafe said Breckenridge was coming back to the island to meet with both him and the mayor to go over this land deal that Rafe's company has been proposing. I'm hoping we can get some face time with Breckenridge before that meeting, as I don't think he's the kind of person who would just come down to the station to speak with us.

Peregrine and I have to shield our eyes as the helicopter approaches, its massive black blades kicking up dirt and blocking out all sound. After what seems like an eternity, the engines begin to wind down and one of Breckenridge's men runs up to open the door.

Breckenridge steps out, still dressed all in white, though his suit today is more formal than the one from the other night.

"Mr. Breckenridge," I call out, holding my badge up so he and his security personnel can see it clearly. Oddly, Roberts and Daniels aren't among them. I assume they must still be back at the house, keeping watch.

"Yes?"

"I'm Special Agent Slate with the FBI. Could we have a moment of your time to ask you some questions?"

The security team tries to usher Breckenridge forward, but he holds them back. The sound from the blades has quieted enough that he can speak without shouting. "You're the ones who were searching my home."

"We were looking for a missing woman, Claire Taylor. Did you know her?"

"I'm sorry," he says. "I don't have anything to say." He allows his team to guide him to the nearby black limo where a driver stands, waiting.

"Went about as I expected," Peregrine says, lighting up. She takes a few puffs before allowing the cigarette to dangle from her fingers.

I watch as Breckenridge reaches the limo. Of course he wouldn't be willing to speak with us. Why would he? But he knows something, and I want to know about that missing footage from that night.

"Dammit," I say and break into a run towards the limo.

"Slate, what are you doing?" Peregrine calls after me.

I'm about ten feet from the car when one of the security personnel notices me and before I can even slow, I have a gun pointed at my head. I stop in my tracks. "That's not very smart. Threatening a federal officer with a firearm is a felony. Even in the Virgin Islands."

He looks to the driver of the vehicle and lowers his weapon. Breckenridge is already inside, witnessing the incident. "I want to speak with Mr. Breckenridge again."

"You'll have to make an appointment," the security officer says, holstering his weapon.

I approach the car and attempt to get in the back, but the man blocks my path. "Mr. Breckenridge, are you aware that all of your security footage from the night in question has been erased?"

"Eladio, step aside, please," Breckenridge says. The man huffs air out through his considerable nostrils like a bull before moving aside. "Agent, please take a seat." Breckenridge pats the seat next to him. I slip into the car, the leather reminding me of Rafe's car from the other night.

"Give us a second, please," Breckenridge says and Eladio closes the door, sealing off the world. Inside the car it's cool, and the tinted windows give the impression it's later in the day than it actually is. "Would you like a water? Or maybe something stronger?" Breckenridge indicates the small minibar next to him. It's stocked with an impressive number of liquors for a limo.

"No, thank you," I say.

"Very well," he says. "Speak." He says it with such authority that I'm a little surprised. Every time I've seen the man he's been jovial, friendly and seems very approachable. But in here, it's like someone has flipped a switch.

"Were you aware?" I ask. "About the records being deleted?"

"We're handling it internally," he says.

"Not good enough," I say. "We found a missing woman's effects not far from your property, and your footage from the party she attended the night she went missing just happens to have been erased. I want to know who did it and why."

"I can't tell you who," he says. "But my guess is it was someone who didn't want their activities of the evening known."

"What activities?" I ask.

He levels his gaze at me. "You saw the rooms. You know

what's down there. Thank you for that, by the way. The entire point of those rooms was to allow people some privacy away from prying eyes. They aren't meant to be public knowledge." He leans his head back against the headrest. "I'll be lucky now if they're ever used again."

"Look, I don't care about what you do in your personal time," I say. "As long as it's not illegal and no one is getting hurt, it doesn't concern me. What *does* concern me is that this missing woman, Taylor, may have not been a willing participant in one of those rooms."

"Yes, I heard you tried to…what was it…dust for fingerprints?" He laughs. "How did that go?"

"As well as you'd expect," I say. "Doesn't it bother you that you have a security leak?"

He draws a deep breath. "As I said, we're handling it internally. The responsible party will be found and dealt with."

"Roberts told me only he and you had the authority to delete those records. You obviously weren't there, so that leaves him."

"Then why haven't you charged him?" Breckenridge asks. "I'll tell you why. Because my people have been cooperative, on my orders. And deleting footage is not a crime."

"It is if it is meant to conceal another crime. Such as rape, or assault."

"Which you believe happened on my property?"

I return his hard gaze. "I know *something* happened on your property because Claire Taylor is missing. And until I know what happened to that footage, just know we are keeping a close eye on your activities."

"Agent, if you had anything on me, we both know I would not be sitting here, listening to a bunch of wild accusations. You are fishing. And if you keep it up, I will wrap the FBI up in so many lawsuits your head will spin."

That's the second time I've been threatened with litigation. Can't these "important" men come up with something more original? But Breckenridge isn't used to bowing down to anyone, and the law wouldn't be any different. I can't believe how different he is from the man I saw the other night.

"I think we're done here," I say.

"I think we are." I open the door and get out, not even bothering to look at Eladio as I head back to Peregrine, who has one eyebrow arched as I approach.

"You've got some balls; I'll give you that. Did he say anything?"

"Stonewalled." I watch as Breckenridge's limo pulls out of the airport and heads towards the main road. "What are the odds he's on the phone with Montenegro right now?"

"Fairly good," she says.

We're never going to get anything on Breckenridge, I have to accept that. He's got too much money to throw in the way. I had hoped to get at least something from him, but he was clever enough to keep the details to himself. He never confirmed knowing Claire Taylor, nor who or what could have been in those rooms that night. I lean back against the Jeep and rub my forehead.

"It's a cluster all right," Peregrine says, looking out past the airport to the ocean.

"I just feel like I'm being pulled in a hundred different directions. First, we have Claire missing, then Marian shows up dead, and we still have two other women no one has seen in weeks." Maybe I should be concentrating my focus on them. Until now, I've been more than a little myopic surrounding Claire, probably because I met her. And I had hoped that she might be the easiest to find. But whoever has taken these women is doing a damn good job not to leave anything behind.

Peregrine takes up a position beside me. "Let's think about this. Taylor goes missing from a party. Stamper from her vacation home. The last place anyone saw Tolluse was a grocery store, and Van Allen went missing from a hotel bar."

"All public places, except for Stamper," I say, trying to find a pattern. "And all of them except Van Allen connect back to Rafe Connor in some form or another. But what do they *all* have in common?"

"Women, aged twenty-eight to forty-six. No similarities in skin, hair, eye color. No consistency with height, weight or personality."

"We're missing something big." I rub my temple again. "Van Allen. She was local, wasn't she?"

Peregrine nods. "The rest were visitors to the island."

"Does Van Allen still have family here? Anyone related to her?"

Peregrine pulls out her phone, searching for a few minutes. "Just a boyfriend. He's the one who reported her missing two weeks ago. The rest of her family lives in Florida." She puts her phone away. "That's right. Her mother came down to look for her, but had to go back to work and could only stay a few days. Montenegro didn't do very much to appease the woman."

"You weren't working the case then?"

"I hadn't realized things were being swept under the rug," she says, pulling out another cigarette. "If I'd known, I would have interviewed Van Allen's mother while she was still here."

"Do you have an address on that boyfriend? I want to talk to him."

"We already have his statement," she says.

"He's the only person on the island other than Rafe who knows one of these women personally. Maybe he knows something he doesn't realize he knows. Regardless, we at least owe him an update. After what happened with Marian. I don't want him to think there's not anyone out here fighting to find her."

"Yeah, okay," she says, putting the cigarette away before she can light it. "But I'm driving."

## Chapter Twenty-Three

As PEREGRINE DRIVES, I read over the statement from Wilson Krantz, the boyfriend of Amy Van Allen, the third woman to go missing from the island. From his statement, Van Allen had an interview at the hotel for a job as a marketing specialist. Krantz stated they were supposed to meet up after the interview was over to hopefully celebrate, but when she didn't come home, he headed over to the hotel only to find no trace of her. He even spoke to the man she was supposed to interview with—a Donald Lasky—but *he* claimed she never showed up for the interview.

Apparently, her cell phone stopped pinging around the same time the interview was supposed to start, and no one has seen her since. The bartender at the hotel also delivered a statement, saying he served her a vodka colins, but he never saw her leave the bar. He even said her drink was only half finished, though there was a twenty sitting under the glass. He figured she had decided not to finish it and left when he wasn't looking. No usable prints were pulled from the twenty.

"Krantz lives at 522 Laerke Street, you know it?" I ask as we head back through town. My failed attempt to coerce something out of Breckenridge has only served to piss me off.

"Yeah, it's in town," Peregrine says, navigating the small streets of the city.

"And you haven't spoken to him since he made his statement," I say.

"Never had a reason to," she says. "I had noticed the case wasn't being pursued, but it wasn't until Tolluse went missing that I finally started getting involved. That was eight days ago. Now Taylor is gone too."

"I guess if Montenegro isn't providing much help, it's a lot for one person to try and take on by themselves."

"Damn straight," she says.

"And no one else was willing to step up to help? I find that hard to believe."

"That's probably my fault," she says. "Once I 'took over,' it put a damper on things. I don't have a lot of friends on the force due to some of my...previous activities."

I give her an appraising look. "Previous, as in...illegal?"

"Not strictly, no. Still, not everyone appreciates *creative* solutions to cases."

I'm not sure I want to know what that means. But it isn't like I haven't bent the rules, or flat out broken them on occasion. Sometimes it's the only way to get the job done, as much as I hate to admit it.

Peregrine pulls up to a row of homes on one of the side streets. There's no parking on the street, so she has to pull around back into a small alley where we both extricate ourselves from the car. The space is tight; a lot of the homes in town aren't built to handle vehicles, the assumption being that the residents are close enough to walk to all their needs.

I check the time on my phone as I follow Peregrine around the building and up a flight of metal stairs on the front of the building. Krantz lives on the second floor, and most of the units up here are lined up more like a hotel than individual apartments. And yet they each have their own addresses. It's just another one of those small differences that comes with living on the island, I suppose.

Peregrine reaches the door and knocks before I can catch up. She strikes me as the kind of person who will take whatever action is necessary to reach her goal, regardless of the consequences. She's a bull, headstrong and always moving forward. Is that what she meant when she said people didn't like working with her? Do they find her too abrasive? I've been accused of that myself in the past, but like Peregrine, I'm not about to let it stop me from doing my job.

"Wilson Krantz, open up," she announces through the door. "This is the police."

"Maybe don't word it quite like that," I suggest.

"Why?"

"Because it sounds like we're here to arrest him."

She considers it a moment, then nods, knocking again. "We need to speak to you about Ms. Van Allen."

A second later the bolt on the door slides and it opens to reveal a man in his late twenties, wearing a white undershirt and dark pants. His hair is matted and his glasses are slightly askew. Immediately, I catch a whiff of alcohol.

He squints in the mid-day sun. "You have news about Amy?"

"Let's go inside, Mr. Krantz," I offer. He looks at me, and from the surprise on his face, I'm not even sure he knew I was there until I said something.

"Yeah, yeah," he says and backs away from the door, holding it open for us. Krantz has a slight southern accent that I would place as coming from somewhere around Atlanta. Whatever it is, he's not a local.

The inside of his place is sparse, but clean. He's got an older couch that sits up against the wall as we come in, but because all of the blinds are drawn, it's a little hard to see.

"Can you turn on a light, Mr. Krantz?"

"Yeah, sure," he says and opens up the curtains over the

couch, flooding the room with sunlight. He heads through to the back where the kitchen is located and opens the curtains there as well. The kitchen is small but looks functional. There's a two-person dining table adjacent to the counters, and on it is a dark red bong beside a half-empty bottle of rum.

Krantz sees me looking at the bong and doesn't even bother trying to hide it. Instead he goes to the fridge and grabs a water. "Want anything?"

"We're good, thank you," Peregrine says.

"Do you want to…uhh…" He looks around but doesn't have sufficient seating for all three of us. The place is obviously built for one, two at most, and feels almost claustrophobic in its size. Though when I look up, there's a surfboard hanging from a makeshift pulley system drilled into the beams running above our heads. Krantz has made the most of his space. "Here," he says, pulling a chair from the table in the kitchen and brings it into the living room. He sits in it, offering us the couch.

"You have news about Amy?" he asks, straightening his glasses again. He seems to have sobered a little as he was moving around the apartment.

Peregrine looks to me as if to say, *It's your show.*

"Mr. Krantz, I'm Special Agent Slate with the FBI. We believe Amy is just one in a number of kidnappings that have taken place over the past four weeks."

"Wait, there have been more?" he asks.

I nod. "We found one of the women yesterday. It wasn't Amy, but her condition suggests she was attempting to escape."

"What did she say? Did she see Amy?" he asks, leaning forward on his chair.

"Unfortunately, she didn't survive," I say. "We believe her death may have been an accident." I catch Peregrine glaring at me. We have no evidence to prove that one way or another, but I'm taking Liam's words to heart. For my sanity and

William Krantz's, I have to believe he could be on to something.

"So what does that mean?" Krantz asks.

"It means we think Amy is still alive," I say. "We think she's being held somewhere here, on the island, against her will."

"But you don't know where," he says.

"We don't. We're hoping you can help us fill in some more gaps about what happened to her."

He sits back, frustration practically radiating off him. "I already gave the police everything I know." He gets up, heading for the kitchen.

"Mr. Krantz," I call after him, but he grabs the bong and returns to the living room. "I know this is upsetting, but I'd like to ask you some more questions about that day."

Fishing a lighter out of his pocket, he lights the end of the bong and takes three or four good, deep breaths before blowing the smoke back out. "Ask."

"That looks like more than three ounces to me," Peregrine says, glaring at the bong.

"Yeah, and?"

"Two and a half ounces is the legal limit for recreational use."

She's focusing on the wrong thing. I just want to get some answers out of this guy before he's too high to respond. "Walk me through that day again, if you would."

He scoffs. "What, like from when I got up?" I nod. He blows out another ring of smoke towards the ceiling. "I got up, got dressed, ate…I dunno, something. Called Amy and wished her luck on the interview and that was it."

"Did you actually talk to her?" I ask. "Or just leave a message?"

"We talked for a minute," he says. "She usually answers. Which was why I knew something was wrong when she wasn't picking up later that day. It was just going straight to voice-mail. She *always* keeps her phone charged. If we go out, she'll find the closest outlet and plug it up, just to make sure it doesn't die."

"What time was her interview?" I ask.

"Eleven," he says, setting the bong aside. He settles back into the chair.

"And she was trying to get a marketing job, is that right?"

"Marketing and Promotions Manager."

"Where was she working before?" I ask.

"Nowhere. She moved down here for this job after college."

Peregrine and I exchange a look. "Before she got it?"

He lets out another strained breath. "Yeah. Is that so strange?"

"It seems like a big risk for a job she didn't have yet. What if she hadn't gotten the job? What was the plan?"

"She was going to get it, no question," he says and grabs the bong again, taking another hit before I can stop him. "It was a guarantee."

"How do you know that?"

"Because that guy told her she would." His eyes are starting to go a little glassy, and I can tell we're not going to get much out of him. Still, I flip back through my notes from the case file. "Who, Donald Lasky? The hotel manager?"

"Nah, nah," he says. "That other guy. Her old boyfriend. The one she had in the states."

"*Who*, Mr. Krantz. I need a name."

He looks back up at the ceiling again, then over to his surf-board. "Copp? No, Connor. Sounds like conman, right?" He laughs like it's the funniest thing he's ever heard.

"*Rafe* Connor?" I ask.

He shoots me a finger gun. "That's him. Rafe Conman."

"You're saying Rafe Connor was involved with Amy Van Allen? Personally?"

He shrugs. "Hey, I didn't ask for deets. She just told me

they were together for a while and he got her a job down here. She just had to interview."

"Why did they break up?" I ask, my head spinning with the possibilities. This means Rafe is connected to every single one of the victims in one way or another.

"Who cares," he says. "She said she still had the job after they were over. I thought maybe the guy would try to get back into her life, but she and I have been together for almost four weeks now and I never even saw the man."

"Mr. Krantz, how high are you right now?" Peregrine asks.

"I guess about fifteen feet?" He glances out the window. "Maybe sixteen?"

She turns to me. "None of this is credible. He was already questionable when we came in. He's obviously not coming down anytime soon. We can't trust a word out of his mouth."

"Hey, you can trust me," he sing-songs. "I got all the information."

"Mr. Krantz, how would you describe your relationship with Ms. Van Allen?" I ask.

"Whaddayamean?"

"How did you meet? How often did you see each other before she went missing?" When we arrived, I could plainly see the concern on his face. But now it's like that has all been wiped away. He's either trying his best to forget the pain of her disappearance, or he never really cared about her in the first place.

"Met down on the beach a few weeks back," he says, pointing to the board. "She's pretty good on the crest. Not as good as I am, but decent."

"And how many times have you seen each other since?" I ask.

"Maybe ten, twelve?" he says.

"And you were never concerned she might be seeing Connor on the side?"

He pinches his features. "Naw, man. Why would she do that?"

"For the job, dumbass," Peregrine says. "So she would still keep the job."

"Oh," he says, like he hasn't considered this before. "But...we like, slept together. Are you tellin' me I was sleepin' with a dude too? That's like, the transitive property, right?"

"I think we're done here," Peregrine says, standing. I wish we could get more details out of Krantz, but he's obviously off to cloud-coo-coo land for a while. Still, he's given us some invaluable information.

"Mr. Krantz," I say, pulling my card out of my pocket and placing it on the table between us. "I would like you to call me when you sober up. We may have some more questions for you."

"You got it, boss," he says, giving me a thumbs up. The odds that he actually remembers this conversation are next to nil, but I have to try anyway.

"Now what?" Peregrine asks as we head back down the stairs to the car. "Arrest Connor?"

"On what basis?" I ask. "As much as I would like to, we don't have any direct evidence that he's behind this, just connection. We don't even have motive."

"Except that he's obscured the fact he knew all the victims in one way or another from us."

"True," I say. "Maybe it's worth rattling his cage a little. Let's see what falls out."

# Chapter Twenty-Four

MY HEAD IS BUZZING as we drive back up the winding road to the Breckenridge mansion. Something about Rafe hasn't seemed right since the moment he approached me at the pool. At first, I thought it was just raw male bravado, but the more I've gotten to know him the more I realize there is more going on under the surface.

For a man who seems to have everything, he's incredibly insecure with women. First his attempts with Claire Taylor, then with me. And then, when neither of those options worked out, he turned to a sex worker to fulfill his needs. And yet he still wears his wedding band. After doing a basic level of research I was able to find that his story about his wife is true. She passed away a few months ago from a boating accident. And because they never had any kids, he was alone when she died.

Maybe that's what this has all been about. Trying to fulfill some deep-seeded need for a legacy. Rafe runs one of the most successful businesses in the world, employs thousands upon thousands of people, is responsible for billions of dollars in economic growth. It makes sense he would want something in place to make sure all that continues after he dies. I can't say for sure, but what if this desire for a legacy turned into something of an obsession? What if Rafe got tired of being rejected, and just started abducting women against their will, to do with as he pleased? Maybe in some way as a substitution for his dead wife? Breckenridge would be able to provide the perfect location to make that possibility a reality.

Yet, when we searched those rooms, they were all empty. Maybe Rafe didn't want the women there during the party. And maybe we didn't find the lowest level of the house.

"You sure this is a good idea?" Peregrine asks as we approach the closed gates of the property. "Showing our hand like this?"

"I think up until now, Rafe has gotten everything he's wanted," I say. "He's been operating unchecked and needs to know that someone is out there watching his every move, making sure he's not about to get away with it. It might even make him slip up."

"You sure don't take things lightly, do you?"

Maybe I wouldn't be so gung-ho if this wasn't personal. But Rafe tried to bring me into his little...club. If he hadn't found out I was an FBI agent, there is a possibility I might be sitting somewhere with the other four women right now. But given how brazenly these women have disappeared, with no one seeming to see or hear a thing, I'm not so confident I could have gotten myself out of such a situation. One thing I'm certain about: Rafe is involved. Everything keeps coming back to him. And if Marian Stamper is any indication, we are on a hard clock here. This investigation can't take another two weeks; I just don't think they have that long.

When we arrive at the gate, Peregrine reaches out to hit the call button, but one of the guards in black appears from behind the wall before she can. "This is private property," he calls out.

I get out of the car, approaching the man. "And I'm a federal agent. I have reason to believe you're harboring a suspect in there." I recognize the man from the night of the party, though he's not one of the house security guards.

"I don't know what you're talking about," he says.

"I see. You'd like to be charged with obstructing justice and aiding and abetting a felon. Easy enough." I pull out my phone and snap a picture of him.

"What was that for?" he asks.

"Just going to have my people at the FBI run a facial match on you, pull all your information so we know who to charge when the time comes."

"Listen, lady—"

"Special Agent Slate," I correct him with a growl.

"I don't care who you are. I have orders not to let anyone in, and that's how it's going to be. Try your intimidation tactics somewhere else."

I stand there, my nostrils flaring. "Fine." After a moment, I get back in the car.

"I'm guessing that didn't go as you'd hoped," Peregrine says.

"No. But it was worth a shot. We'll just have to do this the hard way."

"The *hard* way?" she asks.

I glance down at her footwear. "You're going to need something with better soles."

ROUGHLY AN HOUR LATER, WE'RE BACK TRAIPSING THROUGH the jungle *yet again*. I feel like it's Groundhog Day and my life has become one endless hike in unending jungle. Except this time, I know exactly where I'm going. Peregrine is about ten steps behind me as we scale the hill. She's keeping up, but it's rough going. We've probably covered five hundred feet of elevation and we're not even halfway there yet. At least this time I brought some water.

By the time we reach the stone circle, I am drenched in my own sweat. My hair is stuck to my head and my face is so warm I feel like someone could cook smores on my forehead. Police tape still surrounds the entire area, but it doesn't look like the CSI team has been back to do any more work, not that I blame them. Pulling anything from this jungle is an exercise in frustration.

"We're close," I call back to her.

"Uh-huh," she says, panting. "I just hope this is worth it."

That makes two of us. What I really hope is that we're not too late. It took longer to get back down the mountain and park at the bottom of the trail than I had anticipated, and getting back up here has been a feat in itself. Still, I'm determined to reach the Breckenridge mansion before the meeting has concluded. In fact, I can't wait to see the look on Rafe's face when we get there.

As the jungle falls away and we find ourselves in the brush, the mansion comes into view. The sun is just beginning to set over the ocean, painting the sky in a beautiful flurry of colors that seem to go on forever. Pink and purple hues reflect off a dazzling blue ocean, and for a brief moment I think about just stopping to enjoy the view. Then Claire Taylor's face appears in my head, and I trudge forward, heading for the far end of the gardens attached to the mansion. When we reach the border, I'm surprised not to see any security personnel out here. Especially after I informed them about the possible security risk.

In fact, the gardens are eerily quiet as we make our way through. The lights of the house glow in the distance, and I can even see the pool reflecting off the walls, the dancing lights creating intricate patterns across the home.

I continue to look around for any security, but from what I can tell, there is no one out here. Do they have everyone inside? "This is where the meeting was scheduled to take place, right?" I ask.

"According to the mayor's office, yes. He had the entire afternoon blocked out for it," Peregrine says. We're both on edge out here. I thought we would at least encounter some resistance as we approached, like we did at the gate. And yet, it's like the place has been abandoned.

As we reach the pool deck where, not more than a few nights ago, Breckenridge stood and announced his "amazing night of food," I start to get a deep pit somewhere in my stomach. "Give me your other firearm," I whisper.

Peregrine reaches down and pulls out a .38 special from her ankle holster while at the same time retrieving her weapon from under her coat. She hands me the smaller gun. "You expecting trouble?"

"There should be *someone* out here," I say. "It's too quiet." We make our way around the pool area, looking for an open door into the home. The indoor/outdoor glass plate windows have all been shut. I check the nearest door, finding it locked.

"Slate, what's going on?" Peregrine asks.

"I don't know." The lights are on inside the house, but there's no one milling about. I can even see into the kitchen from here, which looks abandoned. I catch sight of another door on the far side of the kitchen. "Come on."

We make our way around the side of the house carefully until we reach the kitchen door. I try it, and thankfully it opens without resistance. Keeping my weapon down, I step into the house carefully. Like the night I was here before, soft jazz music is playing from somewhere. I can only assume Breckenridge would host this meeting in the boardroom I passed the night I was looking for the basement, which is on the other side of the house.

Something is very wrong here. At the very least, there should be people watching the entrances and exits. For as many people as Breckenridge had meet him at his helicopter, there should be at least as many here. But I have yet to see anyone other than the man at the gate. And because I can't see out that side of the house, I can't even be sure he's still there.

"Could they have left already?" Peregrine asks. "Maybe they changed the location of the meeting. Or it wrapped up early?"

I'm not so sure. They would have wanted a place that was free from prying eyes. Sure, they could have met at the Grand Solomon or somewhere just as fancy, but why not go for the big guns? Breckenridge's house has what must be one of the best views on the island. I can't believe Rafe wouldn't want to use it as a selling point.

Finally, we reach the far side of the house. It's taking a while because we're checking all the blind corners, looking for anyone who might be on the lookout for us. But it's dead silent. No voices from anywhere, no footsteps, nothing. It's like the house has been abandoned.

"Slate."

I glance to my right where Peregrine has indicated, seeing a pair of legs in black suit pants on the ground, sticking out from behind a wall. After checking my lines, I carefully creep over to the body. Peregrine has her weapon trained above my head, keeping an eye out for anyone who might be hiding. When I round the wall, I see it's one of the security guards. He's motionless on the floor, and when I check for a pulse, I don't feel a thing. "Dead," I whisper. I try tapping his cheeks gently, but he's not responding. I don't see any wounds on him anywhere, so it's impossible to know what happened. "Call it in."

Peregrine nods and pulls out her phone as I make my way down the hall towards the boardroom. Last time I was here, this hallway was full of people coming and going, laughing and trying not to spill their drinks. It's as if this place is nothing more than a shadow of its former self.

When I reach the door, I double check the adjoining hallway, which forms a T intersection, but there is no one there.

The hallway is as empty as the rest of the house. The two large wooden doors that seal off the boardroom are closed tight. Peregrine joins me. "I've got EMS and backup on the way," she whispers.

I nod at the doors, and she seems to understand. She stands in front of one door as I stand in front of the other. She places a hand on the handle and mouths, *Ready?* I nod again and she throws open the door. I peek inside quickly, pulling back in case someone is waiting for me. But what I see in the few milliseconds my eyes travel over the room sends my stomach plummeting. I grimace, taking a second look to verify.

At the very end of the table, in the largest chair, sits Jeremy Breckenridge, his throat sliced from ear to ear. And beside him sits the mayor, in the exact same fashion.

# Chapter Twenty-Five

"WHAT A SHITSHOW," Montenegro says, surveying the meeting room. "An absolute shitshow."

The room is buzzing with activity as Montenegro's people work to secure the scene and gather all the evidence they can. After finding Breckenridge and Mayor Williams, Peregrine and I searched the rest of the house, locating three more security personnel. Unlike the man in the hallway, all three of them were in a similar state to the men in the boardroom. Killed indiscriminately. However, also unlike the man in the hallway, they had been hidden in closets or bedrooms. For what purpose, we still don't know.

Montenegro gets in my face. He's a hair shorter than I am, but his attitude makes up for it. "What have you brought down upon us?"

"I haven't brought anything down. You had this problem before I arrived."

"Before you arrived, I didn't have any bodies. Now I have six. *Six.*" He screams the last word, causing some of the techs in the room to jump. But I'm not about to let him rattle me.

"You need to find Rafe Connor. Right now. He's the key to all this."

"If you have any suggestions, I'm all ears. His car is still outside. So unless he trudged down that little path of yours, he could be anywhere on this island."

He wasn't on the path because we didn't pass him on the way up.

"Captain?" one of the officers says, calling all of our attention. "He's ready."

"Finally," Montenegro says, pushing past me. I follow as Peregrine stays behind to monitor the work in the boardroom. "Where do you think you're going?"

"To interview the only person who might be able to tell us what happened here," I state confidently.

"You've done enough. I don't need your help."

"Captain," I say. "I know you don't like me. But you need me there to make sure we're not missing anything."

Montenegro grumbles and turns on his heel. I take that as the best invitation I'm going to get from the man. I follow him back into the kitchen where the man who stopped us at the gate sits, no longer full of bravado. An officer stands close to him while others continue to search the house.

"Mr. Tovey," Montenegro says. Tovey looks up and sees me before returning his gaze to the table. Montenegro sits across from him. "You've been informed of your rights?" Tovey nods. "And you're waiving your right to have a lawyer present."

"Yes," he says.

"Tell me what happened. In your own words."

There's a half-empty bottle of water on the table beside Tovey, who takes it and drains the rest in one gulp. He wipes the back of his mouth with his expensive suit sleeve and pushes the bottle away. "It's all my fault."

"Let's just start at the beginning," Montenegro says.

Tovey nods. "I…uh…I got to work this morning around ten a.m. Breckenridge was due to arrive around eleven. I always get here early to do a sweep of the property."

"Was there anyone else here when you arrived?" I ask.

He nods. "The house security team," he says. "Brecken-ridge keeps some of them on retainer twenty-four seven when he's on or close to the island. They had been here all night."

"And no one had any problems," Montenegro offers.

"No. Nothing. Everything was normal. They were busy prepping the house for Breckenridge; the kitchen staff was preparing meals and the housekeepers were doing their final walk-throughs. I knew it was going to be a long day, what with the meeting and all, so I used the facilities, then headed out to my car where I waited for the convoy to arrive."

"Wait," I say. "Was the whole house security team present?"

He nods.

"What does that matter?" Montenegro asks.

"Roberts and Daniels. They weren't among the victims," I say, turning back to Tovey. "Were they here earlier?"

"I…uh…I think so?"

Montenegro pulls out his phone and makes a note. "Your car is the black Mercedes parked out front? Inside the wall?"

Tovey nods.

"You were on patrol the night of the party too, weren't you?" I ask.

"Yes ma'am," he says. All the fight has gone out of him.

"Okay, keep going."

"Breckenridge arrived around eleven fifteen. The meeting was scheduled for four. I didn't see him only but for a few seconds as his car drove in and he got out and went into the house. My job is to watch the gate. That's it."

"Who arrived next?" I ask.

"Connor. He came by around one. Breckenridge had told us to expect him early. I guess they wanted to talk strategy or something. I know whatever this is, it's supposed to be a big deal for the island. Some kind of land deal? I don't really keep up."

"Keep going," Montenegro says, impatience creeping into his words.

"Right, so Connor gets here around one. Again, I don't see much of him. Then I get a call at three-thirty that Mayor Williams is on his way up. He pulled up around three forty, I think."

"Was he alone?" Montenegro asks.

"Yes, just him."

"No personal security?" I ask. "No advisors?"

"No one else in the car. I greeted him at the gate, asked him how he thought the Buccaneers were faring this year, and we shared a quick laugh. After that, I didn't see him again. He headed down to the house and went inside. That's all I know."

"You didn't have any other communication from anyone else inside the house all evening?" Montenegro asks.

"No sir. I was told the meeting would probably run long, and to be prepared to stay late into the evening."

"And no one else approached the gate?"

Tovey glances over to me. "Just her and that other cop."

"What time was that?" Montenegro asks.

"Around five, five thirty maybe. After they left, I got back in my car, kept an eye on the feeds from the walls, and waited for the meeting to end. The next thing I knew, the ambulance was bearing down on the house, sirens going full blast."

"And you never heard anything from the house. No struggling, no one yelling or calling for help," he adds.

"Nothing. It was quiet. I just thought the meeting was running long."

Montenegro watches the man for a few minutes, as if he's trying to read his mind. "How do you explain what's happened in here?"

"I can't."

"You watch the gate," he says. "You're in charge of keeping an eye on the people coming and going from this

182 • ALEX SIGMORE

property. Someone obviously snuck onto the property and killed these men. How did they do it?"

"The only other way I know of is that path your people found the other day," he says. "The one that leads down the mountain."

"And you didn't think to station anyone there?" I ask. "For such an important meeting?"

"That falls under house security," he argues. "That's not my department. I watch the front gate and the walls. That's it."

Montenegro points at me. "That's how she got onto the property. And you had no idea, did you? You never even saw her coming."

Tovey drops his head again.

"Seems like a piss poor security operation if you ask me," Montenegro says, standing back up. "Plan on being here a while. I'll have someone take your official statement before you can go home."

He nods again.

Montenegro heads back out of the kitchen and I follow. "This place has security cameras," he tells one of his officers. "Pull the feeds."

"They'll be blank," I say.

"What?"

"Roberts isn't here. Which means he is more than likely in on it. He had the security clearance to erase the feeds before they left." I should have seen through it the other day. But the man put on a good show. Either that or I'm losing my touch. "Has there been any word from Rafe's people?" I ask.

"No."

"If he's not here, he must be with the killers," I say. "He could have orchestrated this whole thing."

"Yes, Agent, I'm aware," Montenegro says, exhaustion and frustration competing to dominate his voice. "He's officially a suspect. Does that make you feel any better?"

It should, but it doesn't. Could Rafe have really put together a hit on Breckenridge and Mayor Williams? If so, why? He said he'd been working on this career-defining deal for months. Years even. So did the deal go bad, and the mayor refused to grant the land for his developments? I can't see Rafe as the kind who would fly off the handle and just start murdering people indiscriminately. Not to mention, what was his beef with Breckenridge? And how does all this tie back to the missing women?

I let Montenegro head off on his own. No doubt he doesn't want me on his heels any more than I want to be there. Instead, I head to the secure side of the house, down to where Breckenridge kept his "special" rooms. The door to the stairs is propped open with a book from a nearby bookshelf.

Downstairs, two officers are working on breaking the lock to the lowest part of the house. The door beside it, which contains all of Breckenridge's collection pieces, stands open and the room empty. The golden handle Roberts used on the lock the other day sits lifelessly at my feet.

There's a snapping and the squeal of metal as the door to the sex dungeon is broken.

"Finally," one of the officers says. "Thing is like a fucking bank vault." They manage to pull the door open and step inside. I follow them in, finding the lights down the hallway are already on.

"What the hell...?" the other officer says.

"C'mon," I tell them. "This way." We trot quickly down the hallway, and for the second time, I'm afraid of what I might find down here. "Check each of these doors." I point to each of the six, opening the first one myself. But once again, the room is empty. I *know* these rooms are connected to these missing women in some way, I just don't know how yet.

The other officers head to the rest of the rooms, but they will all be empty.

Frustrated, I head back into the hallway to make sure I'm

not missing anything, maybe a hidden door somewhere that might lead to an even lower level. But after a few minutes, I'm forced to conclude this is as far as it goes. And it's nothing but another dead end.

"Agent?" one of the officers calls out. He's in the third door down on the right. I head inside, finding it's very much like the others. Full of tools for every kind of pleasure and pain imaginable. "What do you make of this?" He holds up a small placard, like the kind you would find at a table setting. Written cross it are only two words: *Black Cat.*

I'm not sure *what* to make of it. I haven't encountered any "Black Cat" in this investigation, so I have to assume it was a pseudonym for one of Breckenridge's guests or associates. "Bag it up," I tell him. "We'll file it into evidence." It looks to be handwritten, so it could be important, but for the moment, I don't know how.

I head back upstairs to find that the same medical examiner who was helping us with Marian Stamper has arrived and is examining Mayor Williams and Breckenridge as Montenegro and Peregrine look on.

"Anything?" Peregrine asks.

"There's no one downstairs," I say. "Do we have IDs on all the security personnel?"

She nods. "They all had their identification on them. We're checking with Breckenridge's people right now."

"Have you ever seen anything like this on the island before?" I ask Montenegro.

"Like what? Mass killings?"

I'd hardly call six people a mass killing. Then again, maybe I'm biased. "I'm talking about the signature. Cutting from ear to ear across the throat. Anything like that before?"

"No," he says, not blinking. He's staring at Mayor Williams.

"We have to assume whoever did this came and left using the trail," Peregrine suggests. "And since we used it as well and didn't see anyone, it at least narrows down the timeframe to before five thirty."

Montenegro turns to Peregrine. "You said she would make this all go away. I should have known better than to trust *you*." For the first time, Peregrine shies away from him, her veneer cracked.

"I'm sorry?" I say, on the defensive. There's no mistaking the vitriol in his voice.

"I was told you would be able to help. But from what I can see, all you have been is a hindrance."

I'm not sure what he's talking about, but I don't like his tone. "Excuse me, but we were the ones who *found* them this way. If not for us, you'd be at least twelve hours behind."

"And what good does it do us?" he asks. "What help has all your 'FBI' experience been? All I have is more missing women and now *this*." He turns back to Peregrine. "I told you this was a bad idea from the beginning. Next time maybe you'll listen to me." He storms off, presumably to yell at someone else.

"What the hell is he talking about?" I ask.

Peregrine's eyes shift back and forth. She motions for me to follow her into an adjacent room. There's no one else in here. She regards me for a moment before her face falls. "It was me," she says. I screw up my features, unsure what she means.

"I was the one who blew your cover."

# Chapter Twenty-Six

IT'S like it takes me longer to understand what she's saying than should be normal.

"Why would you do that?" I ask.

For a brief second, she seemed almost contrite, but immediately she snaps back to the stoic. She takes a step closer. "Don't you see what I'm working with here?"

"I don't understand," I say. "How could you have even known?" I think back to Zara checking the clearances on my operation.

"I clocked you, coming off the plane," she says.

I remember feeling like someone had eyes on me. But I thought at the time it was nothing more than paranoia. "What, did I forget to take off my jacket with the big, yellow FBI letters emblazoned on the back?"

She shakes her head. "It wasn't that. At first, I thought you were a cop from the mainland. You just have this…aura about you. It's hard to explain."

"Yeah? Try." No one else has ever said I have an *aura*. And I wouldn't have been able to get close to Fletch if I did. I worked that case for weeks and no one ever said a word. My cover was perfect…wasn't it?

"I don't know how to describe it," she says, pulling out a cigarette and lighting it, despite us still being inside. She glances to her right, where a series of sliding doors connect the room to the large outdoor deck. She slides one open and steps out into the night air. I follow. She's not about to get off that easy.

"Peregrine, I deserve an explanation," I say, following her out.

She stops, looking out over the dark ocean. "You don't know what it's like. Working under Montenegro and the others. Everyone wants to pretend like bad things don't happen here, like we're immune from all that because we're supposed to be a 'tropical paradise.' That's built into the culture; I see it every day. You think he's mad because he's got multiple dead bodies on his hands, one of which is the mayor? He's mad because if the press gets wind of it, and they will, it means less tourist dollars for the island. It means more scrutiny. It means he'll probably get fired."

"That's all well and good," I say. "But it doesn't explain why or even how you managed to break my cover."

She turns to me. "I did it because I needed someone I could trust. I've tried working with the other officers on the island. All of them want to toe the line. They want to be good little soldiers and fill up their pockets with a little bonus at the end of the month for sweeping things under the rug."

"You're saying they're on the take? All of them?"

"It's not a very big island, Agent. There's an unwritten rule around here. Don't make waves, enjoy the view, and keep the money rolling in."

"That's why the other officers don't want to work with you," I say. "They can't trust you because you're not willing to participate."

She takes a long drag on the cigarette. "I used to be. Back when I first started. Even when I was promoted to detective. But then I realized how many people I was hurting. I learned about all the horrific things that happened here that no one talked about. And I couldn't do it anymore."

The lights around the patio have shadowed her face, but I can tell its drawn...serious. I don't believe she's lying about it. She blows a stream of smoke out of the side of her mouth so it doesn't end up in my face. "Why hasn't Montenegro fired you yet?"

"Because his need for good detectives outweighs his desire to get rid of me. Besides, what was I going to do, go to the mayor? He knew about it. I guess now I could go to the city council, but all that would do is jam up the department for months, allowing even more crimes to go unnoticed."

"So you figured the best thing you could do was stay and chip away at what you could," I say.

"More or less. But most of the cases I work, I do it solo. Including this one. As I said, Montenegro didn't even have anyone working the file. And had bodies not started showing up, I doubt he ever would have. He would have just let those women disappear into thin air, like they never existed."

I work my jaw, trying to wrap my head around this. I knew Montenegro wasn't what I would call a man of stellar character, but this is low, even for him. And now I've been dragged down into all this. "And your solution was to out me from my own investigation," I say, the accusation plain.

"I'm sorry about that," she says. "But I was desperate. I thought maybe a fellow cop could give me some assistance, but when I learned who you really were and why you were here, I *knew* you could help. Believe me, when you arrived, I didn't think you were anything other than a cop on vacation."

"Do you even understand what you did?" I say. "I was in with Rafe. He's obviously the key to all of this and I was *in* with him. I could have blown this thing out from the inside without anyone getting killed. You completely screwed my investigation and you didn't do yourself any favors in the process." It's rare I get mad enough to yell, but this is one of those occasions. For someone to make the decision for me, to not even allow me to do my job? "You're just as bad as the rest of them."

She takes another puff of her cigarette. "I'm sorry. By the time I realized what was going on, I'd already discussed it with Montenegro."

I want to smash something, and the nearby pot with the fern in it is looking pretty good right about now. But I'm not done with Peregrine. "Exactly *how* did you find out who I was, anyway?"

"I swear, when I started I thought you were just a cop. Nothing else."

"You said that."

She sighs. "I have a friend in the CIA. He managed to pull some strings."

"And he was okay with you disrupting an official FBI investigation?"

She looks to the side. "He didn't know. I told him I was gathering information only, and that you had appeared on my radar."

"Let me get this straight," I growl. "You saw me arrive, thought I might be an ally to help you with this case, decided to do some background work on me, and lied to the CIA about obtaining that information. Then, when you realized who I was, you ruined an official FBI investigation for your own selfish needs, because you couldn't work the case alone anymore."

She hesitates, her head down. "That about sums it up, yeah."

"I should have you arrested," I say. "For obstruction of justice. And misappropriation of government resources. Not to mention those *strings* your friend pulled, were more than likely illegal. You don't just blow an FBI agent's cover for your own gratification. That is not only reckless, but dangerous as well. If I'd been in another position, revealing my true identity could have gotten me killed."

"Agent Slate, I'm sor—"

"Save it," I say. "Rest assured I'll be filing official charges against you when I return. And if I had the authority, I would have you removed from duty. But I doubt Montenegro is going to listen to me right now. And given the island's government is in freefall, it's the only thing keeping you from seeing the inside of a jail cell." I shove my finger into her shoulder. "Do. Not. Leave. This. Island. Understand me?"

She nods.

I turn and storm off, heading for the house exit. I'm so furious I can barely focus on keeping one foot in front of the other. Peregrine's actions may have cost these women their lives, not to mention she put me at risk. I fumble for my phone, ready to call Zara to find out who this CIA contact could have been and how they managed to place such a high-level request.

But as I get my phone out of my pocket, I find I am shaking with rage. There's only one thing that will help me burn off some of this energy. I spot the Mercedes parked near the front gates of the house. I make a bee-line for it, slip into the car and press the ignition. The car roars to life and I tear out of the property, barely missing the nearby ambulance as I do.

Within seconds I'm approaching sixty. I press the accclerator even harder, as if doing so will channel all my frustration into the vehicle. The wind whips at my hair as I crest the hills, hugging the curves. The lights illuminate the road in front of me, but it is *dark* out here.

Finally, I ease off the gas a little. The car slows and I find a place to pull off. I get out and stare out at the city below, and beyond that, the ocean.

And I scream harder than I ever have before, my voice echoing through the night.

# Chapter Twenty-Seven

"EMILY, HANG ON A SECOND," Liam says. My phone is sitting on the nightstand in my motel room as I continue to throw clothes into my suitcase. Behind him is our kitchen, where I assume he is preparing another wonderful meal just for himself and probably a few bites for the pups. I just want to be back there. I don't care if it is cold as balls. I need to get off this island.

"I'm coming home," I say without looking back at the phone. "I'm done with this place."

"Will you hang on a second and listen to me?" he says.

I bite my lip and stop, staring up at the ceiling in frustration. "What?"

"Sit down and take a breath."

"Liam I—"

"*Sit*," he commands.

I roll my eyes and I perch myself on the edge of the bed, glaring at him. "There. Happy?"

"No. And you won't be either if you leave right now."

"Did you not hear a word I said?" I say, standing back up. "She stabbed me in the back. She blew my cover. This whole thing is *fucked*."

"So?" he asks. The nonchalant way he does it makes me want to smack him.

"*So?* She could have gotten me killed."

"I understand that. And she'll need to pay for that. But how does you leaving help Claire Taylor or the other missing women? In fact, given everything you've told me, isn't this Montenegro character more likely to refocus the investigation on the mayor and the billionaire, and just quietly forget about the missing women?"

I huff, sitting back on the edge of the bed again. "If what Peregrine says about him is true, probably."

"So then you're the only one who can fight for them now. And I know if you leave, you'll be halfway back here on that plane and realize you never should have left. I'm sorry that happened to you, and I'm sorry she violated your trust. But you still have a duty to perform."

He's right, of course. Leaving now would give Montenegro everything he wants. Not to mention Rafe is still in the wind. I can't let him get away with this. But I can't help but think about how many more answers I would have if I were allowed to remain undercover.

"C'mon Em, I can see the gears turning. Talk to me."

"She said I was an obvious mark," I tell him. "That she ID'd me as a cop right off the plane."

"What? That's ridiculous," he says.

"What if she's right? What if I've been fooling myself on this other job, the one in DC? I'm dealing with some dangerous people there—if they suspect I'm anything other than a socialite who represents—"

"Stop. I'm not going to let you do this to yourself," he says. "You are not an easy mark. Otherwise Caruthers never would have given you this job."

"Then how did she ID me? Trust me, I was *on* as soon as I stepped off the plane. I was aware of my surroundings, and I was vigilant, but not overly so. Not suspicious." Though I did have that feeling at the airport. The one that put me on edge.

"I don't know." Liam gives me a reassuring smile. "But I know it's bullshit. It has to be. You are not bad at undercover work."

All the fight goes out of me and my shoulders sag. "I just don't know what I'm supposed to do. There hasn't been any evidence from any of the women other than the necklace at those damn stones. And I have a very bad feeling that they are running out of time."

"You're going to have to go back to the beginning. What do all these women have in common?"

"Rafe Connor," I say.

"Then start there," he says. "Start with his company. Why these particular women? And is there anyone else on the island that might be a target?"

"I think it's going to be a little difficult finding anything out," I say. "Considering he's already enacted his *final plan*."

"How do you know?" he asks. "You said yourself the killings didn't seem to be connected to the missing women at all. How do you know he doesn't have something else planned?"

A sense of dread rolls over my shoulders like a heavy cloak. "I don't know."

"But you can find out," he says. "I believe in you."

I smile and reach over, touching the screen. "I miss you."

"We miss you right back," he says. "Some of us more than others." He pans the camera down to show both dogs looking up at me, their eyes wide and wanting.

"Hi guys," I coo. "Momma will be back home soon. I promise."

Timber licks his lips while Rocky whines. It both makes me laugh and breaks my heart at the same time. I hate leaving them. Liam appears in the screen again. "You've got this, Em. I know you do."

"Thanks," I say. "I'll keep you updated as I can. I guess I need to go back to square one."

"Talk to you soon," he says. "Love you."

"Love you back," I say before hanging up. I continue sitting there on the bed, contemplating my next move. Everything points back to Rafe. But Rafe is missing, presumed on the lamb. No doubt Montenegro has shut down all traffic off the island, which makes my threat to Peregrine a little redundant. Still, Rafe isn't going to take public transportation to get off the island. He's going to find another way. A private charter of some kind.

I still believe he's the key to finding these women. He was at that meeting. He knows what happened.

I just need to find him.

"DON'T WORRY, WE'RE GOING TO GET TO THE BOTTOM OF this," Zara says. I'm speaking to her as I head down one of the main streets of Queen's Bay, looking for a particular building.

"I just don't like not knowing who I'm dealing with," I tell her. "I didn't realize Peregrine was that desperate or that ruthless."

"See, this is why I should have been there," she says. "Something I plan on emphasizing to Caruthers for the next month."

I chuckle. "Go easy on him. He's got a department to run. How's it going over there anyway?" I check the numbers on the nearby corner. I'm close, but not there yet. I head down the next block.

"Fletch is back in Croatia, big surprise," she says. "No doubt he's meeting with his contacts again. Maybe even buying brand new batches of information to sell. We're trying to trace who bought the info you copied, but it's been tricky."

And we still don't know the full impact of what it means. But I'm willing to bet when he heads back here in another week or two, he'll be looking to connect back up with Emily Agostini."

"Great, can't wait to go *back* undercover," I say. "Assuming I make any progress here."

"Caruthers and I have been discussing our next moves. I think you're going to like the direction we're going in. And don't rush. Work the case there. Fletch isn't going anywhere. If you don't snag him this time, we can get him the next."

"Yeah," I say. "Assuming he doesn't catch on to my *aura*."

"I don't care what that woman says, that's a bunch of BS, capital 'Bull.'"

I tell her. "I just don't like how this all feels." I glance up. "You said 5813 LaRue Boulevard?"

"That should be it. Connor Investments International's address there on the island."

As I look up at the building, I have to admit I'm unimpressed. I guess I was expecting a much larger, grander building for someone as rich as Rafe. Then again, this is only supposed to be a temporary office while he worked the deal.

That's one thing that's sticking in my craw about all of this. Why would Rafe go off the handle and murder two people? Surely not because they rejected his bid. He's an established businessman, I'm sure he hears the word "no" all the time. So, what was different this time?

"I'm here," I tell her. "But it's like any other building on this street. Mostly stucco and bright shutters. Barely even looks like a commercial building."

"Yeah, according to the map that sounds right," she says. "As best I can tell, the office was set up five months ago. Just somewhere he could work without needing to travel back to New York or Atlanta all the time."

"Okay." I take a deep breath. "I doubt they'll be open, but I'm going to give it a shot."

"Best of luck," she chirps. "Let me know if you need anything else."

"Tell you what, if one more person stabs me in the back, I'm demanding Caruthers send you down here."

"Now that's an idea I can get behind," she replies. "See ya."

"Thanks, Z." I hang up and pull the earpiece out of my ear. The door to the building isn't marked, but nor is it locked. And when I pull on it, I find it opens quite easily.

The first floor of the building is made up of four different businesses, each occupying one corner of the building. A dentist, a jeweler, a taxidermy office and an accountant. There are also two sets of stairs on each side of me leading up to the second floor, forming a natural barrier between the offices on each side. I take the left side of the stairs up and find four more offices above, though two are vacant. The one right in front of me is what looks like an artist's shop of some kind, while the last one is marked by a simple *CII* on the glass door. Inside, I can see a young woman sitting at a reception desk, looking flustered. She's on the phone, but her tight hair has fallen out of place and her bun is coming loose.

I open the door and catch the end of her conversation.

"—n't say. As I've already told you, he hasn't been in. I will notify you if that changes. Yes. Yes, I understand. Thank you. You too." She hangs up then looks up at me. "Welcome to Connor Investments." She pushes her blonde hair back into place, but it falls right back out. "How can I help you?"

I show her my badge and her face falls. "I'm Special Agent Slate with the FBI."

"Before you say anything," she says, holding out her hands. "I haven't seen him. He hasn't been in since yesterday morning. I don't know where he is, and he hasn't called in. Okay?"

"Been fielding a lot of calls from the police today?" I ask.

"You wouldn't believe how many," she says. "And no one

will even tell me anything. What's going on? Where is Mr. Connor?"

"That's the million-dollar question," I tell her. "You said you saw him yesterday morning?"

She nods. "Yes, before his meeting with the mayor. He was making sure he had everything for the meeting. We went over it probably a dozen times."

"How did he seem?" I ask. "Was he nervous? Anxious?"

She scoffs. "You obviously don't know Mr. Connor. He doesn't get nervous before meetings. If anything, he gets calmer. It's kind of scary."

I perk up. "Scary how?"

"Just how he can turn off his emotions like that," she says. "It's like nothing can rattle him. I wish I could do that sometimes."

"And that's how he was yesterday morning?"

She nods. "I met him early to make sure all the notes for the presentation were in order. He then went over the presentation while I watched, as like a practice run. It sounded good, but he wanted to do it again."

I look around the office; pictures hang on the wall, mostly of Rafe with important people, but also standing with larger groups of people in front of large, impressive buildings. The office itself is a simple setup. The reception desk and a few chairs with a small couch, and there is a larger office behind her. I can see Rafe's desk through the glass door. "I don't suppose I could get inside his office, could I?"

She gives me a sympathetic look. "Do you have a warrant?"

"No, I don't."

"I'm sorry," she says. "I could lose my job if I let you in there. Mr. Connor is very private about business matters. He's told me time and time again about intellectual security, whatever that means. I just know I'm not to let anyone in without official documentation or word from Mr. Connor."

I nod. "I had to ask. Unfortunately, Mr. Connor is missing. I'm sorry, what's your name?"

"Cassandra," she says extending her hand. I take it and give it a quick shake.

"And how long have you worked here, Cassandra?"

"Here? Or for Mr. Connor?"

I cock my head. "Both."

"I started working for him back in 2018," she says. "But when he needed someone for this office, I volunteered. I figured free room and board on an island for six months to a year? Who wouldn't take that deal?"

"Yeah, makes sense," I say. "Where did you work before?"

"In the Atlanta branch," she says.

"Would you say you know Mr. Connor pretty well?"

She hems and haws, shrugging her shoulders. "I guess. He's usually a private person."

He didn't seem so private to me, but then again, I didn't have to work with the man day in and day out. Maybe he maintained a different persona with his direct work colleagues than he would in a more social setting.

Without access to his office, I don't think there is much more I can learn here. I could always try to force the issue, but I don't think I would get very far. Not to mention, Montenegro is probably already working on obtaining a warrant to toss the place. I had hoped I might be able to learn something before he screwed it all up, but I guess I'm out of luck. Just another dead end for Emily.

"Okay, thank you for your time," I say, giving her a polite nod. "If I were you, I'd brace myself. The police are going to be in your hair a lot over the next few days."

"Thanks," she says. "Maybe I should just close the office and go home." If she's looking for permission from me, I'm not about to give it. They'll need access to the office, and I'm sure Cassandra is about to endure hours of questioning. I feel for the girl, but I can't impede the process.

As I turn to leave, something catches my eye. A face, in one of the pictures. I move closer, noting the picture looks to be in front of a large plot of land in what looks like the Midwest somewhere. Connor is standing in front of the sign noting it as a CII project, and around him are a dozen or so other people, all smiling.

But what's drawn my eye is one of the women. I pull out my phone and bring up the picture of Vicki Tolluse, comparing the two. She's the woman who went missing from the grocery store—the one Caruthers knows. But what strikes me is I can just barely see Rafe's hand cupping her waist.

I take the picture off the wall and return to Cassandra. "Do you know where this was taken?"

She takes the picture and looks at it. "Sure, this was the Weddington Project. It was a large land development deal outside of Atlanta. Big enough that people called it a miniature city within itself. CII made the whole deal happen. Mr. Connor worked for years procuring that property."

"And this woman?" I ask, pointing to Vicki.

"Ms. Tolluse," Cassandra says, her face going the slightest shade of red. "I believe she used to work for CII, but by this point she represented Bulls Union Bank, which financed the project. She's also working with us here on the development deal for the island."

The son of a bitch lied directly to my face. "I can't help but notice she and Mr. Connor are…friendly," I say.

She nods. "They dated for a few months. It didn't work out, but they maintained their professional relationship." She leans forward. "The only reason I know is because sometimes I listen in on Mr. Connor's conversations. Just in case I need to make notes of anything."

I nod, showing her I'm a willing co-conspirator. "Have you spoken to Ms. Tolluse in the past few weeks?"

"I haven't personally, but I believe Mr. Connor has. I know she's been staying on the island."

I snap a quick picture of the photo, then hang it back on the wall where it was. "Great, thanks again for your help, Cassandra. Maybe you should take the rest of the day off. It's not like your boss is going to know."

She smiles. "You know what? I might do that."

# Chapter Twenty-Eight

OUTSIDE THE CII OFFICES, I take a moment to duck into a shady alleyway and go back over the notes I took from the case. Rafe was in a relationship with Amy Van Allen. And he tried to start a relationship with Claire Taylor. Now I find out that he and Vicki Tolluse were involved for a short time.

I'm willing to bet he had a similar relationship with Marian Stamper. *That's* the connecting piece of all of this. Rafe had been in a relationship with, or at least slept with, every single one of the missing women. So then what was he doing? Why would he round them up and hide them away somewhere? What was he after?

It's not much, but it's a start. And it's more information than I had before. Thinking back, only one of the women was married: Marian Stamper. Her husband works for CII, but when I confronted Rafe with that fact, he seemed unfazed. Then I remember what Cassandra said about him being able to regulate his emotions. He might have just been playing me this entire time. Or am I looking at something else here? Did Marian Stamper's husband find out about Rafe?

I call Zara back as I head back towards town.

"Yo," she says. "How did it go. Find anything interesting?"

202 • ALEX SIGMORE

"I think so," I tell her. "I need you to look something up for me. I need you to find out as much as you can about Henry Avecido. You know, the guy married to Marian Stamper?"

"Already way ahead of you," she says. "I pulled it the other day, but I wasn't sure if you'd need it or not."

"Really? You could have told me," I say.

"Hey, I'm not the one running the investigation," she says. "I just figured I'd save myself some time in case you needed it."

I stroll down the narrow sidewalk, shielding my eyes from the sun. "So what do you have on him?"

"He works for the Atlanta offices of CII, been an employee for almost twenty years, going back to the beginnings of the company. He's been married for eighteen of those years, however six months ago he filed for divorce. That wasn't in his original file, by the way. I had to search the Georgia court records for that one."

"Divorce," I say. "What was the reason listed?"

"Irreconcilable differences," she replies.

"Cheating." I nod. "He found out about Rafe and Marian."

"Whoa, Marian was having an affair?" Zara asks.

"That's my working theory. Do we even know why she was on the island to begin with?"

"I can look into it," Zara says. "But if they were having an affair, I can't really think of a better place than a tropical island, can you?"

I think back to the picture of Tolluse, and of Claire Taylor. And of Amy Van Allen, waiting for her "job interview." Could Connor have been seeing all of these women *at once*? "Jesus," I say. "I think this guy might be a real player." I explain my theory to Zara.

"That's one hell of a juggling act," she says. "Why go to

all the trouble? I mean, why not keep one in a different city and just do a round robin kind of deal."

I have to hold back a snort at the mental image. "Because men are stupid. And they too often think with what's in their pants instead of what's in their skulls."

"You'd think for someone that rich, he could afford to make his life less complicated," she says.

"Who knows? What I do know is that of all the women missing from this island, I have at least some proof he was dating two of them. Anecdotal proof of three and a suspicion of all four. He took them, stashed them somewhere and then pretended like he didn't know a thing. The man stood there and lied to me without even breaking a sweat."

"To be fair, he was coming off post-coital activities," she says.

"Ugh, don't say that." I shudder, thinking of the image of him standing there in nothing but a towel. I should check on the young woman who was in his hotel room yesterday afternoon. Though I'm not sure she fits in the same category as the other women. It seems he had *relationships* with these other women. She could have been nothing more than a means to an end.

"Okay, but if he still had access to them, what was he doing with the sex worker?" Zara asks. "Why not just go to his secret hidey hole and have his way with them?"

Again, my mind does somersaults over the mental images trying to appear in my head. "That's a good point. Maybe he didn't have access to them anymore."

"What, like he dropped them into the bottom of a well?" she asks.

She's right. None of this makes much sense. Why gather the women on this island just to dispose of them? Why not keep them in Breckenridge's basement if he wanted them around for his "needs"? It would have been the perfect place. "I'm still missing something. Something big."

As I'm walking, I pass one of those souvenir shops that sells everything from hats to postcards. And one of the post-cards happens to catch my eye. It's a picture of the standing stone circle, except it's not the one near Breckenridge's house. It's a different one. "Z, I'll call you back. If you find anything let me know."

"Sure," she says, though I hear the hesitation. I think this case is confounding her as much as it is me. I hang up and pick up the postcard, taking it up to the old man at the desk.

"Excuse me, can you tell me where this is?" I ask. The image shows the stones out in the middle of what looks like a field. On the back there is a description mark: *Stones of the Native Kaltano People. St. Solomon, VI.*

The man barely glances at the postcard. Instead he pulls out a paper map of the island. He points to a particular peninsula on the northern side. "There," he says, his gnarled finger near the tip of the island. It's the other one Peregrine told me about.

A thought occurs to me. "How many of these are there on the island?"

His white eyebrows raise. "This one here, this is the one for tourists."

"I'm no tourist," I tell him. "I've seen these somewhere else. Deep in the jungle."

He smiles. It's a kind gesture. "Ah. There were five, spread over the island. One was here in Queen's Bay, but it was removed long ago. When my grandfather was still a child." He gestures to the street behind me, which I take to mean they were removed or destroyed to make way for the city. "Four remain." He points out the locations of the other three, one being near Breckenridge's home. And another close to where Marian Stamper died.

"What are they, exactly?" I ask.

He shrugs. "No one can know for sure. Some secrets die with history."

"I've heard them as being referred to as killing stones." I watch his reaction carefully. His eyes darken.

"Ignorant people speaking of what they do not know." He bends down, rooting around under the counter before pulling out a piece of paper. He places it on top of the map and makes small dots at the location of each of the five stone locations, including the one that used to be in Queen's Bay. He then connects the dots to form a symbol unlike any I've ever seen before. It almost looks like a figure holding its hands up to the sky, though they are connected by a single line.

"This," he says, holding up the pictures. "This is the Kaltano symbol for life. For abundance. That much I do know."

"Then the stones weren't used for sacrifices?" I ask.

"No. Not the Kaltano. They were not those kind of peoples. My family, my ancestors. I know the history of my people. Before the colonialists, they lived in harmony with each other and the land. Look around. This place is a paradise."

"And you're sure," I ask, floating Peregrine's idea. "Maybe they sacrificed animals?"

He shakes his head again. "No. I do not believe it. There was no need for blood. Plenty to eat, without eating the animals."

As best I can tell, the man believes what he's telling me. Whether he is a historian or not, I don't know. But I have no doubt his family has lived here for generations, maybe even going back as far as when the island was settled. He would know the island as well as anyone.

And it makes sense what he's saying. Why arrange the locations of the stones in the symbol for life if they are to be used for death? Besides, I feel the stories about native cultures being "savage" are generally ideas that come from colonists, scared of what they didn't understand. And those stories are then passed down as fact, when the truth may be far different.

Not to say there weren't some cultures that did practice sacrifices, but I'm not sure this was one of them.

What's more concerning is Claire Taylor went missing near one of these locations, and Marian Stamper appeared near another. I have to wonder if they are connected to the missing women...but how? What I really need is to locate the other two stone monuments to see if there are any other pieces of evidence I'm missing.

"May I buy this?" I ask, indicating the map. "And could you mark those locations for me again?"

"Of course," he says, using a red sharpie to circle the areas of the island where the stones stand. "If you want to visit, these are the roads you'll need to take. Be careful though, they can be treacherous. And you will be spending a lot of time in the wilderness. No coverage out there." He holds up his cell phone. "It's dangerous to go alone."

"I understand," I say, handing over a ten. He goes to make change but I stop him. "Keep it. You've been very helpful."

"Thank you," he says, nodding. "Why don't you grab a water on your way out. You'll need it out there." He smiles again.

I thank him and do as he suggests before heading back out to my car parked a few streets over. It looks like the jungle and I aren't done with each other just yet.

## Chapter Twenty-Nine

THERE'S NO PARKING LOT, so I'm forced to find street parking a couple of blocks down. I then have to trudge back up the hill to my destination. I can see why a lot of people don't bother with cars on the island. The infrastructure for them here really isn't very good.

Once I reach the building, I head inside. The door itself is propped open with a large rock, and a sign hangs on the door advertising the day's specials. Despite the open windows that look out on the town beyond, it's somehow still dark in here. Some yacht rock song from the eighties is playing on the jukebox and a breeze drifts through the open windows, blowing out past the bar, which is open on the backside. A television is mounted on the far wall, showing a soccer game in another country. The place only has about five tables and the bar itself, and right now the crowds are low. There is one couple sitting at a table sharing a pair of bright cocktails, but the person I'm looking for is hunched over a beer at the bar, a cigarette hanging from her mouth.

I take a seat one stool over and wait until she realizes I'm there. Peregrine furrows her brow. "Slate?"

"Drowning your sorrows?"

She glances at the beer. "Figured if I was about to get fired, I might as well enjoy it. Come here to give me another ear full?" She takes a long drag of the cigarette and blows it out as the bartender—a man in his late forties—comes over.

"Get you anything?" he asks.

"Just a water," I tell him. I turn my attention back to Peregrine. "You can't seriously believe I was too hard on you."

She takes a deep breath and puts out the cigarette in a nearby ashtray. "What are you doing here?"

I contemplated this moment multiple times. As much as I would rather do this on my own, I know how bad of an idea that would be. And considering I don't trust any of Montenegro's people to have my back, I'm not left with a lot of choices. It's either Peregrine, or I wait for someone to get here from the Miami office. Someone who probably won't know this island as well as she would.

"Let's call it a last resort," I say. "I've found some information that may lead to the women, but I need some help."

"And you think that person is me," she jeers.

I square my shoulders as the bartender sets the water in front of me and heads to the back. "First, you don't get to take a tone with me. You endangered my life. Second, you owe me. And third, I don't think you want to give up on those women. You're getting a second chance here, Detective. Don't throw it away."

She turns to me. "Are you saying you won't have me arrested if I help you?"

"Let's see how it goes," I tell her. "Look at it this way. I'm less likely to be pissed off if we find those women."

"What about Rafe?" she asks.

"He's not my priority at the moment." I give her a quick rundown of what I found at his office. "Montenegro is chasing him down. But no one is looking for these women. And I'm not sure how much time they have left."

She looks at her drink, which she's barely touched. It's like she wants to say something else but is holding back. I don't need her to open up to me. What I do need is for her to help me find these other stones. There may be more evidence out there.

"Maybe I shouldn't," she says. "You were right. I did endanger you. And I haven't been completely transparent with you."

"What do you mean?" I ask.

"When I said before that I clocked you at the airport, that was a lie. I knew who you were before you got here."

Dammit, I was afraid of this. I told Caruthers my cover would only go so far. I've been too visible as an FBI Agent over the past two years. I've worked too many high-profile cases. "Let me guess, you saw me on TV?"

Her eyebrows shoot up. "You were on TV?"

"Briefly," I say. "It was to do with that big case a year or so ago, the big scandal with the FBI. I was one of the agents that helped bring it down."

"Oh," she says. "I didn't really...well, congrats, I guess. I didn't know about that."

"Wait, so if you didn't see me on TV, how did you know who I was when I got here?"

Peregrine stares at her glass a moment. Her shoulders are bunched, and she still hasn't made eye contact with me. What is going on here? I take a quick sip of water to combat the dryness in my throat.

"I...uh...I wasn't supposed to say," she replies.

"Detective, what are you talking about?"

She bites her lip and turns to me. "The day before you arrived, I received an anonymous email informing me an FBI Agent would be coming to St. Solomon, undercover. I was told that you were being watched, and if your cover remained intact, you would in fact become a target."

"I'm sorry, *what?*"

"I was also told not to give you this information, that if

revealed, I would lose my job. As 'proof,' a copy of my employment record was attached to the email. Along with a picture of you."

"I need to see this email," I say.

"It's gone from the server," she replies. "I was preparing to tell you the morning after your arrest, but when I woke up, the email and all the contents were gone."

"You didn't think to download them?" I ask. "Or copy them?"

"That was the frightening part," she says. "I did. And they too, were gone. Which means someone was in my apartment. Someone came in and physically deleted those files."

"I don't understand," I say. "How could someone have known I was coming here?"

She holds up her hands in defeat before pulling out another cigarette.

"So that whole story about knowing someone in the CIA, that was all bullshit?"

"It was the only thing I could think of that might make sense," she said. "I didn't want to lose the only job I've ever cared about. But I guess now it really doesn't matter anymore."

"So you exposed me...when? After I was arrested?"

She nods. "I figured that was as good a time as any."

"But who sent the email?" I ask. "Montenegro?"

"If he did, he's the best actor on the planet. Because when I informed him who you really were, the shock on his face was almost comical. Before it turned to rage, of course."

This is not good. Someone has eyes on me. Someone with enough power and influence to expose my operation. My immediate thought is James Hunter, the man who infiltrated the FBI and rose within its ranks to become a deputy director. But that's not possible. He's in prison and his activities are being closely monitored. He wouldn't have the access.

Then I remember what Zara said about Fletch's possible

government-level documents. Possible encrypted FBI files including personal information on high-profile field agents, being siphoned off and sold to the highest bidder. It's the only way someone could have known what I was doing.

"I need to make a call." I excuse myself and find the quietest corner of the bar.

"Hey, long time no talk," Zara says. "What's it been, like an hour?"

"Listen," I say. "I think we may still have a security leak. Peregrine just told me she received an anonymous email informing her I would be coming to the island undercover, *before* I arrived. *That's* how she knew who I was. Not some bogus CIA request. What if the info we pulled from Fletch were classified FBI documents after all?"

"Shit," she says. "We've run into a roadblock and I haven't been able to finish the decryption. This could be a major problem."

"Yeah. A big one."

"Okay," she says, and I can see her thinking in my mind's eye. "Don't…don't say anything else. We can't trust this line or any other until we figure out what's going on. I'll be in touch." She hangs up. It isn't often I hear panic in Zara's voice, and the times I do fill me with dread. The thought of someone having that kind of access to our classified information is unfathomable.

The question remains though, what is the purpose behind it all? Why target me? Or am I just one of a hundred agents who are right now, having their days ruined by information leaks?

"You okay?" Peregrine asks as I join her back at the bar.

"No, not really," I say. "What you've told me has grave consequences for the Bureau. And if it's accurate, then we have a much larger problem than I thought."

"What are you going to do?" she asks.

"What can I do? I'm here, the women are still missing, and

without the email that was sent to you, I can't really help, can I?"

Peregrine forgoes lighting the cigarette and instead takes a sip of her beer. "I guess not." She regards me. "You know, for someone who just learned that someone is tracking them, you're taking it pretty well."

"I have a lot of experience in this area," I say, my hand curled into a fist on top of the bar. First Camille, then my aunt, and now some bidder on the black market. Except this time, it may not be just me. It might be all of us.

"Sorry to hear that. And I'm sorry I lied to you. I thought —I don't know what I was thinking. There was no way this situation was going to end up going my way." She turns to me. "You're really not giving up?"

"I'm not going to let my personal problems get in the way here. These women need our help. And if there is anything we can do to find them, we need to do it."

"Okay," she says. "So, what do you need me to do?"

I pull out the map, showing her the locations of the other standing stones. "We need to look at these. *All* of them."

"Why?" she asks. "We didn't find anything else at the ones near Breckenridge's house."

I tap the location close to where Marian Stamper was found. "I think they have something to do with the kidnappings. I don't know what. But I don't believe it's a coincidence two of our victims are tied to these locations. These stones, they aren't *killing stones*. They're something else."

"What?" she asks.

"That's what we need to find out."

## Chapter Thirty

AFTER LOADING up on more supplies, given we have no idea how long we're going to be out there, and after I swing by my hotel and grab a change of clothes into something more appropriate for traipsing through the jungle, we make our way to the Standing Stones Monument on the north side of the island. Even though it's a tourist destination and likely not to provide any crucial information, I think it's worth checking out if for no other reason than to mark it off our list.

On the way, I inform Peregrine about my theories surrounding Rafe, along with what I found out about the stones so far. Thankfully, she isn't married to the "sacrificial" idea either, recalling it was something she heard when she was young but never really investigated.

Now that I know she was compelled to out me, I'm less angry. And I'm trying my best not to think about the ramifications of what that may mean. But Zara is on the job, and there is no one else I would rather have working behind the scenes on this. She will put her head together with the team and Caruthers and maybe even loop Janice in. All of us have experience with this in the past. I know they can handle it. I

214 • ALEX SIGMORE

need to focus on the case in front of me and not worry about what I can't control.

The road to the standing stones monument is thankfully paved, and there's even a small parking lot nearby. The stones sit on the edge of a cliff overlooking the north side of the island. A well-worn path leads from the parking lot to the stones where people are standing near, either taking photographs or admiring the view. As best I can tell, the stones look similar if not identical to the ones we saw near Breckenridge's house. They aren't shaped in any way, instead they seem to have been pulled from the ground somewhere and stood on their ends, as if they are pointing to the sky. Each one ends in a ragged tip. Maybe that was the inspiration for the stories about them being used for sacrifices.

Peregrine and I give the site a thorough look. A couple of people shoot us curious glances, but many are so involved with their own pictures they barely notice us, except when we get into one of their shots. After going over the site multiple times, I'm forced to conclude there is nothing there.

I can see the draw to this place. It's calm, tranquil, even amongst the tourists. As the wind blows through my hair, I can't help but feel a sense of peace despite the heaviness that hangs over me. The ocean beyond sparkles with a bright intensity, almost like it is winking a thousand wishes in my direction.

But I don't believe in wishes. Especially not when people's lives are on the line.

Five minutes later, we're back on the road, heading for the next location. Since we've already seen the one near Breckenridge's house, we head straight for the next-closest location, which is near the middle of the island.

I keep thinking about how these locations are arranged. It always surprises me what people are able to do without the aid of modern technology. Presumably, the Kaltano people had no way to get a bird's eye view of the island, and yet they managed to arrange the locations of these stones in a way that if seen from above, they would form a symbol that was obviously very important to them. While the feat itself is amazing, I believe the intent behind it is even more impressive. It tells me that this idea, this concept of abundance or life, was so important that the Kaltano tried to turn the island into the symbol itself.

It also makes me wonder who we might be dealing with here. If I'm right, it's someone who knows this island well. Who knows its history. And is looking to connect that history to kidnapping women. But then, if these monuments were to represent life, why are they being used in this manner? It all makes me think maybe I'm way off on this one. Maybe Claire Taylor's necklace and the location Marian Stamper appeared were nothing more than coincidence. And given we didn't find anything at the stones on the hill, I'm starting to have doubts.

"Okay," Peregrine says. "Turn off here. We'll have to go the rest of the way on foot."

"How far?" I ask.

She opens the map, checking the distance. "About three-quarters of a mile."

I pull out my phone, and sure enough, there's no reception here. Grabbing a couple of waters, I shove them into a makeshift pack and sling it over my back. At least this time I'll be hydrated, though the walk will be farther than when we tried to find the cliff where Marian jumped.

I lock the car and follow Peregrine into the woods, at first following a small trail that's barely visible. Immediately, we're surrounded by dense forest, unable to see more than fifteen or twenty meters into the jungle.

Soon enough, the trail fades away and we're left without a guidepost. Peregrine pulls out a compass and in conjunction with the map, leads us forward. I find myself checking her route every few minutes, as I want to make sure I know where we are at all times. Thankfully, I still have the firearm on loan from Peregrine. I'm not about to be caught unprepared again. Peregrine was right about one thing: this place lulls you into a false sense of security, making you believe nothing bad can happen without you even realizing it. You kind of just fall into the natural rhythm of the island, and you have to keep reminding yourself that it can be just as dangerous as anywhere else.

An hour into the walk, we're ascending what has to be one of the steepest grades I've ever climbed. Every few feet, it's like we're making our way up an unending mountain and its slowing our progress considerably. I have to hand it to Peregrine, for someone who smokes all the damn time, she has pretty good lung capacity. She's not huffing and puffing, which means neither can I, though I kind of want to die a little inside. I've let my training lapse ever since I moved in with Liam, falling into that comfort again. At first, it was just cutting back to a few times a week because I wanted to spend more time at home with him. When it was just me on my own, finding the time wasn't a problem. But with the two of us, it's become more complicated.

Not to mention all those damn tasty meals he won't stop fixing. They're not helping my endurance either. As soon as I get back, I'm starting a new regiment at the gym. I can't let myself get too soft, even if it means I need to spend a little more time away from home.

"I think we're getting close to the top," Peregrine says, hoisting herself up another rock. This path is much more treacherous than the one down past Breckenridge's home. I can't imagine anyone *forcing* someone to come up here, or even carrying them; it's just not practical. All of which is chipping away at my confidence. This could all be nothing more than a giant waste of time.

"Yep, here we are," Peregrine says as she jumps up on the last outcropping. She reaches down for my hand. I take it and she pulls me up, helping me over the edge. As I straighten, I glance back down at what we just climbed. Even the rock face has succumbed to the jungle here; the trees obscure the difficulty of what we just endured.

I crouch down and pull a water from my pack, draining half of it. My entire body is covered in sweat. I've probably lost half a gallon of water out here. Peregrine takes the chance to do the same.

"I guess I see why this isn't the tourist attraction," she says.

"Mm-hmm," I say, my mouth full of water.

"Need a minute?" she asks.

"Nope, I'm good." I stand back up, the pack on my back again.

"Don't feel bad," she says. "I've been climbing these hills since I was little. That and being out in the water all day. You get used to it."

"Let's just keep moving," I say. She pulls out the compass again, and after comparing it to the map, continues forward.

"We should still be right on track," she says. "Maybe another two hundred feet or so?"

I squint, trying to see a break in the woods anywhere, but there's nothing ahead of us.

"You've never been here before?" I ask.

"This particular part of the island? No. Never had any reason to. We've got plenty of hiking trails all over the island. I'll hit those all the time. But bushwacking into the wilderness? Nah."

"You're not afraid of getting lost, are you? The island isn't that big."

"Getting lost, no. Spraining an ankle, getting stranded, falling down a cliff? You better believe it."

"Yeah." I'm so used to being able to call someone at a

moment's notice and have them respond to me, I keep forgetting about the inherent dangers of being out of contact for extended periods of time. "So no one really comes out here?"

"I doubt it," she says. "Though I'm sure there are always going to be those nature nutjobs who just *need* to explore everything."

We walk for another ten minutes, stepping over branches, rocks and everything else that seems to be in our way before Peregrine stops me with an arm. Ahead of us is what remains of a crumbling stone structure, but it's nothing like the standing stones. It looks more modern. There's not much left, but what remains is in a circle, and one of the walls is still partially standing, curving around the side.

"What is it?"

"Remnants of a sugar mill," she says. "Sugar was a big export crop on the islands back in colonial times. There used to be mills like this all over the place.

"So where are the stones?" I ask.

"That's a good question."

We proceed carefully, the entire time I'm wondering if the old man made a mistake. But as we get closer to the mill and peer over the edge, I realize the mill is not just sitting on the ground. Instead, it seems to encircle a large hole, about fifty feet in diameter. Remnants of wooden beams tell me there was probably a floor here at one point which has long rotted away.

"Look," Peregrine says, peering down into the hole. About fifteen feet down at the bottom of the hole are the large stones, all standing in a circle. A stone staircase leads down to them, though thanks to the canopy, not a lot of light is reaching all the way down there.

"The colonists built the mill over the stones?" I ask.

"Looks that way." The hole itself looks like a natural formation, but I can't even fathom a guess as to how the

Kaltano managed to get those stones down there in the first place. Did they have a pulley system? "What do you think?"

I stare down into the dark hole. Even though I can't see anyone down there, it would be the perfect place to hold someone who you didn't want found. "I hate to say it, but I think we need to go down there."

"Yeah," Peregrine says. "I hate for you to say it too."

# Chapter Thirty-One

NEITHER OF US thought to bring flashlights, so we're limited to the lights on our phones. But first, we take our time descending the stone staircase. The staircase itself doesn't look like it was part of the mill, instead it seems that the Kaltano constructed them to reach the stones and get back out.

Thankfully, due to the size of the hole, some light does reach us when we get to the bottom. It's damp down here, and a bit cooler than up above. The cool air feels refreshing on my skin, but I'm not the kind of person who does well when she's down in something. Most people would call it claustrophobia, but I just call it a healthy appreciation for open spaces.

"Hello?" I call out as Peregrine finishes making her way down the staircase. I pull out my phone and begin shining it in all the nooks and crannies of the hole, avoiding the stones in the middle. I'd love to know how they got here, but I'm more concerned with the likelihood someone might be trapped down here. What if Rafe left one woman at each stone location? Maybe Claire was at the other stones and managed to escape like Marian. She could be out in the woods somewhere, lost or hurt. Peregrine herself illustrated how treacherous that could be.

"Anything?" Peregrine asks as I look over the walls. The remains of old burlap sacks litter the ground. Other than that, I don't see any indication of life down here.

"Just some old sugar sacks. When did the mills go out of business?"

"Probably early eighteen hundreds," she says. "Obviously this one hasn't been operating for some time."

"Why build it *over* the stone location?"

"Maybe they used this place for storage." She picks up the remains of one of the sacks. "A cool, dry place to store sugar. Once it was covered from the weather, it probably kept them from needing to build a storage facility."

It makes sense. An underground location with access already in place? For people who were trying to make a living, not having to haul a bunch of lumber up here or clear a huge swath of trees could have made all the difference. Still, there has to be another access road or something. Otherwise this mill would have been completely improbable.

Unfortunately, other than a few sacks, I don't think there's much down here. I don't see any indication anyone was ever being held here against their will. No restraints of any kind, no cages. Not even food or waste remains.

"Well?" she asks.

I'm forced to admit it's another dead end in a seemingly endless line of dead ends. I'm about to say as much when I pick up a scent in the air. It's foul, almost like sulfur. "Do you smell that?"

She turns to me. "Sargassum."

I nod, recalling the smell from when we found Marian Stamper. "You said it sits in the bays. So what's it doing down here?"

We look around more carefully, trying to find the source of the smell. It's not very strong and it takes us a few minutes to find it's coming from one of the dark corners behind the stairs. As I shine the light from my phone on it, I realize there's actually a passage back there I hadn't noticed before. The way the rocks are arranged makes it particularly difficult to see unless you already happened to know about it.

"Is that—"

"Yeah," I say. "It's a passageway." Ducking my head inside, the smell of sargassum is stronger in here. "Definitely the source of the smell."

"Is it big enough to go inside?"

I step back out for some fresh air. "Ceiling is low. We'd have to crawl." Though the prospect of crawling through rank underground caves is not high on my to-do list. I step aside so she can inspect the passage. Peregrine gets herself all the way in, then backs out again.

"Yep, I think you're right. But it looks large enough that we could get through it. Should we give it a try?"

The fact that I don't want to go crawling around small holes that I might not be able to get back out of notwithstanding, I'm beginning to have serious doubts about my theory. "I might be completely wrong about these stones. We didn't find anything at the public site."

"No, but consider Marian Stamper. What if she escaped a pit like this? It makes sense, right? She could have crawled her way out in a desperate attempt to find food or water."

"It's not much to go on," I say. "She could have just as easily escaped a cage or something similar." I crane my neck back up to look at the canopy of trees shielding the site. Still, if someone did want to hide people, a secret passage inside a hole deep in the jungle would be a good way to do it. No one would ever find them out here.

"I don't suppose you brought any string with you?"

"String?"

"To run behind us, so we won't get lost in there. There's no telling how deep this goes. Or if it connects to any others."

"At some point it will have to empty out to the ocean," she

says. "It's the only way that smell could have made it all the way up here."

I take a deep breath. There isn't a lot that fazes me. I can handle life and death situations without it tearing up my psyche, most of the time. But crawling into a dark little hole that goes God knows where is an entirely different animal. I don't like small spaces and I don't like feeling trapped. Even when I was a little kid and we'd visit caves hundred of feet tall near my hometown, I was always apprehensive about going inside. I remember thinking I would get stuck and there would be no way to ever get me out.

"Don't like cramped places, huh?" Peregrine asks.

It's ironic, on an island where almost every view is endless, that I'm about to trap myself in stone. But at the same time, I don't have a better idea. I can't underestimate whoever is hurting these women, in much the same way I shouldn't have underestimated colonists who built a sugar mill in the middle of unreachable jungle.

I take a few more deep breaths then pull out my phone. "I'll go first."

"You sure?" she asks. "I don't mind."

"No, I got it," I say, getting down on all fours. Facing the inky blackness of the passageway, I flip on the light on my phone and begin crawling forward. If it can't get a signal, it's going to at least be good for something.

Thankfully, the passageway is small enough that the light illuminates pretty much everything. The ground is slightly slick with moss, and rock surrounds me on all sides. Looking closely, I feel like I can see tool marks of some kind on the walls. The ceiling is low, but after the first ten feet or so, it opens up a little and I'm able to crouch instead of crawl, which makes going a little easier and quicker.

"I think this is a man-made cavern," I call back to Peregrine. "Tool marks in the rock."

"Shit," she says somewhere behind me. "You're right."

The question is, who carved it? Was it the sugar millers, or the Kaltano? Or someone else entirely? The passageway isn't nearly as cramped as I originally thought, and I manage to relax my breathing a little. The further we go, the more it opens up, but I have no way of knowing how far we've gone or where exactly we're going. It does feel like we're descending, but it's a gentle slope—nothing that would be hard to get back up. Still, the floor is slick and treacherous, and I take care with every step. The last thing I want to do is slip and hit my head.

"Good back there?" I ask Peregrine.

"Still breathing," she replies.

I am glad she's here. This would have been a lot harder without her. She's a good wayfinder. And maybe I was a bit too harsh on her before. But I can deal with that later.

As the cavern opens up more and more, I find I can stand up completely and walk. The drawback is my light no longer reaches all the walls. It also doesn't reach all the way to the floor in front of me. I happen to be looking down at just the right moment and stop, holding my hand out behind me so Peregrine will see it.

"What?"

"There's a drop off," I say. I crouch forward and sweep my phone over the ground, finding it falls away to my right, dropping off into the darkness. "There's a ledge over here. Looks wide enough we can walk across. Just stay close to the wall."

"Uh-huh," she says. "I'm starting to think you might be right. There's no way someone could have forced someone down here against their will."

"Probably not," I say. Even though the smell of sargassum is stronger, I'm also beginning to smell sea air. I press my back to the wall while at the same time keeping my light out as much as I can, though it just dissolves into the darkness before me. I slide along, testing the ground with every step. If it gives way, I would slip into who knows where. But one thing is for sure, I wouldn't be able to get back out.

Finally, the drop off ends and the path widens again. I wonder if perhaps the drop off wasn't always there and is just a result of geologic activity over time. I take my first deep breath since coming in here as Peregrine reaches the end and takes a moment for herself on the other side. I really hope we can just follow the shore back to civilization because I do *not* want to do that again.

"For someone who doesn't like cramped spaces, you're doing a pretty good job," she says.

"Thanks."

I'm about to turn when I hear the rustling behind me. It's like the quick shuffling of feet and I turn, though it's too late. Something strikes the side of my head and the darkness that fills the cavern envelops me completely.

I don't even feel myself hit the ground.

# Chapter Thirty-Two

I WAKE to the sounds of what I think are screams. At first I think it's coming from a terrible dream, that I'm stuck somewhere and I'm the one who is screaming to get out, like I am being crushed by something large and unyielding. But as soon as my eyes snap open, I realize it's the scraping of rock against rock somewhere far in the distance. I'm on my knees, though my legs are bound together and my arms are tied behind me with a thick rope. When I'm conscious enough, I feel the needles in my lower legs and knees from being on them for so long. I've been tied in such a way that I can't move or even sit up straight. My wrists are attached to my ankles and the restraints are *tight*.

I can move my head, and the scene before me unfolds like something out of a horror movie. We're still underground, but this is a much larger cave than the passageway. Someone has brought in large floodlights that are strategically situated around what I can only describe as a room, filling the place with bright light. Beside me is Peregrine, still unconscious and tied like me.

On the other side of me, inexplicably, is Rafe, bound in the exact same way. However he is fully conscious. His eyes are sunken in, and his lips are dry and chapped. It looks like he's been here much longer than I have. "Rafe?" I say and realize my throat is dry and scratchy.

He doesn't respond, instead he continues looking forward. In front of us sits what looks like a portable folding table, like the kind a masseuse would use. However, what's most concerning is the fact it is *dripping* with dark, crimson stains. To the point where the original color of the fabric isn't visible anymore. The color has also drained down to the supports beneath and there is a significant amount on the floor. Some of it is dried while more is fresh.

The sound of the scraping grows louder.

As I take in the scene, I realize we're not the only three people in the room. Across from us, on the other side of the cavern, are two other women. I recognize them both as Amy Van Allen and Claire Taylor. Claire still has her evening gown on from the night she went missing. Both women look terrible. Their hair is matted and dirty and both are barely on the edge of consciousness. Unlike us, they are restrained with their arms above them, chained by thick metal chains that have been driven into the rock. Beside them are two empty pairs of chains. One, I assume, once held Marian Stamper. A chill runs down my back as I realize Vicki Tolluse is nowhere to be found and my eyes return to the crimson stains on the folding table.

The whole place is an honest-to-god torture chamber. And that sound is louder still.

"Alyssa," I hiss, hoping to wake Peregrine up. "*Alyssa.*"

She winces, her eyes still closed, but she begins to move. Though, like me, she finds she can't get out of this position. She glances over at me, her eyes going wide, then takes in the room. "What the—?"

"Can you move at all?" I ask her. "If you can get to my restraints—"

The scraping ceases and footsteps from behind us silence

me. From the cadence and the echoes off the walls, I hear three distinct sets. One is lighter than the other two. A figure passes between me and Peregrine, and I realize, with some surprise, that it's a woman. She has dark brown hair that's been pulled back into a high ponytail and is wearing a white business suit. The legs of the suit are covered with dark stains, probably from the caverns. In her hand is a long, serrated knife, which she must have been dragging along the cavern walls as she approached. She walks wordlessly to the table and circles around before facing us.

I have to hold my tongue as she does because the entire front of her suit is coated in crimson red. That can only be blood. Nothing else has quite that color. And the splatter pattern would suggest something violent happened. Some of it has dried on her face, but she doesn't even seem to notice. Instead, she's watching us. Watching *me*.

Two more people walk past us, and I realize I know both of them before they even turn around. Roberts and Daniels, the two men who worked for Jeremy Breckenridge. The two men who provided access to Breckenridge's house when we came to serve the warrant. Roberts was the one who showed me Breckenridge's "special" rooms and insisted no one could have erased that footage other than him or Breckenridge. And neither was at the house after the massacre.

"Do you know who I am?" the woman asks, her question directed at me.

"Should I?" I ask.

The response seems to cut at her, but she grins despite it. She turns to Rafe. "Why don't you tell her, honey? Maybe it's better if it comes from you."

Rafe doesn't move, doesn't speak. He only stares straight forward. If I didn't know better, I would almost say he's comatose.

"Fine, if you want to be coy about it," the woman says. She walks around to the front of the table and hops up on it.

Whatever fresh blood coated the surface now soaks into her clothes, but she doesn't seem to care. "My name is Felicia Dawson. Formerly Mrs. Felicia Connor."

"You're his wife," I say. "But you're supposed to be dead."

She chucks her head back and laughs, though it seems forced. "Yes, I very much am, aren't I, honey? Why don't you tell the FBI agent all about it?"

Rafe remains motionless.

"No? I guess it's up to me then." She hops off the table again and sure enough, her white pants are covered in even more blood. "He called it a 'boating accident.'" She uses air quotes to emphasize her point. "When in fact, he was the one who sabotaged the boat, weren't you?" She glares at him. "We took the boat out, just like we had every weekend for the previous year. I fell asleep on the deck and the next thing I know, I'm underwater and the boat is sinking below me. My *husband* is nowhere to be found." She walks over closer to him. "But this was no small sailboat. No, this was a fifteen-million-dollar yacht. The *Black Cat*. Complete with its own escape craft. And wouldn't you know it? The escape boat was missing." She turns her attention back to me. "So there I was, treading water in the middle of the ocean, with nowhere to go. I still don't know how he sank it, because they never recovered the ship. It's somewhere at the bottom of the Atlantic, right now. After all, why look further into an accident that involved a distraught husband and no life insurance policy or motives in any way?"

She turns and walks back to the table. "Of course, it doesn't hurt when you have the local police in your pocket."

I glance at Peregrine. One look from her tells me she knows nothing about this. But I'm willing to bet Montenegro does.

"How did you survive?" I ask.

"I'm a good swimmer," she says. "But no one is that good. As luck would have it, a fishing boat spotted me after a few hours. The only drawback was the boat was from Cuba. So that's where I ended up. Of course, by the time I managed to barter my way back to the US, I had already been dead for three weeks."

She glares at Rafe, who still hasn't moved or said a word. A long silence stretches out and the only sound I can hear is Felicia's breathing becoming more and more rapid. It's like she's winding herself up for something. Finally, she turns to me. "He tried to seduce you too, didn't he? Thought he might have a chance with you. But it's a good thing he didn't, otherwise you might find yourself on *that* side of the room." She motions to the two women behind her. Neither of them move at being addressed.

"Felicia, what have you done here?" I ask.

"What have I—" she asks, incredulous. "Don't you mean what has *he* done." She says it with such vitriol I think for a moment that she caught him in some kind of act down here with these women and stopped him, tying him up for his own good. But then she brandishes the knife at him. "This is all *his* fault. I'm just cleaning up his mess."

"Where is Vicki?" I ask. "What have you done with her?"

I catch Roberts's posture falter for a brief second.

"With any luck, what's left of her is drifting out to sea," she says. "These caves, they connect all over the island. The Kaltano used them to traverse the island, almost like a rudimentary subway system. Carved out from millions of years of erosion underneath with a little human assistance, they form a labyrinth of pathways right under everyone's feet. And they lead to underground pools, which connect back out to the ocean. My grandmother would bring me here when I was little and show me these ancient places. We would swim in the protected pools and watch the fish underwater. It was a perfect paradise." She steps forward and runs the edge of the knife along Rafe's cheek. The blood on the blade smears across his skin, though he doesn't bother turning away.

"But some people just aren't satisfied with paradise," she adds in a lithe voice. "Some people are obsessed with progress, unchecked and unending."

"The land development," I say. "You opposed it."

"Why do you think he tried to kill me?" she asks. "My mistake was keeping quiet and only professing my objections to him. It was when I threatened to use my platform to rally against him, to stop him from even attempting to develop this island that I think he first got the idea. He backed off, initially. I thought I'd gotten through to him. But apparently, he was just placating me until he could get rid of me."

She slaps Rafe, *hard*. It is so sudden it sounds like a gunshot. The sound echoes off the walls of the cavern. "I was the one who first brought you here," she hisses. "And you wanted to destroy it all."

"You were born here, on St. Solomon," I say.

"My family goes back generations," she replies. "Back to before the first settlers. It was bad enough when they came, bringing their diseases, their farms, their wars. My people worked hard with the government to make the island a preserve. To keep anyone from doing what *he* was trying to do. But money greases wheels. And eventually, things fall apart. I knew I couldn't count on the local government turning away all those tourism dollars forever."

She returns to the table and sets the knife down. She nods to Roberts, who nods back then unshackles Amy Van Allen's chains. She's so weak she can't even stand. He has to practically pick her up and carry her over to the table.

"Felicia," I say, watching with horror. "Whatever he's done to you, whatever he planned on doing to this island, you don't need to blame these women. We can find another solution to all of this."

"Can we?" she asks, picking up the knife again and "cleaning" it against her pant leg. "Because I can think of no better pain than to make him watch as I flay each and every one of the women he was with in front of his eyes, before doing the same to him."

Vicki Tolluse is dead. There is no doubt in my mind now. And if I don't do something, Amy and Claire will be next. "But why punish them too?" I ask. "What did they do?"

"What did they do?" she yells. "What did they *do?*" Her voice seems to bring Amy to consciousness, and she tries to kick herself away from Roberts. But the big man is no match for her and he places her on the table, strapping her down as she struggles. "Not only did they fuck my husband, but they all helped him in this little land deal of his."

"No," I say. "Vicki Tolluse quit CII. She wasn't involved. And Marian Stamper's husband is the one who worked for your husband, not her."

Felicia gives me the most pitying look. "Oh, not a very good detective, are you? Vicki quit CII to run Rafe's little banking project. She came here to soften up Mayor Williams with some well-placed *donations*, courtesy of the bank's best client. Marian may have not worked for CII, but she introduced several key players into my husband's sphere. Including the Secretary of the Interior Department in Washington. That's your area, I believe."

She looks down at Amy, who is trying to say something, but if her throat is as sore as mine, I doubt she'll be able to get anything out. She's been down here for too long without water. It's a wonder she hasn't died already. "And this little tart was to be in charge of marketing all the new condos my husband was about to build on the island." She smiles. "Weren't you, darling?"

"Okay!" I shout, getting her attention. "But that doesn't mean they deserve to die." Felicia is completely unhinged. There is no reasoning with her, only stalling. But she's also determined, and she isn't going to wait around forever. I glance at Peregrine, but the woman seems too horrified to even comprehend trying to escape. Her gaze is locked on the knife, which is hovering precariously over Amy Van Allen.

I'm the only one who can do anything about this situation. "Felicia, you don't have to do this anymore. With your testimony about your husband, we can make sure he goes away for a long time. He'll never have the chance to do anything to this island."

"No, there is only one way to make sure he can never do anything to the island." Light glints off the knife before she points it to me. "You should feel lucky. Your death will be much swifter."

Before I can say anything else, she plunges the knife into Amy's midsection and her screams fill the caverns.

## Chapter Thirty-Three

I TURN AWAY as Felicia cuts into Amy, unable to witness the carnage before me. Peregrine does the same, but Rafe just continues to stare forward, seemingly unaffected. I struggle against my bonds, but find they only grow tighter the harder I pull and given how quickly Felicia is working, Amy doesn't have long.

Without warning, Rafe jumps up, his ropes falling away. He runs and slams into Felicia as Roberts and Daniels dogpile on him. They're all fighting each other, and I look over where Rafe was bound and see a small sharp piece of rock near his restrains. He must have been working on them for a while, slowly cutting and lulling Felicia into a false sense of security.

As they tussle, I throw myself on my side and scoot with some difficulty to where he was sitting and feel around for the piece of rock. I get it in my hands and begin working at my rope as fast as I can.

"You *bastard*!" Felicia yells as Roberts and Daniels finally get Rafe off her. They both hold him back as she punches him in the face. Something cracks—most likely his nose. Peregrine, meanwhile, is trying to make her way over to me as I saw furiously at the restraints.

"Who do you think you are?" she yells again. "You think just because you have money that gives you the right to destroy anything in your way?"

"I never should have married such a hippie piece of trash," he spits. "Look at you, pretending like this island is more important than people. Look at what you've done."

"It *is* more important, you idiot. The future of this island is worth more than a few bodies. Who is going to miss them? There are eight *billion* people on this planet, and you're worried about a select few? There is nowhere else like this place. *Anywhere.* And you want to turn it into another vacation destination, just so you can squeeze more money out of it for yourself. How much is enough, Rafe? When will it ever be enough? Or are you willing to turn the entire planet into one giant condo unit so you can make your *fucking money*?" She screams the last words and slices at Rafe, cutting through his midsection. His shirt flaps open and blood spills out, coming fast and dark red. I work harder on the rope, feeling it begin to give.

Rafe cries out in pain as she cuts at him again and again, slashing giant swaths across his body. Finally, the rope gives and my hands are free. No longer bound, I make quick work of the ropes around my ankles before cutting away Peregrine's restraints.

Felicia is feverishly hacking away at Rafe, blood splattering her face and hands, practically dripping off her. Rafe, dead from the loss of blood, hangs like a ragdoll in Roberts and Daniels's arms as Felicia works out her frustration. My first concern is Amy, but it's three against two and I don't know where our firearms are, if they're still even here somewhere.

I reach the table, and find Amy is still breathing, despite the loss of blood. It looks like Felicia only had the opportunity to stab her once, but there's no way she's not bleeding internally. We need to get her out of here and to medical attention.

"Ma'am!" Roberts yells and Felicia turns, her focus locked

on me. Her face is crimson red, the blood dripping down her brow like sweat, but she has a gleam in her eye and her eyes are blazing with fire. She runs at me with the knife held high above her head, intent on turning me into something resembling Rafe. I see Roberts and Daniels drop Rafe, their hands going into their jackets.

"They're armed!" I yell.

Daniels turns at the last second to see Peregrine slam into him as Roberts pulls out his gun, aimed at me. I move just enough to the side to put Felicia between me and Roberts as the woman slashes at me with the knife. I manage to dodge her clumsy attempts; she's not skilled with the weapon. But that can sometimes make for a more dangerous opponent. She's hacking and slashing at me with no rhyme or reason and it's only by the fact I've had training in dealing with knife attacks that I'm able to dodge. Finally, I manage to block her arm and twist her wrist, causing her to drop it. I turn her around, one arm around her neck as I continue to use her as a human shield.

"Drop it, Roberts," I say. "It's over." Peregrine and Daniels are still struggling for his gun, and Roberts looks like he might turn his weapon on them.

"Shoot her, you idiot!" Felicia screams.

"I—"

"Remember your oath to me. To your people!" Felicia yells.

Roberts winces and squeezes off a round. It goes wide, missing us both. He's clearly not ready to shoot his boss—his *real* boss. I think Felicia realizes too she can't count on him to kill me, because in that instant she shoves her head back, smashing into my skull. I see stars for a brief instant, but that's all she needs to get out of my grasp.

I stumble back into the table while Felicia goes for the nearby knife. I also see Roberts with a renewed focus, and he's trained his weapon on me. He squeezes the trigger at the same moment Felicia straightens back up to come at me with the knife. The bullet plows right into her back. She cries out, falling forward on me so I'm practically holding her up, both of us against the table still bearing Amy.

"Don't let them take it," she says, her voice losing its power. "Don't let them destroy this place."

"Drop it!" Peregrine says. I glance over and see Daniels is unconscious and she has Roberts in her sights. "Drop it or I drop you."

The fight goes out of Roberts's eyes. He tosses the gun in her direction. When I look down, Felicia is still hanging on to me, her eyes pleading. Finally, she loses her grip and tumbles to the floor. She rolls onto her back to stare up at the ceiling of the cavern and whispers something, but it's too soft for me to hear. It sounds something like a melody, and then I see the light leave her eyes as she stops breathing.

"We need to get Amy medical attention!" I tell Peregrine. "How do we get out of here?" I start unstrapping Amy from the table. Her face is ashen, but she's still breathing. Still, given how deep underground we are and how difficult it was to get down here, I'm not sure we have a chance of saving her. She's lost a lot of blood already, and she won't survive a lengthy trip through the caves.

"What's the quickest way out of here?" Peregrine says, her weapon still trained on Roberts. She bends down and picks up the second gun without taking her focus off him.

His hands are up, but his head is down. "Immunity," he says.

"What?"

"I want immunity. No charges, and I get to walk free."

I don't see we have much of a choice. Without him, we might be lost down here forever. I look around at the carnage before us, blood and bodies everywhere. He'd be content to let the rest of us die down here, I'm sure of it. "Fine. I agree. No charges and no jail time. In exchange for a full confession."

"In exchange for leaving this place."

I wince. I'm out of options. "Agreed."

"What about him?" Peregrine asks, motioning to the unmoving Daniels.

"Stay here with him until I get back," I tell her. "And see if you can't help Claire." I begin to lift Amy up off the table.

"No," Roberts says. "Leave her there."

"I'm not—"

"You can push the table, it's on wheels," he says. His hands are still up, but he points with both index fingers to his right. "There's a ramp. No stairs."

Leaving Amy on the table would be preferable, as it would minimize additional blood loss. I take her hand and have her press it to the wound. "Hold this as tight as you can," I tell her. "I'm going to get you some help."

She smiles weakly as I go over and retrieve one of the guns from Peregrine. "I'll be back for you." She nods and I motion for Roberts to show us the way. He takes a few tentative steps, and when he realizes I'm not going to shoot him, he finally turns his back to me and leads the way.

I get behind the folding bed and begin pushing. It's a little slow at first, but eventually I'm able to get it moving. Amy continues to take shallow breaths as she holds her wound tight.

"How far is it?" I ask as we leave Peregrine and Daniels behind in the main cavern.

"Not as far as you think," he replies.

I'm hesitant about leaving Peregrine behind, but Amy needs help and I doubt I'd be able to find my own way out of here. At least not before she bled out.

I think I hear the ocean as I continue pushing the table, careful of the floor underneath us. It's bumpy, but she's hanging on. And as Roberts described, there haven't been any steps yet, though it feels like we're ascending.

"It's up here," he says. I still have my weapon trained on

his back, which I'm sure he knows. Roberts isn't stupid, and he's a surprisingly good liar. I should have pushed harder the day we came to look at the security footage. Maybe then I could have figured out. But then again, I had no idea how deep all of this went.

Roberts turns around, taking hold of the end of the table. "What are you doing?"

"You're going to need help getting her around this corner," he says.

"Step back," I tell him.

He puts his hands up and takes a step back.

"He's…" Amy says. Her voice is weak. "He's…lying."

I see it in an instant. His eyes flash and his hand goes into his jacket. I pull the trigger twice. Both rounds slam into his chest. He falls to the ground, twitching once before his hand comes loose. His jacket lays to the side, revealing a second weapon hidden in a holster.

I'm breathing, hard, but I shove the gun back into my waistband and turn back to Amy. It seems she used the last of her energy to save me, because she's lost consciousness. I work my way around the table, only to find that around the corner is nothing but a dead end. There's no passage out this way. Apparently, Roberts thought if he could get me alone and distracted, he could gain the upper hand. I guess he didn't trust me when I said I wouldn't go after him.

"Amy, c'mon now, I need you to stay awake," I say, tapping her cheeks, but it's no use. She's losing too much blood. And I doubt there's a way out of this place that doesn't involve climbing stairs at some point. The best I can do is try to stop the bleeding and leave her with Peregrine before going for help.

But it's too late by the time I get the table back into the main chamber. Amy has stopped breathing, and no amount of CPR is going to replenish her blood supply. Peregrine has managed to restrain Daniels with what remained of our ropes and unlock Claire, who is sitting up against one of the rocks.

Peregrine looks up as I leave the table, feeling like a failure. No words pass between us. No doubt she heard the gunshots. Looking around, I survey what's turned into a royal mess. I double check Rafe's non-existent pulse then attend to Claire. Physically, she seems fine, other than the fact she's probably dehydrated. But her eyes are bright, and she's watching me carefully as I quickly monitor her vitals.

"You were at the party," she says, her voice somewhat hoarse.

"I was. I'm an FBI Agent. I was undercover."

She nods. "What happens now?"

"Now we get you out of here," I say. "I'm hoping you can show us the way."

She nods. "I left a trail to follow."

## Chapter Thirty-Four

IT TOOK the better part of two hours to get out of the caverns because not only did we have to keep stopping for Claire to catch her breath, we had to ensure Daniels wasn't loosening his restraints. By the time we finally made it outside, I realized we were back at the stones adjacent to the Breckenridge mansion. Claire explained along the way that she'd dropped a ring every time they reached an intersection, so she could always find her way back out. I'm sure Felicia, knowing this island as well as she did, wouldn't have needed guideposts. Thankfully Claire never gave up hope.

She also explained that Roberts snatched her from the party late that evening, taking her down the trail and through the caverns, leaving her chained up until Felicia showed sometime later to berate her. The other women were already there when she arrived. And while Marian managed to escape sometime later, Vicki was killed not long before Peregrine and I showed up. Claire wasn't sure how he got there, she just woke to find Rafe had been captured as well, which was apparently what Felicia had wanted all along. Then she made him watch she slowly tortured the women he'd been involved with.

The entire time we were searching those stones near Breckenridge's house, Claire was right under our feet, we just didn't know it. The entrance to the caves was so well disguised it would have taken someone with experience to find it, at least from that end.

But as we exited a hidden compartment near the standing stones, I realized that all five monuments must connect to the same network. Marian Stamper must have gotten lost in the caves and found an exit near the stones on the other side of the island. No telling how long she'd been in there, trying to find a way out.

Once we have cell service again, Peregrine calls Montenegro while I call Caruthers to give him a full update, but he reminds me the line may not be secure and for me to hold off until he can arrive in person. With everything that's happened, I'd almost forgotten about what Peregrine told me. I also advise him to send a contingent of agents down from Miami, as soon as possible. Rafe and Montenegro were in league, and I don't trust the man to perform a thorough investigation.

Regardless, by the time we make it back up the hill, a police cruiser is already waiting for Daniels. Peregrine accompanies him while I get in the ambulance with Claire. They start her on fluids, and by the time we reach the island's only hospital, she's already looking better. They admit her for dehydration and one of the nurses happens to notice the dried blood on my head. They end up admitting me too, to make sure I don't have a concussion.

By the time I finally sign my discharge paperwork, I'm surprised to find Caruthers and Liam trotting up to the hospital. I slam into Liam's arms, wrapping myself into him as hard as I can, unaware until this moment just how much I've missed him. He doesn't say anything, he just holds me, and I find my shoulders relax for the first time in a week. The two of us stand there, the world melting away before Caruthers finally clears his throat.

"Sorry, sir," I say, pulling away from Liam. "It's been a day."

"I understand. Agent Coll wouldn't let me leave without him."

That doesn't surprise me. Given everything that's happened, I'm surprised I was able to keep him away as long as I did. "I'm glad."

"I convinced Zara to stay back in DC, though she fought me like hell," Liam says. "She's still trying to take care of..." He glances at Caruthers.

"Slate, we have a serious problem at the Bureau. And as of right now, we are proceeding like all internal communications are being monitored. We've had to resort back to in-person meetings, emails may or may not be secure. It's slowly turning into chaos."

"Has Zara or anyone else made any progress?" I ask.

"I have Agent Foley working on an independent communication system for the moment. We don't know who or what might be out there monitoring our actions. I don't have to tell you, this isn't good. I'd like to speak with the detective who received the email about you."

"She should be back at the station."

"Good. But first, we need to get a handle on what's going on here. The Bureau is still operating and we can't let anyone think different. I need a full report. Right now."

"It's absolute clown shoes," I say. "The mayor is dead; the police captain is more than likely involved and there is a trail of bodies a mile long. Your only survivor is back in that hospital, and the only remaining culprit is with the one officer on this island that I trust."

Caruthers calls over one of the agents at the nearby car. "Stay with the victim until you hear from me." He turns to me.

"Her name is Claire Taylor. She's about five-four, blonde hair and green eyes. I rode here in the ambulance with her."

The agent nods and heads into the hospital.

Liam holds open the back door to the black SUV while Caruthers gets in the passenger side. Liam follows me in, touching the spot on my head. "Are you okay?" he whispers.

I take his hand once he's inside. "It's just a bruise. Nothing more. And I'm a lot better now that you're here."

"Give me everything you've got so far," Caruthers says.

I give him the full rundown of everything we'd discovered over the past few days. I explain how Rafe was connected to each of the missing women, who also apparently had some crucial part to play in the island development land deal that Rafe was here to seal. But it was actually his wife that had captured the women to send Rafe a message before finally capturing him as well. Felicia subscribed to what I'd call a scorched-earth policy, killing everyone who could have been involved with the deal. Considering what she was trying to save, I find that somewhat ironic.

"And these other two men, Roberts and Daniels?" Caruthers asks.

"I assume they are either locals she recruited to her cause, or they all knew each other and had the same ideals. They were both in a prime position to report on Breckenridge and get close to him *and* Rafe. Who knows how long they'd been planning this."

"And Montenegro, how does he fit it?" Caruthers asks.

"I believe he was intentionally ignoring the missing women on Rafe's orders," I say. "Rafe made a big show about Claire going missing, but I think that was more for my benefit than anyone else's. Once he found out I was FBI, I think he tried to throw me off his trail. He knew someone was targeting him, but I don't think he wanted anyone looking into it. Did he know it was his dead wife? Maybe. And maybe that's why he didn't want people looking too closely, or else they might figure out what he did."

I take a breath, going back over it in my head. "Actually, if Peregrine hadn't alerted Montenegro to my true identity, there's a good chance I might have ended up like the other women."

I reach forward and place a supportive hand on Caruthers's shoulder. "I'm sorry about Mrs. Tolluse. I never had the chance to even see her."

He nods. "Do you know where her body is?"

"Somewhere in that maze of caves," I tell him. "It's going to take an entire contingent down there to map them. But I'm sure Daniels can help us with that."

"Let's just see how cooperative he is," Caruthers says.

THE THREE OF US HEAD INTO THE MAIN St. SOLOMON POLICE station with two additional agents at our backs, causing everyone to look up.

"Where's Montenegro?" I ask the desk sergeant.

"He's in the back, with the suspect," the sergeant says.

"Alone?" Liam asks.

"I…uh…"

"Dammit," I say under my breath and reach around, pressing the button to release the door.

"Hey!" the sergeant says, but one of the agents from Miami approaches the window and the sergeant sits back down. Caruthers, Liam, and I head into the back, and I wind my way through the desks and offices, everyone looking up as we do. We find Daniels in the exact same room I was in when I was here, charged with trespassing. However, Montenegro isn't in the room with him—instead he's in the hall, in the middle of a shouting match with Peregrine.

"—I have to remind you that I am your boss!" he yells as we round the corner.

Peregrine looks up. Her face is flushed from arguing. But it breaks into a smile when she sees us. "Thank God, took you long enough. I've been trying like hell to keep him out of there."

"You insolent—" Montenegro says.

"Are you Captain Montenegro?" Caruthers asks, walking up.

Montenegro looks him up and down. "And you are?"

"SSA Caruthers, DC." He pulls out his badge and shows it to him. "This is a federal investigation, and you are being put on notice. If I find you intentionally ignored an official investigation at the request of a private citizen, I will bring charges against you and this office."

"You can't do that," Montenegro says. "I'll go to the governor."

"I have already spoken with Governor Blackwell, and he agrees with me that this is a very serious situation. Believe me, that is only the start of the charges. We will need to investigate your connection to Rafe Connor and what other *requests* you may have acquiesced to."

"This is ridiculous," he spits. "I would never—"

"He's been trying for the past hour to get in there alone with Daniels," Peregrine says.

"Looking to cut a deal before we could speak with him?" I ask. "How much did you share with Rafe about the investigation? Was he the one running it?"

"I'm calling my legal representative," Montenegro says, storming off. "You won't come in here and tell me how to run my precinct."

I turn to Caruthers. "Was that true about the governor?"

The tiniest hint of a smirk appears on the man's face. "I'm sure when I speak with the Governor, he will be appalled. But I'd like a little more evidence first."

I have to admit, I'm surprised. I didn't peg Caruthers as the deceptive type. Not that I'm complaining. Instead, I turn to Peregrine. "This is Detective Alyssa Peregrine. She was the one who helped me with the investigation. And the only one in this office, I believe, not under Montenegro's thumb."

Peregrine shakes hands with Liam and Caruthers. "You're the one who received the email about Agent Slate?"

Peregrine nods. "I never should have revealed what I knew. I admit it was for entirely selfish reasons. And I'm ready to accept the consequences of that action."

Liam's body posture has gone stiff, a clear indicator he thinks Peregrine may be a threat. But I place a soft hand on his back and he relaxes a little. I'm sure with everything, he's been on edge. No doubt everyone on the team is.

"Given what we've learned, you may have inadvertently saved Agent Slate from a worse fate," Caruthers says. "When I assigned her to go undercover on the case, I didn't realize just how…extreme it was. Had I known, I may have made a different decision."

"Still," Peregrine says. "I know it was wrong. And I want to answer for that."

Caruthers nods. "We'll take care of that in due course. After we speak with the suspect."

"Please," Peregrine says, stepping aside. "He's all yours."

"Agent Coll, would you stay out here and keep an eye on Montenegro? I don't want him going too far out of my sight," Caruthers says.

"No problem. Good luck in there." I give his hand a supportive squeeze before following my boss into the interrogation room. Daniels is sitting at the table, rubbing his temple. He looks up when we enter.

"Mr. Daniels," Caruthers says. "I'm Supervisory Special Agent Caruthers, with the FBI. I believe you already know my colleague."

Daniels takes one glance at me before turning away again.

"You're in a lot of trouble," Caruthers says. "Accessory to murder, kidnapping, conspiracy, resisting arrest, trespassing, aiding and abetting...shall I go on?"

"Just tell me what you want," Daniels groans. He knows he's fucked. I'm just curious how much fight he has left in him. He didn't seem particularly rowdy as we escorted him out of the caverns. I think once Roberts was down, Daniels became a ship adrift on the ocean.

"A full confession would be a start," Caruthers says, pulling a digital recorder out of his pocket and placing it on the table between us.

"I never wanted this," Daniels says. "This wasn't the plan."

"What *was* the plan?" I ask.

He leans forward, his elbows on the table as he laughs, but it's devoid of any real humor. "She had this grand idea. Kept saying over and over her life never amounted to anything. That she had always been someone else's trinket. First her father, then her boss, then Rafe. Said she had never been in charge of her own destiny. And her life had never meant anything. Not really."

"This is Felicia Connor you're referring to, correct?" Caruthers asks.

Daniels nods. "I knew Felicia when we were little. Growing up on the island together, she was always so full of life, of energy. But all of that slowly drained away as she got older. Her dad, he was a big deal here. And she was trotted around like a doll, always just an accessory. She never really made her own choices in life. He had decided where she would go to school by the time she was ten. When she was fifteen, they'd already found her a job. They rode that girl so hard to keep her grades up, to do all the extracurriculars, to go above and beyond. I didn't see her much during high school. She was too busy. Then I find out she's off to college, then law school. Then married. I honestly thought I'd never see her again."

"When did she first contact you?" I ask.

"About seven months ago," he says. "I had read about the accident, thought she was dead. And then I get this letter out of the blue. Roberts got one as well."

Caruthers leans forward. "Did he know her too?"

"I think they had some kind of fling when they were younger. He didn't go to our school, but I remember seeing him around. She got us together and told us what had happened. I wanted to go to the police then, she refused. She told us the police would be no help, and that Rafe would just get away with it. She had something much bigger planned."

"She worked on this plan for seven months?" I ask.

"We all did. She was well aware it would take a while for us to be hired by Breckenridge. But it was surprisingly easy. Since both Roberts and I were locals, and he had bouncer experience, it was a quicker process than we thought. He was actually the one who recommended me for the job."

I take a deep breath and sit back in my chair. "Tell me about the rooms under the house."

Caruthers arches an eyebrow.

"They are exactly what they look like. Private rooms for rich people to entertain each other, in any way possible."

"What were they to Felicia? Why leave the placard with the name of the boat down there?"

He swallows, hard. "Rafe would use those rooms from time to time with the women he met. The women—" He pauses, looking away. "The woman we took. He would take them there to impress them. To seduce them. Felicia didn't like that. He had never tried that hard with her."

"She took it as an insult," I say.

"That's...one way of putting it," he replies. "Of course, Roberts would report back what was happening to her. That's how she decided on her targets."

"Each of the targets has been in those rooms?"

"All of them," he says. "Ms. Taylor was in there the night

before the party." He stares at me. "Before we knew who you were, we figured you'd end up down there."

"And that's how Felicia chose her victims," I say. He nods. That explains why she didn't go after the woman I caught Rafe with in the hotel. She was looking to send a message, and he had probably figured it out by that point. Still, it amazes me he was willing to risk another young woman just to get his rocks off. It shows exactly what kind of person he was.

"Were you in charge of the abductions?" I ask.

"Roberts was," he says. "I only helped when necessary."

"Whose idea was it to use the caverns?" Caruthers asks. "Not an easy place to reach."

"We used to play in those caverns as kids," Daniels says. "Felicia thought it was only fitting that the people trying to destroy the island should be taken within it."

Caruthers pulls out a notepad and pen. "We're going to need you to lead us back down there to retrieve the bodies."

Daniels nods again. Over the course of the investigation, he's gone from defeated to almost eager, like he can't get the words out quickly enough, as if it's some sort of catharsis.

"What happened last night during the meeting?" I ask. You left a lot of bodies for us to pick up.

Daniels takes a deep breath. "I know. After Mrs. Stamper escaped, Felicia...well, she kind of lost it. She said there couldn't be any more screw ups, and we had to make sure this deal couldn't go through. She was determined, absolutely determined to make sure of it. She told us to do whatever it took to capture Rafe. Roberts and I knew the property, and we knew the personnel. So surprising them wasn't difficult. We managed to take them all down without the big wigs knowing what was going on."

He swallows, hard. "I didn't know what was in those syringes. I thought it was just going to knock them out. I didn't realize...I didn't realize I'd killed someone until it was too late."

"You'll forgive me if my sympathy is in short supply," I say. "Keep going."

He nods, getting ahold of himself. "After we took care of all the guards, Felicia came in, brandishing that big ass knife. She could move so quick and so fast, she got behind Mayor Williams and slit his throat before anyone knew what was happening. By then we were in there. Roberts held down Breckenridge while I held Rafe. I thought she might do it right there. The fire in her eyes was burning so hot. She went and did the same to Breckenridge but stopped short of killing Rafe too. She told him he didn't deserve something so swift."

"Had Rafe known she was alive before then?" Caruthers asks.

Daniels shrugs. "I don't know. I think he knew someone was taunting him, whether he knew it was actually Felicia or someone pretending to be her, I don't know. But the look in his eyes when she held that knife to his throat was of pure terror."

"And that's when you took him down into the island," I say.

Daniels nods. "She made him sit there and listen to the pleas of the four women, though that Taylor woman never said a word. Never yelled or screamed for help. But the others..." He trails off. "She took her time with Tolluse. It took her hours to die. And we had a place to dispose of the bodies." He looks up. "That's when we heard you coming."

I notice Caruthers wince at the mention of Tolluse. He takes the recording and stops it, putting it back in his pocket. "Mr. Daniels. I am charging you with first-degree murder, first-degree kidnapping, and conspiracy to commit a felony. Do you have a lawyer?"

He gives his head a small shake.

"I suggest you get one. Your cooperation will be taken into account, but I would not expect things to go well for you."

"No," he says, though he almost sounds relieved. Like it's a weight off his back. "I guess they won't. I'll show you where we dumped her. She deserves a proper burial, at the least."

As Caruthers and I join Peregrine back outside, I have to admit I'm conflicted. I almost feel sorry for Daniels. He was roped into this, hoping to help out his friend. And he ended up a murderer because of it.

But my thoughts keep coming back to Felicia Connor. A woman searching so hard for a purpose that she went too far over the edge to try and save the place she loved. No doubt the trauma she sustained as a child and a young woman contributed to her mental state, but in the end, it boiled down to a woman who had been betrayed over and over and was looking for retribution. And she took it the only way she knew how. She not only got revenge, but she also managed to save the island.

Yet, when I look at the trail of bodies it took to get there, I don't see how she ever justified it.

"Well?" Peregrine asks.

"He's cooperating," I say. "He's going to take us back down so we can retrieve the bodies."

She lets out a breath. "That's great news. What do you need from me?"

"Help us get this situation wrapped up," Caruthers says. "Then we'll need you to come back to DC with us. I want my people to do a deep dive on the person who contacted you, see if we can't figure out who that could have been. And where they received their information. We'll need your statement as a witness."

"Of course," she says. "Whatever I can do to help. I have some things I need to make up for."

"May I use your phones?" Caruthers asks. "I have a governor to call."

# Chapter Thirty-Five

"MY FREAKING BACK." Zara stands up, places both hands behind her back and stretches until it pops. I'm watching from my desk directly across from her.

"You're going to get a hump if you're not careful," I tell her.

"What? No, I'm not," she says, but she looks over her shoulder anyway. Her face turns sour when she sees me grinning at her. "You're mean."

"I need some way to entertain myself," I say.

"You don't need to stay, you know. You can go home anytime."

"And miss a chance for payback? Never. Plus, Caruthers told me to hang around. I'm not sure what he's waiting on, though."

It's been six days since we came back from St. Solomon, and Zara has been working nonstop, along with the rest of the Intelligence division, to determine exactly how someone could have identified me. Using Peregrine's laptop, Zara was able to find a record of the original email, even though it had been erased, and managed to use that information to trace it back through a dozen different sources. Unfortunately, it all led to a dead end in the system. Whoever contacted Peregrine, they knew what they were doing.

Not only that, but Intelligence still hasn't made much progress on the data recovered from Fletch's computer. According to them, the encryption algorithm is incredibly complex. Which means we may need a key if we ever want to unlock it.

"I think you just feel bad you got a week on a tropical island while I was stuck here," Zara says, walking around our desks while popping her back again.

"I only felt a little bad about that. Honestly, most of the time I was either sweating my ass off in the jungle or crawling through caves. I spent very little time on the beach and only managed one fruity drink."

"Shame," she says. "If I'd been there, I would've insisted on at least three. I just wish you and Liam had gotten some down time."

"Me too," I tell her. Unfortunately, because of the breach, we couldn't take that time off like we'd discussed. But we did at least get *some* time together, even though a lot of it was gathering evidence for the case and helping to locate bodies. It turns out Roberts and Daniels had taken Vicki Tolluse deeper into one of the caves, down to a small little oasis fed from the ocean. Because her body had been flayed open and the lungs no longer had any oxygen in them, she sunk like a stone. When we finally pulled her up, she had already been partially devoured by the local wildlife. But we were able to recover the bodies of Rafe, Felicia, and Roberts.

In addition, Caruthers eventually did bring charges against Montenegro after we found evidence on his computer proving he'd been taking a bribe from Rafe to keep the investigation about the women quiet. Apparently, Rafe had been greasing a lot of wheels, including that of the mayor's office.

So instead of allowing the lieutenant mayor to take over, the governor had to step in and appoint a temporary mayor for Queen's Bay. He also had to appoint a temporary police chief, though his selection was limited to mostly Montenegro's own people.

Before she left to go back, Peregrine promised me she'd throw her hat in the ring for a permanent position, but that'll be up to the local legislature. Regardless, once the media got hold of the story, all hell broke loose. From what I understand, tourism is already down twenty percent. It will take the island a long time to recover, and it looks like Felicia will get her wish; any future development is off the table for the time being.

Peregrine has also promised to open the investigation into Felicia's "accident" again. It falls within the jurisdiction of the nearby island of St. Croix, but she thinks given everything that's happened, she'll be able to convince them to take a second look at what really happened. Given everything Felicia told us, I wouldn't be surprised if Rafe really did sabotage that boat. And even though he's dead, it would at least provide some closure to both the case and her remaining family.

My phone buzzes, and I hit the speaker button. "Slate."

"You and Foley report to my office." Caruthers hangs up.

"Finally," Zara says. I wiggle my eyebrows at her and follow her down to Caruthers's office. We close the door behind us as Caruthers pulls out a paper file and sets it on the desk between us.

"You know why I've asked you here," Caruthers says.

I share a quick glance with Zara who seems as bewildered as me. "Not really, no sir."

"I'm pulling you from your assignments." He's staring directly at me.

"What?"

He holds up one hand, obviously having anticipated this

response. "Hang on. I'm not putting you on leave. But we have a security breach. You can't go back undercover with Mr. Fletch, nor do I think it's a good idea for you to work on your other assignments. Somehow, someone knows who you are. For the time being, I'd like, with your permission, to use that."

I narrow my gaze. "Use that how?"

"To draw out whoever sent Detective Peregrine that email," he replies. Caruthers closes his eyes for a moment before resetting his gaze. "You weren't the only agent whose cover was blown. There are five other agents in different divisions all across the Bureau who had a similar experience at nearly the same time."

"Why didn't we know about this?" Zara demands.

"Because the director doesn't want it to be common knowledge. He believes whatever information you stole from Fletch's computer may have something to do with this breach of intel. And for the moment, he wants it kept quiet."

"Why? Whoever sent the email isn't stupid. They'll expect us to respond in some way."

"Precisely. Which is what the director *doesn't* want to do. He's hoping that by showing no response whatsoever, whoever sent that email will take an even bolder move. One that will help us figure out this mess."

"Okay, so how does pulling me from my cases accomplish that?"

"We're pulling all the affected agents from their cases. It's a security issue," he replies. "Nothing personal."

"Sure feels personal," I say.

He glances at the thin file folder on the desk between us. "For the time-being, you're being reassigned. Out of this office, on lower-priority cases until this has been resolved with the expectation that whoever is keeping an eye on you may try to interfere again. When and if that happens, I want you ready for it. You're to report back anything that could lead us back to whoever is behind all this."

"Great, so a demotion," I say, sitting back. "This is DelMarVa all over again."

"Don't think you are unique in this situation, Slate," he says. "The other five agents are also being given similar treatment. But given the severity of what's happened, what is the alternative?"

He's right. If I were in his position and someone on my team had been compromised, I couldn't exactly keep them running some of our most important cases.

"So why am I here?" Zara asks.

"Because you're going to be her backup. Your familiarity with the encrypted files will be an asset in the chance these events are connected and someone does try to interfere with Agent Slate again. I also want someone watching Slate's back. I don't want her in another situation like St. Solomon again. That was my mistake, and I accept it."

"You didn't know my cover was blown before I even arrived on the island," I say. "It's not your fault."

"But it is my responsibility," he says.

"Wait, so what about Theo?" Zara asks. "I've been the primary point of contact when he brings us information."

"Until further notice, we're putting our…association… with Mr. Arquenest on hold. We need to determine how big our problem is and where it came from."

She leans forward. "You don't think—"

"We're not making any assumptions right now," he says. "Just being cautious. Let us figure out how bad this thing is first, then we can proceed."

Zara sits back, deflated. I know having Theo assist the FBI was a big win for her. It's as if both of us have had our legs cut out from under us.

"So what happens now?" I ask.

"You'll receive your first assignment in a few days. Until then, coordinate with your team to make sure all your other cases are covered. Button everything up. Odds are you won't be working out of this office for a while."

I don't even want to think about what that means. How long is this going to go on? What about Liam? Our time together is already short enough as it is. Does this mean it'll become non-existent?

"I know this isn't what you wanted to hear," Caruthers says. "But hopefully it will be a temporary situation until we can resolve the matter. Until then, I can't make any promises."

"I understand," I say, though it doesn't mean I have to like it.

"Okay, that's it. Get home and pack your suitcases. I'll have everything arranged for you in a few days."

Zara and I head back to our desks, our moods noticeably darker. The last thing I want to do is leave this office. It's where I'm comfortable, and the people I trust are here. Starting over in a new place, even temporarily? Not my idea of improvement.

"This sucks," Zara says, throwing her badge down on the desk. "What am I supposed to tell Theo?"

"The truth," I say, thinking about the same conversation I'm going to have with Liam.

"I guess it could be worse," she finally says after some of the frustration has gone out of her.

I nod, though there's a pit in my stomach about this whole situation. Someone is targeting FBI agents, and I'm one of them. Not to mention, we still don't know what is going on with the data from Fletch's computer. And on top of that, I can't even investigate the issue.

"Yeah," I say, though I don't really believe it.

If there's one thing I know for sure, things always get worse before they get better.

The End?

. . .

To be continued....

*Want to read more about Emily?*

**WHERE THE HIGHWAY ENDS, THE NIGHTMARE BEGINS.**

*Reassigned to a quiet field office in Albuquerque after a mysterious data breach, FBI agent Emily Slate is restless. But when a string of highway robberies in the New Mexico desert turns deadly, she's thrust into a case that feels far more dangerous than it seems. With only her partner Zara for backup, Emily quickly realizes that these aren't just random heists—they're part of something much bigger.*

*As they dig deeper, Emily and Zara uncover a twisted conspiracy of treachery and betrayal, a plot that stretches across the barren desert and threatens to claim more lives. Racing against time, they must unravel the deadly scheme before the killer strikes again—and before they become the next targets.*

*In the vast emptiness of the desert, danger is closer than it appears.*

*JOIN EMILY AS SHE DISCOVERS **THE PASSAGE**, EMILY SLATE Mystery Thriller book 16.*

To get your copy of *The Passage*, CLICK HERE or scan the code below with your phone.

New Series Alert!
Dark Secrets Await…

I HOPE YOU ENJOYED *BLOOD IN THE SAND*! WHILE YOU WAIT for the next installment in Emily's story, I hope you'll take a chance on my new series which introduces Detective Ivy Bishop. And as a loyal Emily Slate reader, I think you're going to love it!

Detective Ivy Bishop is celebrating her recent promotion with the Oakhurst, Oregon Police Department when she receives her first big case: a headless body that's washed up on a nearby beach.

Jumping into action with her new partner, Ivy is determined to show she has what it takes to make it as a detective. But she's harboring a dark secret, one that happened when she was young and continues to haunt her until this day.

Little does Ivy know this is no ordinary case, and will tear open old wounds, and lead her to question everything she ever knew about her past.

Interested in learning more about Ivy? CLICK HERE to snag your copy of HER DARK SECRET!

***Now Available***

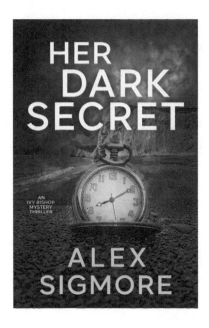

I'm so excited for you to meet Ivy and join along in her adventures!

CLICK HERE or scan the code below to get yours now!

### The Emily Slate FBI Mystery Series

Free Prequel - Her Last Shot (Emily Slate Bonus Story)

His Perfect Crime - (Emily Slate Series Book One)

The Collection Girls - (Emily Slate Series Book Two)

Smoke and Ashes - (Emily Slate Series Book Three)

Her Final Words - (Emily Slate Series Book Four)

Can't Miss Her - (Emily Slate Series Book Five)

The Lost Daughter - (Emily Slate Series Book Six)

The Secret Seven - (Emily Slate Series Book Seven)

A Liar's Grave - (Emily Slate Series Book Eight)

Oh What Fun - (Emily Slate Holiday Special)

The Girl in the Wall - (Emily Slate Series Book Nine)

His Final Act - (Emily Slate Series Book Ten)

The Vanishing Eyes - (Emily Slate Series Book Eleven)

Edge of the Woods - (Emily Slate Series Book Twelve)

Ties That Bind - (Emily Slate Series Book Thirteen)

The Missing Bones - (Emily Slate Series Book Fourteen)

Blood in the Sand - (Emily Slate Series Book Fifteen)

### Coming soon!

The Passage - (Emily Slate Series Book Sixteen)

The Killing Jar - (Emily Slate Series Book Seventeen)

A Deadly Promise - (Emily Slate Series Book Eighteen)

Solitaire's Song - (Emily Slate Series Book Nineteen)

### The Ivy Bishop Mystery Thriller Series

Free Prequel - Bishop's Edge (Ivy Bishop Bonus Story)

Her Dark Secret - (Ivy Bishop Series Book One)

The Girl Without A Clue - (Ivy Bishop Series Book Two)

Coming Soon!

The Buried Faces - (Ivy Bishop Series Book Three)

Her Hidden Lies - (Ivy Bishop Series Book Four)

# A Note from Alex

Hi there!

I hope you've enjoyed *Blood in the Sand*. This book is the official stat of "Season 3" for Emily and opens up a brand new world of intrigue and danger.

Also, I have to confess I had a blast writing this book. There's just something about the combination of sand, surf and murder that just makes my heart patter. But I also have a deep love for the Caribbean, so having the opportunity to set a book there was a dream. I just wish I could have been there while writing it!

As you've already seen, there is plenty more coming for Emily. What will these developments mean for her relationships? Especially now that she has two dogs?! You'll have to read on to find out. I hope you join me for her next adventure, coming soon!

Sincerely,

Alex

P.S. If you haven't already, please take a moment to leave a review or recommend this series to a fellow book lover. It really helps me as a writer and is the best way to make sure there are plenty more *Emily Slate* books in the future.

As always, thank you!

Made in United States
Troutdale, OR
10/24/2024

24076790R00163